COMPLEMENTARY COLORS

CHARM CITY CONNECTIONS

BOOK ONE

ROXANNE BLACKHALL

BLACK LABEL PRESS

A little love letter to a town that gets a bad rap.
With undying love and thanks to my amazing family!

CONTENT NOTES

This book is intended for adults and contains content that may be upsetting for some readers. Detailed information can be found on the author's website.

www.RoxanneBlackhall.com/content

COMPLEMENTARY COLORS

Nicky Bisset is a sassy art teacher who looks like she just stepped out of a fairy convention.

Ty Lake is a preppy type with his eyes set on becoming a museum director.

She gravitates toward the alternative art crowd while he's courting Baltimore's elite to help support the museum.

On the surface, they're all wrong and their views on art are polar opposites, but when they're together, everything feels so right.

Unless Nicky is willing to mold herself to fit Ty's world and rebuild bridges with the grandfather she can't stand (who happens to be his boss), dating her would spell career suicide.

The trouble is, Ty likes her just the way she is.

CHAPTER 1

Nicky Bissett pushed through the glass doors into Ceremony Coffee and paused, trying to decide if she loved or hated the place. If the Apple store went into the cafe business, this is what it would look like. All clean lines, light wood, smooth surfaces, and no visible menu. The rich smell of heaven—or coffee, same thing—urged her on.

Splurging on a cuppa when job hunting and living on savings and whatever art pieces sold on her Etsy page wasn't the smartest choice, but Gramps was a tea drinker and there was no way she was doing an interview without her preferred caffeine-delivery mechanism.

Nicky approached what looked like the place to order and gave the person standing there her best smile. At least they had a name tag. Complete with their pronouns—they/them. Cool.

"Hi Jace. I've never been here before. Help?"

She braced for the cooler-than-you clerk to roll their eyes at the noob. Instead, she got a warm smile.

"Welcome." Jace pointed to a little easel on Nicky's left. "Menu's there. Or tell me what you want. Whatever pastries we've got are on display."

The rumbling of her stomach at the mention of pastries was a not-so-pleasant reminder she'd exited the house in a hurry this morning. Not the way she wanted to go to an interview.

The bell over the door jingled, pulling Nicky back to her caffeine need.

"What's good?"

"Everything. I'm fond of a flat white, but I'm betting that's not your style. You like it sweet, or less so?"

Nicky leaned over for a closer look at the pastries and caught sight of a polished tan leather shoe tapping behind her. She cast an eye back at Jace, who showed no signs of impatience.

"A little on the sweet side."

The shoe tap-tapped again. Nicky dared a quick glance over her shoulder. That shoe belonged to a pair of crisply pressed royal blue trousers.

Great. An impatient suit type.

"I'm thinking salted caramel latte with a vanilla coffee." The voice came from the cloud of steam by the espresso machines.

"Perfect! Thanks." Nicky straightened up and Jace typed in her coffee order.

"Gabe's our barista and they have a talent for making the right drink for people. Did you want a pastry?"

The unmistakable sound of shoe tapping penetrated Nicky's brain through the hum of conversations in the shop. She shot another look back. The edge of a camel overcoat, flung over the owner's arm, and long fingers that twitched in time with the toe tapping.

Nicky decided on a cinnamon roll, paid for her order, thanked Jace, grabbed her pastry and prepared to skirt past Mr. Impatient and wait for her coffee.

She turned and stopped in her tracks. The polished and pressed everything didn't end with the shoes and trousers. The man was so model perfect he could have been on the cover of a magazine.

He stepped past her, swiped his card, said something to Jace and called a hello to Gabe before turning a megawatt smile on Nicky, sending a little shiver of pleasure along her spine.

She had zero interest in getting to know yet another Joe Preppy, but there was no harm in admiring.

And there is a lot to admire.

Which she did, from the tips of those shoes to the top of his head. His rich buttery cream shirt looked so crisp it had to be starched, and a tie in swirling blue tones was in some complicated knot and centered with mathematic precision. Dude even had a pocket square—shades of gold and blue and red.

Lush sandy hair swept back from a strong brow and pale green eyes that were focused on Nicky with a look of amusement that said he'd caught her checking him out.

Feeling a little guilty for ogling, she squeaked an apology and hurried to the end of the counter to collect her coffee. She gave a nod of thanks to Gabe and turned to go. The faster she got away from those dangerous eyes and devastating smile, the better.

Something hard thwacked into her back and the unthinkable happened. Nicky's hand tightened on her cup, the lid popped off, and the hot vanilla-salted-caramel concoction sprayed down her top.

"Jeez lady, watch where you're going!"

A man in a rumpled suit and badly done tie hitched his backpack onto his shoulder. The same pack that had hit Nicky.

Coffee dripped down her hands, and her shirt clung to her chest. The smug expression on the man's face said he knew whose fault this was, but wouldn't admit it.

The buzz of conversation from the tables didn't stop. No one gasped or gawked. Except for Joe Preppy. He stood there with a worried look on his face, probably concerned he'd gotten coffee on his impeccable outfit.

She dropped her now empty cup onto the counter and glared at the man who'd caused the whole mess. He shifted his backpack and scoffed, turned away and walked toward the exit.

So much for Baltimore being Charm City. More like jerk city.

"Dude," she called after him. "Seriously?"

The guy flipped her off and shoved through the door.

She grabbed the napkins Joe Preppy offered and muttered a thank you before trying to mop herself up. It was only her shirt; she'd figure something out. She did not want to go home and change. Her grandfather would use it as an opportunity to get more jabs in.

"Are you okay?" Joe Preppy leaned in and spoke in soft tones. Up close, those eyes were mesmerizing.

Great. First hot guy I see in the city and I'm dripping latte.

"Oh, yeah. Twelve ounces of hot coffee to the chest is a great way to start the morning before a big interview." She needed to dial down the sarcasm. She held the handful of now soaked napkins up. "Thanks for these."

Gabe came over with a trash bag and an offer of more napkins. They apologized for the rude customer before they started wiping the spill.

"I'm good, thanks. Rude dude isn't your fault. May I use the restroom?"

Jace handed her a towel. "It's down the hall."

Safely in the bathroom, Nicky cleaned up as best she could. Luckily, it was a chilly morning, and she had a button up cardigan in her bag that covered most of the coffee stain. Too bad she hadn't grabbed a scarf.

This would not ruin her day. She hadn't gone through the last several months of hell to move back to her grandfather's house for everything to go south like this.

She came out to find Joe Preppy leaning on the counter chatting with Gabe. A bag of cookies and two coffee cups at his elbow. His short, perfectly groomed beard seemed at odds with the preppy look. Okay, maybe Mr. Preppy had a wilder side.

"Thanks for the help there." She fumbled her wallet from her bag, ready to order another coffee, but he pushed a cup toward her.

"Gabe already made a fresh one." His voice was rich and deep, and lacked the distinctive Baltimore accent. He shot a smile at the barista then stood and the friendly grin didn't just transform into the megawatt beam from earlier. It became pure, panty-melting smolder.

Good grief, he's tall. Long and lean and hot AF. Nicky returned his smile.

"I don't know how much help I was. I should have stopped the guy and made him pay for the cleaning bill. But I can do this." He pulled a scarf from somewhere—big surprise, it coordinated with the rest of his outfit—and handed it to Nicky.

Oh great. On top of being drop dead gorgeous, he was the savior type. Not her thing. The preppy Ivy League look more often than not went with a personality to match. Witness her grandfather and her ex-fiancé. No thanks. She was here to put her life back in order after that disaster of a relationship.

Her fingers closed on the soft and silken scarf. "Thank you, but I can't..."

Joe Preppy's lips curled into a half smile. "Please. You said you had a big interview. It shouldn't be ruined by a coffee shower." The half-smile cranked up to near blinding levels, and Nicky grinned in response. His deep voice somehow soothed her frayed nerves. "I'm guessing you're not from around here."

He was all legs, and that suit was so well tailored it should be a sin. There was the dash of cold water she needed. It didn't matter how hot he was. Finding a job and a place to live were her priorities. Men were not on her radar.

"Sort of. I spent my childhood here, but I've been in DC for years." She hauled in a deep breath. "You did the right thing. My battle to fight. That kind of jerk? Being him is its own punishment. Thanks for guarding my coffee."

The colorful scarf now spilling across her lap would cover what the cardigan couldn't. She sighed and looped it around her neck, trying not to get distracted by the scent of pepper and nutmeg.

"And thanks for this. See you around."

Nicky boogied for the door before she was tempted to stay and chat with hot Joe Preppy.

"Hold up." His voice stopped her in her tracks. She turned to find him waving a napkin at her.

TY

Bright blue eyes bored into his and Ty Lake forgot how to speak. He needed to get control of himself. It wasn't like he hadn't seen a pretty woman before; this one happened to be beyond pretty. She looked like an elf princess who'd stepped out of some Tolkienesque fantasy.

"You've got coffee on your boot." Ty pointed down and her gaze followed his finger. *Oh, screw this.* He knelt and swiped at the coffee splotch on a pair of well-worn but shiny yellow Doc Martens. *Where in the hell is she interviewing?*

"Oh." A nervous laugh sounded above his head. The utter ridiculousness of the scene clicked, and Ty stood.

"Nice boots. I'd hate to walk into the office with coffee all over my shoes."

As silly as he felt, it must have hit the right note for her because her laugh changed to something richer and throatier.

"I've got a lot to thank you for today." She held up her booted foot as if admiring the impromptu polish job. "I'd shake your hand, but..." She spread her arms wide—laden with a cup of coffee, a sparkly umbrella, and an eye-searingly bright yellow raincoat. Silver bangles jangled on her wrists and the turquoise streak in her hair matched the stone in her necklace. The same shade as her eyes, which were an uncanny blue.

She was out the door in a swirl of color and the world got a little less bright as she disappeared around the corner.

He'd come in early to have time to sit and enjoy his coffee before his day started, but now he didn't have time to hang around. Thanks to a pixie looking whirlwind in human form.

"Who, or maybe what, was that?" Ty gave a quick glance toward the door as Gabe slid a full drink carrier across the counter at him.

"Figured you'd be ready for these, and I dunno. First time I've seen her."

Ty grabbed the coffees and his bag of cookies and headed out, pausing at the door. "First, I thought MICA student, but..." He glanced down the street the way she'd gone. "She was headed the wrong way for that."

Jace came in wielding a mop and swiped at the last of the coffee spill. "She did mention an interview." They gave a one shoulder shrug as they dipped the mop into the bucket. "She seemed nice."

Jace was right. Even after getting hot coffee spilled down her front, on what was an important day, she'd been all smiles and charm. Ty pushed out the door and broke into a brisk walk.

At the Walters Art Museum, he swung through the front lobby, his footfalls echoing on the hard marble, and dropped the extra coffees and cookies with Bill, the morning guard. Ty waved at the crew staffing the information desk before hurrying out the back, then down the street to the rowhome that housed the museum offices.

He couldn't get the coffee shop woman out of his head. Which was ridiculous. He didn't go for the Bohemian type. She'd looked amazing, but where was she interviewing, dressed like that? What adult bought a bright yellow coat?

The same adult who wears bright yellow boots for a job interview.

Ty gathered his notes and headed to the director's office. Being late to a meeting with the notoriously particular doctor was not a good career move.

"Have a seat," Dr. Mason greeted as Ty walked through the door of the oak paneled office lined with books, framed photos of distinguished museum guests, and a surprising lack of art. He took the seat across from Mason.

"You're looking to leave development." Mason's tone of voice made it clear it wasn't a question. Ty had been clear from the beginning that he envisioned a career in museum work but he'd never told anyone here that it included leaving development.

"You've worked with Hopkins on repatriation research," Mason continued. "We have a divided board here. We've done quite a bit of work and about half in favor of more research, while the other half is content with what we've already done."

Ty already knew the board was split between traditionalists who avoided change, and a more progressive group seeking ways to keep the museum relevant to a younger crowd.

"I don't disagree, sir." *Where the hell is he going?*

"I'd like you to dig into our options from all angles—including PR and long-term cost-benefit analysis."

Wonderful. More work. Great start to the weekend. What Mason was proposing was a full-time job, one which was well above his pay grade.

"I know it's a lot, and it's outside your normal duties," Mason said, as if reading Ty's mind. "The work you do is impressive. Don't think it's gone unnoticed."

Dismissed. Without a chance for discussion and without Ty agreeing to take it on. Not that he'd refuse. It wasn't a title he could put on his CV, but the work would look good as he moved out of development toward his goal of a director-level position at a major museum.

Ty didn't have time to think about that today. His next meeting was in less than thirty minutes, and he still couldn't shake the image of the woman in the coffee shop.

CHAPTER 2

NICKY—TUESDAY, APRIL 2

The step squeaked and Nicky froze. *Dammit. Forgot to stay to the left.* She shifted and hurried down the stairs, already running behind, which meant she'd have to take her scooter instead of the bus and there'd be no time to stop for coffee and maybe catch Joe Preppy.

She tried to tell herself returning his scarf was the only reason she cared, but she wasn't that good at self-deception.

"Well, it's good to see you can at least get up early."

The booming voice stopped her halfway down the hall and she turned to face her grandfather. Pushing seventy and still handsome, with a square jaw, strong features and still more sandy blond than silver. She didn't resemble him at all. Except the eyes. She'd gotten his eyes—piercing and bright blue.

He held out a stiff-looking card. At least he wasn't calling her into his office—a place of dark wood and the smell of rich leather and old books. And the ever-present sense she was simultaneously not enough and too much.

"You should attend this event," he said as she took the embossed card. "It's an excellent networking opportunity. I would ask you to please observe the dress code. This is black tie."

Nicky scanned the invitation to a retirement party for Chris Fields, the Director of Education at the Walters. *Shit.* Mr. Fields had been a fixture of her youth and was the primary reason the museum had become her refuge after her mother passed. She had to go, even if it meant an evening under her grandfather's watchful eye.

"Of course, Gramps," she replied. He had already returned to his desk. There was no point in saying anything else. Gramps had spoken and she was dismissed.

One short, chilly ride later, she pulled her Vespa into a space behind the American Visionary Art Museum and hurried inside. Sabrina Clements met her at the elevators with a big smile. "Glad to see we didn't scare you away. You ready to jump in?"

During the interview, Nicky had realized whatever Sabrina's official job title, the reality was she was responsible for keeping a staff full of artists and free thinkers organized and on task. From what Nicky had seen, she accomplished that without ever raising her voice. It didn't hurt that at six feet tall, with colorful braids cascading to her waist and dark ebony skin, all Sabrina commanded attention simply by entering a room.

"I don't frighten easily. You don't know fear until you try teaching art to middle school children at a private school." She swallowed those memories.

Her new boss chuckled and handed over a printed schedule. "Into the fire today, I'm afraid. I apologize for the split schedule. In the future, we'll try to avoid that, but

Tuesdays are also our slowest days. I'll show you around before you dive in."

Nicky skimmed her itinerary—an architectural tour, then a class making bird or egg mosaics from found materials and discarded mechanical parts. No doubt inspired by Andrew Logan's Cosmic Galaxy Egg that perched outside the building.

Nicky's childhood memories of the museum were of a twisting maze-like space, and the back halls were not any different.

"During your interview, we didn't get around to what made you leave the private school life." Sabrina set a slow pace, allowing plenty of time to talk. Not something Nicky wanted to delve into.

"Oh, y'know..." Nicky feigned a much lighter tone than she felt. "When you realize something you thought you wanted doesn't live up to your expectations."

That was some vague bullshit, and in truth was more about Jeremy than the job. She'd loved the job. Sabrina nodded but paused and fixed Nicky with a penetrating gaze.

"The only reference from your last place of employment was a teacher's aide, which seemed odd considering your otherwise perfect resume. So, what gives?"

Nicky hauled in a deep breath. Sabrina's eyebrow went up, but her expression was kind and soft. Nicky made the call.

"My ex-fiancé and I worked at the same school." In the past, she'd tried making it about the breakup, but that led to follow-up questions—why not go to another school, why look outside the school system. No one wanted to hire someone they figured was temporary and would be around until their heartache, or their relationship, mended.

Not happening here. Not after what Jeremy did.

She swallowed and looked down at her feet. "We had an argument. It got nasty and I left. He didn't take too kindly to rejection. It escalated and I called the police. Next thing I know, the school fired me because someone sent them old photos from when I was dancing."

"Oh, I bet that went over well." Sabrina's face registered disgust and nothing about it said it was aimed at Nicky.

"About like you'd expect."

Sabrina's mouth thinned and her eyes narrowed. For a moment, Nicky feared she'd been wrong about the source of disgust, and she was about to be fired before starting. Then Sabrina shook her head, her face all soft eyes and heartache.

"Your ex sent them."

There was no question and no judgement. Nicky hadn't bothered to confront Jeremy. The damage was done.

"High likelihood. I'm not ashamed of my previous jobs, but not everyone agrees."

Sabrina placed a hand on Nicky's shoulder. "Thank you for being honest with me. For the record, this stays between the two of us." She dropped her hand and resumed walking. "Not that I'd worry about anyone here caring, but it's your choice to make."

TY—FRIDAY, APRIL 5

The loud music and flashing lights were giving Ty a headache. He rarely allowed himself this kind of time off, so when he did, he made the most of it. Not tonight, though.

Deke Wallace flopped into the booth across from him. "What the fuck, man? It is Friday night. Relax."

Ty shrugged and signaled for another drink. He'd pay it in the morning but fuck it.

"Bored, I guess. Tell me that same group of ladies isn't in here every week." He didn't wait for Deke's response. He knew he was right. "Zach is up to his usual."

He tipped his chin at the corner where their friend was making out with a lanky blonde. Zach always went for the same type—tall, athletically built, blonde. Bonus points for large breasts—real or fake. The relationship would last a few months. Right about when the girl wanted to get serious, he bounced.

At least Deke admitted he was in it for sex. The women never seemed to mind, and he had a few repeats, but always kept it super casual.

"You've never been Mr. Party, but either fix this shit or take off. You are a buzz kill right now." Deke flashed a smile at a stunning brunette in a bright yellow dress. The look she shot back would melt the pants off an ice sculpture in the arctic. All Ty could think of was the woman with a yellow coat and boots

"Well, there's your evening's fun." His beer arrived and he shoved it toward Deke. He wanted out of here and off the merry-go-round that passed for a social life. "I'm heading out."

Not one to turn down a free drink, Deke snagged the glass. "I'm gonna regret asking, but what's going on?" He took a long pull on the beer, eying Ty over the rim. "You got maybe two minutes before that gorgeous lady makes her way over here."

Deke had confidence to spare, and he was rarely wrong. Ty couldn't put a finger on what was bugging him, much less put it in words.

"So, I met this girl." *What the fuck.* He'd sort of met her. The only reason he knew her name was from her coffee order. Nicky, with a Y. He'd only seen her that one time at the coffee shop. She'd peered into the pastry case as if everything there was the most delectable thing she'd ever seen.

It had taken him about two seconds to decide that bit of brightly colored dynamite in female form was the most delectable thing he had laid eyes on and his entire world went sideways. He needed to focus on his career, not an achingly beautiful woman who could pass for a mythical creature.

"Uh huh." Deke smirked and sat down the beer. "That's what has you all quiet and fucked up? She put a spell on you or something?"

Ty lifted a shoulder. The thought had occurred to him. She looked the part. "Or something, I guess. She's quirky. And cute. And I dunno, perky."

Deke's eyebrows reached for his hairline. "Perky? Are you serious?"

The brunette cruised by their table, her gaze traveling over Deke with obvious lust. "Right on cue." Deke gave the woman a long appraising look and finished with a wink before turning back to Ty. "Man, whatever has you worked up, spit it out. Because that woman is hot. I am not giving up hot to discuss fucking perky."

Ty tossed cash onto the table. That would more than cover his drinks and share of the tip. "Yeah, never mind. I don't know where my head is right now. Text tomorrow if you're up to a game."

Outside, the cool evening air pulled him away from the bar entrance, making him realize how hot and stuffy it had been inside. Maybe that was the reason for his grumpy mood. The night was clear and mild for early April. Home wasn't too far to walk, but there had been some muggings recently. Maybe a ride was a better idea.

A high-pitched horn sounded, pulling his attention away from his phone as a cherry red Vespa pulled to the curb in front of him. As if summoned by his thoughts, there she was.

Nicky. With a Y.

Tight pants hugged her long legs and a colorful scarf poked out of her leather jacket.

"Fancy running into you." She laughed and whipped her

helmet off. Her hair hung in a long braid over one shoulder and earrings—several pairs by the looks—sparkled in the streetlights. Unbidden, he found himself wanting to know if she had any other piercings.

"Oh, hey, did you get your scarf back?"

It took him a little too long to process her question. His scarf? Oh.

"Yes. You didn't need to return it, but thanks." He'd been baffled when Jace handed him the painted bag containing his dry-cleaned scarf and a note written in sparkly purple ink—and handwriting so pretty it didn't look real. Then disappointed that she hadn't given it to him personally. Which was a shitty attitude.

"That place any fun?" Her voice cut into those thoughts.

Ty gave half a glance to the bar behind him and decided in an instant it was not fun at all.

She was dressed for a night out and she was wearing makeup—though she might've been when they'd met. He hadn't noticed anything beyond her impossibly blue eyes and pouty mouth.

"It's uh..." Ty fumbled over what to tell her. "A bit of a meat market, to be honest." Which was why he was leaving. "Not my scene."

Her nose scrunched up, then she gestured at his phone where the ride app still glowed. "You need a ride?" She tipped her head at the seat behind her.

"Do you have a second helmet? It's kind of the law here."

Fuck if that didn't make him sound like a major stick in the mud. It wouldn't be the first time he'd ridden a motorcycle without a helmet.

"Nope, sorry, but if you don't live that far away..." She held her helmet out as she trailed off.

The idea of getting on the scooter behind her, feeling her

trim curves between his thighs, was too much for his brain to process. His cock processed things just fine and started throbbing in a way that said it had been too long.

Ty shook his head. He'd take her thinking he was afraid. Or too goody-goody. Anything that saved him from admitting he'd popped a woody like a teenager at the thought of touching her. Never mind what she'd feel if he were pressed against her back.

Her gaze traveled his body and the smirk she shot him suggested she'd noticed. *Fuck.*

"Suit yourself." She slipped the helmet back on, buckling it under her chin. "See you around."

With a wave, she was off, leaning in as she whipped the little scooter around the corner and then out of sight. He thumbed the ride app and ordered a car, wishing he'd sucked it up and climbed on the seat behind her.

CHAPTER 3

Light sparkled off the mirrored wings of the spinning Black Icarus statue in the stairwell and Nicky couldn't stop smiling. She hadn't expected an invite to the quarterly staff social at the American Visionary Arts Museum, but here she was. After less than a week on the job, it was clear the small staff was more like family than coworkers.

"This is about to wrap up, but something tells me you're not ready for home. Wanna come meet the wife?" Sabrina propped her lanky frame against the wall next to her.

"That obvious?" Nicky made a habit of staying out until she was reasonably sure her grandfather would either be in bed, or locked in his office.

"Let's go." Sabrina led the way down the stairs and through the thinning crowd. Fifteen minutes later, Nicky was curled on a cushy sofa with a cat on her lap, laughing as Sabrina's wife Anne told a story about last year's Kinetic Sculpture Race.

"Oh, that's amazing!" Nicky loved the KSR—the perfect

melding of engineering and art. She especially loved the wackiness of the people-powered sculptures. It was a few weeks away and Sabrina was neck deep in planning. For Nicky, it meant she'd be getting a few extra shifts while the rest of the staff prepped for the race.

"Okay," Anne said. "What's the deal with you and home? Or more accurately, I suspect, your grandfather?"

Nicky cringed and wished they could go back to talking about anything but that. She looked at the black void of a cat purring away in her lap instead of her hosts.

"We never had a good relationship. Gramps is..." Nicky struggled to find the right words. People who only knew the man professionally tended to like him.

"Gramps is a strong personality. He likes his music and his art classical. He wants his world to be a library—hushed and reverent. Above all, respectful and proper."

"Why are you living with him?" Leave it to Sabrina to go straight to the deep end.

"I made the mistake of putting all my eggs in one basket." When Sabrina and Anne both raised their eyebrows, Nicky looked down at the cat before speaking.

"Well, I mean, you know the story of my ex," she said, looking back up at Sabrina.

"I don't," Anne replied.

"I told you it would stay between us." A soft smile lit Sabrina's face.

"Yeah, well..." Nicky cleared her throat, trying to figure out what to say. "Sabrina can fill you in on everything. My ex and I lived and worked together, so when we split, I was single, jobless, and homeless. I couch surfed for a bit."

That last was glamorizing things, as most of her college friends still lived in makeshift artist's lofts at places like the Copycat and often didn't have couches. Or did, but they'd been scrounged from the free bin of discarded furniture. Or worse.

"I called my grandfather because I had no other options. The devil you know, right?"

Nicky swallowed over a dry throat. A few weeks ago, even thinking about all of this would have reduced her to tears, but she saw no judgement or pity from Sabrina and Anne.

Sabrina rose and wrapped her arms around Nicky in a fierce hug, disturbing the sleeping cat. "Well, you have better friends now." Sabrina's tone gave no room for argument, and Anne chimed in her agreement.

For the first time in a long time, perhaps ever, Nicky felt comfortable and at home.

Later, as she stepped into the brownstone, she couldn't help but compare the two spaces.

Sabrina and Anne's small row home was warm and charming, filled with love and laughter. The walls alive with color and art. Her grandfather's entry was like a mausoleum—dark walls rose to a high ceiling and the hard marble floor had no rugs to soften your footsteps.

No art hung on the walls. Nothing personal, except the brass plate that marked his home office. The place she'd been called into for every grade less than an A. Every infraction—real or perceived. Her grandfather behind the big desk, berating her for being too much like her father.

She instinctively rose to her toes to keep her heels from striking the marble.

Walk softly. Don't rush about so. Children should be seen and not heard. Hush, a young lady should speak gently.

The refrains of her childhood. Nicky made her way up the stairs, wishing she'd been able to find something, anything other than this. She'd asked about staying in the pottery studio her father had installed in the carriage house out back. Gramps refused.

If Nicky were in a self-reflective mood, she might admit that her questionable relationship with her grandfather went a long way toward explaining her complicated thing with preppy guys. Like her first boyfriend. Or Jeremy. Or the guy from the coffee shop.

Feeling childish, Nicky turned and glared at the closed office door, then stuck her tongue out at the brass plate bearing the name of one Dr. Richard Mason.

TY—MONDAY, APRIL 8

Several rounds of one on one with Deke over the weekend had left Ty with aching muscles. A point driven home when he hauled open the heavy coffee shop door. It had done nothing to get his mind off Nicky-with-a-Y. He scanned the shop and saw a sea of beige and gray and denim. No Technicolor pixie-like woman.

Ty was about to open his mouth, ask Gabe and Jace if she ever came in, when the door opened again. He didn't need to turn to look. He knew.

"Morning!" How on earth was anyone that cheery on a Monday? "And good morning to you."

Her smile broadened, crinkling her eyes in the corners. The blue streak seemed a little lighter today. The impossibly bright yellow coat flung over her arm and of course, the matching Doc Martens on her feet.

"Happy Monday." *Where did that shit come from?* This woman turned him into a clueless teenager. Her smile got even wider, then turned into a laugh.

"I like Mondays. It's a fresh start to the week. You've had the weekend to decompress and let go of anything negative."

She shot him a sidelong look. "Did you get to unwind? You seemed a little on edge Friday night."

Of course, she would remember that. "I should have been working, but you're right, sometimes you need time off. I caught up with friends, played a little ball. It felt good to relax. What about you?"

Ty kicked himself. What would he talk about next, the weather? Nicky didn't seem to mind the inane conversation starter. She gave a little wave of her hand—so-so.

"A very social weekend. The Friday night fiasco was followed by a staff event on Saturday." She took a moment to place her coffee order, poring over the pastry case as if there was something new or different in there. As if life, to Nicky, was one big opportunity for wonder.

"I need to find time and space to set my easel up," she continued when she turned back to him. "Maybe once I find full-time work and a place of my own, I'll look for a studio space."

There it was—the perfect opening to get more personal.

"Or a live-work place. They're all over Baltimore."

Her face clouded for a moment before she closed her eyes for a breath. When she opened them again, it was back to a cheery, open expression. Huh. Maybe all was not sunshine and roses.

"In a perfect world." Her smile quirked up on one side and her eyes gave a half roll. Maybe art wasn't a safe topic. Oh well, he'd opened this box, and dammit, he was curious, in spite of himself.

"What do you paint? I assume you paint, with the easel and all."

"I do," she replied with a grin. "A little of everything, really. My abstract oils sell well in my Etsy shop. But my biggest business is pen and ink pinup art."

The smile that curled her lips made Ty wish he could hang around, but he had a meeting to get to. He picked up his order from Gabe and waved at Nicky before heading out the door. Fifteen minutes later, he sat in his boss' austere office, mentally kicking himself for not introducing himself—and getting her name in return. He held back a groan as Richard Mason's voice penetrated his brain.

"I want you to set up a fundraiser at the retirement party."

He'd been warned that Mason was a hard ass who demanded a lot from his subordinates. The man also thought everyone was at his beck and call, whether or not they worked for him. Still, he was likely the fastest route to Ty's goals, so he held his tongue.

Besides, tying donations to a retirement event made sense. The donors got their tax write off, the museum got the funds, and the retiree got a nice tribute.

"Are you bringing anyone to the event?" The question nearly made Ty choke on a swallow of coffee.

"Um... No, I wasn't planning to."

He crossed his fingers that Mason would not suggest he needed a date—to look respectable, or something like that.

"Good."

Well, that was a surprise.

"Mixing social and professional life is unavoidable in this business. Sometimes, it's best to attend alone."

That plan was just fine with Ty. His career was one big reason he didn't date. All but the most casual relationships chafed at not being invited to social events that for him were all about work. He didn't have time or attention to give to anyone else when he was working, and that always caused disappointment or resentment.

Mason flipped his wrist and gave his watch a quick glance. "I've got to cut this short, I'm afraid. Coordinate with

Lizabeth so she can get the fundraiser up on the webpage as well."

He was on the phone before Ty could rise from his chair. He sketched a quick salute and went off in search of Mason's assistant. *Might as well get this over with. This is going to be a long week.*

CHAPTER 4

NICKY—TUESDAY, APRIL 9

"Hey, you're becoming a regular." Jace, the ever-patient clerk at Ceremony, flashed a smile. "What can we make for you?"

Nicky breathed in the coffee-scented air and leaned over the pastry case. She needed the caffeine as much as she needed out of her grandfather's house, so she'd decided a cup of coffee was a reasonable indulgence. And maybe a pastry. She'd also decided that this choice had nothing to do with Joe Preppy, but she should at least get his name.

She pointed to a bar filled with nuts and dried fruit. "One of those, and something that would go with it. Surprise me." Jace nodded and said something to Gabe then poked a few things on the register before quoting an amount that didn't have Nicky cringing.

In no time, Gabe slid a cup across the counter. "Caramel praline and cardamom. I think you'll like it." They turned back to wiping down the espresso machine.

Jace's head twitched toward the door, but Nicky had

already caught a flash of perfectly put together outfit and knew it had to be him.

Something about him made all her senses came alive. His hair was still damp as if from the shower and the scent of nutmeg and pepper enveloped her as he passed by. The same scent that had been on the scarf he'd loaned her. She'd noticed it on him yesterday as well. It had to be his cologne. Or maybe his soap. Either way, she liked it.

"Good morning." That warm, rich voice carried in the open space and Nicky turned to watch him pay for his order—an Americano and an oatmeal cookie, plus four more cookies and a bunch of coffees to go—Jace hadn't even asked what he was getting.

Joe Preppy may be hot as hell, but he seems as predictable as time.

Which was a damn good reason to rein in the silly fascination she had with him instead of admiring his gray suit and crisp white shirt with cufflinks that glinted as he reached for his coffee.

He turned to Nicky and flashed that megawatt smile, pulling her from the examination of his wardrobe.

"And good morning to you." He headed toward the door, giving Nicky a moment of panic, fearing she'd missed the chance to ask his name. Not that she should care what his name was.

Then he paused, turned back to her, and arched an eyebrow. The effect was devastating. "Got anything big going on today?"

Nicky shook herself, grabbed her pastry, then took the half-dozen steps needed to bring her next to him.

"Just work," she replied. She looked up—he was tall. A bit over six feet, she'd guess. And so handsome. And so not her type.

"I keep seeing you around. It's pretty clear you either work or live around here. Maybe both." She was babbling. Nicky took a deep breath, screwed up her courage, and stuck her right hand out. "Hi, I'm Nicky Bissett."

A smile twisted one corner of his mouth upward. He balanced his coffee and the cookies on top of the drink carrier in a precarious tower and took her hand. "Ty Lake. Nice to meet you."

She gave a quick squeeze, careful to avoid toppling the cookie-coffee Jenga going on in his other hand, then let go. Nicky opened the door and held it for him.

Outside, she pulled her sunglasses down over her eyes, letting the door swing shut behind them. He was re-stacking the coffee tower, squinting in the bright spring sunshine.

"Hang on." Nicky hooked a finger into the bow of the glasses sticking out of his suit coat pocket.

The sun turned his eyes a pale, translucent jade shot through with veins of deeper green that radiated from his pupils. Nicky took a step closer as she unfolded his shades one-handed then reached up to settle them on his face.

Her fingers brushed his cheek, and the brief contact made her skin tingle. *Oh hello. That's unexpected.* Ty's lips parted in a gasp and Nicky stepped back. Whatever spark she felt, it looked like he felt it, too.

Nope. Not thinking about sparks with this guy.

"Five coffees and a bag of cookies. Is that your order every day?"

His eyes were hidden behind the mirrored aviators she'd just put on him—of course he wore aviators—but color flushed his cheeks. Was the man blushing? Then his smile bloomed.

"I get them for the front desk and security on duty. It's a little thank you."

Great. So, Joe Preppy—no, Ty—was hot, and chivalrous, and sweet. He was still probably just as uptight and straight as his tie. A silvery thing with a darker gray stripe. His suits were always dark colors—blue, gray, black. His ties and pocket squares, though, they had some flash. Today the pocket square was a purple paisley, and like always, he looked like he'd stepped off the pages of a fashion magazine.

They reached the sidewalk and with nowhere to be for another couple hours, Nicky turned and walked with him down the street. He moved to the outside of the pavement and adjusted his stride.

"If it's not too personal, what do you do for work?"

She chuffed a laugh at the apparent similar pattern of their thoughts. She'd been racking her brain trying to figure out what sort of job required a suit and cufflinks.

"I'm teaching part time at the American Visionary Art Museum." She braced herself for a polite reaction. Instead, he gave her a genuine and bright smile.

"Not surprised. First time I saw you, I thought you were a MICA student."

That made her laugh. She had attended the Maryland Institute College of Art, despite her grandfather's refusal to help with tuition. Which was what led her to busting her ass to pay her way. And gave Jeremy the fuel to get her fired, but Ty didn't need to know any of that. Ever.

"The paint stains kinda give it away, I guess." She waved a hand at her bag.

Ty gave a crooked smile and lifted one eyebrow. "You think?"

"What about you?" If she had to guess, she'd say an attorney. Or an accountant. Or something like that.

Ty tipped his head at the big building on the corner. "That's the office."

Nicky's breath caught in her throat. The Walters Art Museum. It was a place of respite, but also conflict. Hours spent sketching or doing homework in the museum were hours away from the cold house.

"I handle a lot of the fundraising and work with donors."

Oh no. Oh hell no. That means he knows Gramps.

Nicky suppressed a shudder. Well, she wasn't interested in Joe Preppy, anyway. She plastered a smile on her face and zipped her coat against a sudden chill that had nothing to do with the brisk April wind.

"Cool job." She cast a glance down at her watch. "Oh crap! I've gotta run. See you around."

She caught his raised eyebrows and startled expression before she darted across the street. A tide of disappointment surged through her. He was hot and nice, and she'd enjoyed talking to him. Not to mention whatever chemistry they seemed to have. None of that mattered. The perfectly pressed suit should have been a clue—Ty Lake was not her type.

Well. Shit.

TY

The sway of her hips as she hurried down the street set the bright purple skirt in motion and Ty was mesmerized. Something he'd said had changed her. It was like a door slammed closed over her face and her once open and friendly expression turned flat and distant.

All he'd done was tell her where he worked. Not that it mattered. He wasn't looking for a relationship to complicate his already over-scheduled life. Still, there was no denying he was attracted, and more than that, he'd enjoyed Nicky's company.

He dropped the cookies and coffees at the security desk

and headed straight for Mason's office. The director was out, but Lizabeth had roped Ty into helping her prep a few things for the upcoming event.

Not exactly the best use of his time, but it seemed to be what Mason wanted. Unfortunately, it wasn't consuming enough to keep his mind from churning over how Nicky had practically bolted when she found out where he worked.

After lunch, Ty knocked off early and headed for the gym, hoping a workout would take his mind off of her.

"You still mooning over cute and quirky?" Deke's eyes were glued to the mirror, watching his form as he did curls. He rigorously maintained a physique that was ripped, but not too ripped. Girl bait, he used to call it. And it worked.

Ty flipped him off as he wiped down the weight machine. He worked out to keep from looking like a string bean. One of the best things he'd learned in lacrosse—a good diet and working out were the difference between skinny and lean.

Fuck, who the hell is she?

"Dunno who you're talking about," he lied before straddling the lat pull down machine. His friend was so focused on his biceps that he missed Ty's line of bullshit.

Deke racked his weights and leaned onto the machine next to Ty. "You're a terrible liar. Always have been. Spill."

So much for Deke missing something.

"It's the quirky part that has me hung up," Ty grumbled. "That is not my norm."

Deke practically burst into laughter. "So what, man? Nothing wrong with friends with benefits."

Ty fired off a set of reps, but every inhale called up the sharp intake of breath she'd made when he told her where he worked. Every time he blew out a breath, he felt the sucker punch to his solar plexus when she'd walked away.

"Screw that," Ty replied. "I want more than that. I'm not

in a hurry to settle down or anything. I've got too much going on, but I don't want disposable relationships."

"Man, whatever." Deke shoved away from the machine, uncrossing his arms. "Get over it. You've got that work thing coming up. Take a date."

"Can't," Ty grunted out the word as he did another set of reps. "I'm gonna be working and the boss made it clear I should come alone."

He finished his set and wiped the machine. "I'm gonna hit the cardio room."

He didn't need Deke pestering him to get laid. Or about Nicky. He got the treadmill set up and cranked it up to a run, but thoughts of her would not let go. He brought the speed back down and thumbed his phone browser open and searched for Nicky Bissett. An Etsy page with her name on it was the first result. He tapped the link and scrolled to her About page.

An art degree from MICA. *Impressive.* A handful of awards, some prestigious. A list of previous events, but nothing upcoming. No website or blog. Nothing personal.

Her Insta account was an echo of her Etsy—images of her artwork. Plus, some in progress and behind-the-scenes shots. One that fascinated him was a plaster torso mold she'd done, painted in intricate patterns, then shattered and put everything back together—only slightly wrong. It was beautiful and oddly disquieting.

That was the extent of her online presence. A carefully curated, narrowly focused window that revealed nothing except that she was a very talented artist who did a lot more than paint and draw pinups.

"Who the hell are you, Nicky Bissett?"

CHAPTER 5

NICKY—THURSDAY, APRIL 11

The brownstone's steps loomed large and imposing. Nicky glanced down at her paint-splattered clothing—most of it old stains that had been through multiple washes. The kind of things she kept on hand for certain classes.

"Well," she spoke at the imposing front door. "Maybe if I run for the stairs."

The shrill whistle of the teakettle punctuated the air as Nicky stepped into the hall, spurring her to move faster. Her chances of getting upstairs unnoticed grew slimmer by the second.

"I put you down for tomorrow's event since you can't seem to be bothered to RSVP. I hope you'll at least tone down the ridiculous streak in your hair. There will be people there I think you should meet. It will do you some good to make decent connections in the serious art world for once."

His voice carried in the still house and Nicky instinctively made herself smaller, softened her footfalls and prayed he would stay in the kitchen.

"What in the world?" Richard Mason stood in the dining-room door, a cup of tea in one hand while he gestured at Nicky with the other. "Don't even think of climbing those stairs until you've cleaned some of that mess off."

"I was teaching a large-format painting class today. It's all dry. I won't get paint on the carpet or the woodwork."

His mouth turned down in an expression of distaste. *You'd have thought I offered him a jellyfish to hold.*

"Moira." He breathed out as a sigh as he shook his head. "I cannot understand why you insist on refusing to apply to local schools and instead are doing things where you come home looking like... like..." He waved his hand at her again.

She had thought she was prepared for her grandfather's quirks, but his criticism was never ending. She planned to stay with him only until she had a solid job and rebuilt her savings enough to manage a place of her own. While she appreciated the free rent—free was a relative term.

"Whatever you think of it, this is my job. It's in a field I enjoy, and I love every day I go to work."

"You are a babysitter and not making anywhere near enough to live on." His words sliced into the air, and then he laughed. Actually laughed. Had he always been this heartless and cruel? "You are far too much like your father. Were your mother still alive, she'd say the same things."

Nicky clamped her mouth shut over the desire to yell at him. She had believed that maybe she and her grandfather could rebuild a positive relationship.

"You and your father both refuse to use your skills for anything substantial, and he tried to drag Coco down that same path. His idea of a career consisted of making pottery to sell at local craft fairs. Instead of doing something with himself, he was content to play with mud."

Her parents divorced when she was six, and her mother packed up their small apartment and moved them back to this house where Nicky's childhood promptly died. The last time she had seen her father was at her ninth birthday party.

She hauled in a slow breath and blew it out on a count of ten and then repeated. She would not take her grandfather's bait. She would not sink to his level.

"I will not have this conversation with you. Enjoy your tea." Nicky hefted her bag and made for the stairs.

"Where are you going, young lady?" The ring of authority in her grandfather's voice gave her a half second pause, but Nicky squared her shoulders, turned, and looked him directly in the eye before she answered.

She waved her hand at her clothes. "Unless you want me to hose off outside, I need to go upstairs to change and shower."

Nicky pounded up the steps without waiting for a response.

"Come back here." His voice echoed in the room and she cringed. Yeah. That she remembered. Her grandfather, always scowling. Always grumpy.

"Or what?" She muttered the words as she flung open her bedroom door and slammed it behind her, thankful the tears waited until she was safely in the room.

She had to find somewhere else to live, but all she could afford right now was a room, and she'd have no space to make art. No, she needed more hours, or a second job so she could find a place where she could put up her easel. She needed that income.

A sob wrenched through her, the sound rough and ragged

in the still air. Not for the first time, Nicky questioned the wisdom of coming here, but she'd made this choice, and she had to make the most of it.

35

CHAPTER 6

TY—FRIDAY, APRIL 12

A shock of bright blue caught Ty's attention. In a sea of black evening wear, the vivid color stood out. He angled his head, trying to get a better view. He could only think of one person daring enough to wear that shade. Nicky.

She'd been on his mind all night. Hell, all week. Ever since her abrupt departure on Tuesday. He'd seen her in the coffee shop occasionally and they exchanged polite good mornings, but that was it.

He excused himself from the group before anyone started in on another anecdote about Chris Fields. He wove his way through the crowd, intent on finding her. Her laughter chimed above the hum of chatter in the room and he turned.

She'd swept her hair into a sleek high ponytail, and the usually bright streak seemed toned down—a deep blue that subtly blended into her dark brown hair and complemented the shimmering brocade she wore. Traces of an intricate floral tattoo peeked out at her shoulder, making Ty wonder how far down it went. But it was her wide eyes and full mouth that held his attention.

When she'd tugged his sunglasses from his jacket and put them on for him, he'd read that as an invitation to flirt. Everything pointed to interest. Maybe he was wrong, but he didn't think so.

She left whatever conversation she'd been having and leaned against one of the big pillars, looking for all the world like she was at home. Ty offered his best smile as he approached.

"After our abbreviated conversation on Tuesday, I assumed you weren't a fan of this place."

Her eyes traveled up his body, clearly assessing. It wasn't the first time he'd caught her checking him out. He stuffed his hands in his pockets and waited for her to get to his face. Then he winked. She rolled her eyes, but her lips curled into a smile.

"I love the museum." She beckoned him closer. "Even if there are some mixed feelings."

That felt like a huge opening to learn more about her, but before he could say anything, Richard Mason's voice boomed into their little bubble.

"Tyler, I see you've met my granddaughter, Moira Bissett."

Nicky's eyes narrowed and a look of irritation flashed over her features as he processed Mason's words. *His granddaughter?* This fairytale creature was related to a man who thought navy blue was quite daring enough, thank you very much?

Not good. Shit. Though it explained a lot.

"I was just saying how good it was to see him again." Nicky flashed a dazzling smile at Ty. Screw everything else. He wanted to see her smiling like that more often—at him.

Mason looked confused for half a moment. "Oh, you are acquainted?"

"We see each other at Ceremony Coffee pretty regularly." Ty cut his eyes to Nicky and caught the subtle amusement on her face.

"Moira moved to DC shortly after college, but now she's back in Baltimore. I keep trying to convince her to pursue graduate work at Hopkins, but apparently, she has no inclination for proper education or serious studies." He sighed, effectively communicating this was a great weight upon his soul.

Nicky's lips pressed tightly together as if she was biting her tongue.

"Oh, we've never talked about college. Nicky's online portfolio said something about MICA, I believe. Is that right?" Richard Mason be damned; Ty wasn't about to call her Moira when she chose to go by something else.

"Combined BFA and master's in education at MICA." Nicky shot her grandfather a tight grin before looking back at Ty. "How about you?"

He leaned in close and pitched his voice low. "Yes, I googled you. Love your work, by the way, and I went to Hopkins, I'm afraid." He straightened up and included Mason in the rest. "I'm a Baltimore kid, through and through. I wanted to be an archeologist, but the moment I realized you could make your living by helping keep places like this alive?" He spread his hands wide and looked around the broad marble sculpture court. "Well... here I am."

Mason held his glass out toward Nicky. "I need a refill. Moira, would you be so kind?" He wiggled the glass when she didn't take it from him.

Nicky flagged down a passing server, snagged Mason's glass and dropped it onto the tray. "Dr. Mason needs another Scotch and soda, please." The server took off like a shot and Nicky turned back to them with a pleasant smile.

"Ty, it was nice to see you again." Then she turned on her grandfather and the smile dropped. "If you'll excuse me, I've got networking to do."

She didn't huff off, but it was a damn close thing. Ty ignored Mason's apologies for his granddaughter's behavior; he was too busy trying to track where she went in the crowd.

"She can be quite bright and charming," Mason said. "When she wants to be. Unfortunately, she's also impetuous and prone to frivolity. I was hoping moving back home would convince her to change."

As far as Ty could tell, Nicky was a force of nature and he'd have better luck trying to convince the sun to rise in the west. Mason pointed out an older couple and insisted Ty should meet them.

One conversation led to another, and another, and it went on for over an hour before he could extricate himself from Mason. Though it was an hour well spent, Ty had been on autopilot. His brain was too busy mulling over how to salvage his budding friendship with Nicky.

He chewed his lower lip as he slipped into the quieter space at the perimeter of the room.

She sat on the bench furthest from the festivities. Her sandals on the floor and her feet tucked up under her. He was struck again by how comfortable she looked. Ty sipped his drink and contemplated the stunning woman in front of him.

His original assessment of quirky and perky held. She was also bright and funny, with a quick wit that could lean to sarcasm.

Even at a formal event, tamed down from her usual, she could have been at a fairy convention. Hell, she could have been a fairy—just give her wings. Or an elf. Or pixie. The only thing he was sure of was that she could not possibly be of this world.

He didn't know what kind of bad blood circulated between her and Mason, but it was clear there was a lot of it.

Which sucked. Because Ty was enthralled. Getting himself involved with his boss' granddaughter seemed like a bad idea on a good day. Considering their complicated relationship, one wrong step could end his career in a snap of Richard Mason's fingers. Ty dropped his empty glass on a nearby table and moved closer.

She tipped her head back to rest against the wall and her eyes caught his. Even in the soft light, he caught the flash of sadness before her face transformed into a neutral expression.

"Mind if I join you?" Ty gestured at the bench next to her. She lifted her head and looked around at the empty benches nearby. Then she slid her feet further out of sight—how she managed that in the form-fitting dress, he had no idea.

"Knock yourself out." Her head sank back, but her eyes stayed on him as he sat, carefully keeping a polite distance.

He needed to know just how deep that rift was. She was like some sparkly creature who suddenly made him realize how gray and dull his world was.

"I thought we were developing a friendship..." Ty paused. A pleasantly blank look seemed bolted onto her face as if concealing anything real or true underneath. He'd tried telling himself she wasn't his type, but he didn't know what his type was anymore. What he did know is he enjoyed the times he'd been around her and her brand of perky, and until she'd found out where he worked, he felt confident the feeling was mutual.

"I'm sorry if I did or said something wrong, but I don't think that's it. I'm thinking it's got something to do with that guy." He pointed across the room where Mason was just visible among a group of guests. Her cool expression didn't budge. Not even a flicker to let him know if he was hot or cold.

"Here's the deal." He leaned forward, still careful not to encroach on her space. "Unless one of us finds a new coffee shop or changes our schedules—which I don't see happening—we're going to keep seeing each other. I don't know about you, but I think our conversations are a great start to the day."

A minuscule crack formed in the stone of her face. Tiny. A barely perceptible lift of the corner of her lips. He risked continuing. "Everyone can use a friend."

The crack widened, softening her eyes. "I'll give you points for not calling me Moira after that's how he introduced me."

A cool hand landed on his and her pale blue eyes locked on his face.

"You didn't do or say anything wrong. That's all on me. And him." Her hand retreated, and Ty resisted the urge to grab it back and hold on until she spilled her story. Even sitting curled on a narrow bench, clearly hiding from her grandfather, she radiated confidence. Like she knew who she was and was comfortable with it.

She bent forward and slipped her shoes back on her feet with a grimace. "I'm going to call it a night." She rose and brushed imaginary wrinkles from her dress. "I'll catch holy hell for it, but tomorrow is a big meeting for the Kinetic Sculpture Race." Something in her face triggered every protective instinct he'd ever known, and then some. Even as he was cringing over the idea of the strange race that was a Baltimore tradition.

"Why not take a tour of the upcoming exhibit with me?"

A look of concern crossed her face, then she sighed. "You sure you want to risk that? Because a certain someone will hear about it." A short laugh escaped her lips. "I'm used to his attitudes. Are you?"

"I'll manage." He stood and offered his arm. Nicky tucked her hand into the crook of his elbow. "Maybe if we cut through the Ancient World and take the stairs on that side, he won't notice."

NICKY

She wanted to tell him they had a snowball's chance in hell of her grandfather not noticing his Golden Boy taking off with his wayward granddaughter, but Ty's laughter was infectious and she found herself grinning along with him. And the route he suggested would bypass the main lobby, which meant maybe it was possible.

They slipped out the doors and miraculously found few people outside the sculpture court. Ty navigated through the dimly lit space like he'd done this all before. He'd just opened the stairwell door when a passing security guard shone his light on them and Nicky's breath stilled in her chest.

"I'm sorry, folks, this part of the museum is closed during the... Oh. Sorry." The light switched off. "Mister Lake, I didn't realize it was you."

Well, there's a first.

In the past, the staff would have recognized her—it was a coin toss whether they'd report her to her grandfather or quietly admonish her to be more careful before pretending they didn't see her.

The guard walked away. Nicky blew out a breath that turned into a laugh as they made their way along the stairs. When they came into the special exhibit hall, Ty pulled his phone out and hit the flashlight, illuminating a colorful model of a castle sitting on a field of green and a leaping cat in boots coming through the gate.

"Walter Wick." Nicky took her own phone out and lit up the wall. More of Wick's fantastical images, some with models, stretched the length of the gallery. They strolled along the brightly colored space, admiring the images and models.

"Everything isn't always so serious here," Ty said. "This exhibit has been making the rounds and it's very popular. We lucked into being able to schedule it around spring break, so we anticipate a lot of families coming in, plus there's a day camp for kids."

Nicky skimmed the placards—someone had done a good job including a gold mine of educational information. Not that it should be surprising. This wasn't the first time the author had produced an educational retrospective of his work. She'd attended one while in college, and had toured his studio in Vermont.

Ty stopped in front of the Jolly Roger from *Can You See What I See?* He leaned down, taking a closer look. A tux was never high on Nicky's list of hot looks for a man, mostly because she associated them with boring. Seeing Ty in one was enough to change her opinion. She had to resist the urge to highlight his ass with her phone's flashlight.

"I grew up on these books," Ty said as he straightened. There was a look of childlike glee on his face that she wished she could capture. Her grandfather saw exhibits like this as pandering to the masses, but Ty was delighting in it. Maybe she'd judged him wrong. Very wrong.

"So did I," she replied. "They're fun. They're also full of combinations of art and science—like forced perspective. I use Wick's work frequently when teaching young children, and their parents, about art. He's a very accessible introduction to the art world."

She expected Ty to scoff at that. Instead, he nodded. "I can see that."

He turned to her with a small smile. "I was serious earlier.

When I said everyone can use a friend. No ulterior motives. No expectations. Just... I like your company."

The instinct to say something sarcastic rose up and Nicky clamped her mouth shut before something like "yeah right" could slip out. Guys who looked like Ty were not the type to accept platonic friendships with women. Never mind the fact that some not-so-buried part of her was all for things being very non-platonic with Ty.

"No ulterior motives what-so-ever, huh?"

His smile shone bright even in the dark exhibit. "Motives and desires are two different things."

"Are they really?" She crossed to a bench situated next to what looked like an interactive exhibit for young children. Hard to tell in the dark.

"Related, sure," he replied as he sat next to her. "Desire is what you want. Motive stems from that. It's the transformation from desire to action."

What she desired right now was to take her shoes off and swap out for the flats in her bag. But that was in coat check and that meant going into the main lobby, and by the sounds drifting through the echoing space, people were starting to leave. Plus, she was enjoying the banter.

"I see your point," she replied. "What about the ulterior part? No hidden agenda?"

Ty spread his hands out and adopted a look of innocence. "Would you believe me if I said no?"

Nicky gave it a moment of thought. Or at least pretended to. Then shook her head.

"I'm not much of a hidden agenda type," he replied. "I prefer being open and straight forward, just like I've been with you tonight."

Their fingers brushed on the bench and a gasp escaped Nicky's lips. Ty's just-right cocky smile had disappeared.

Instead, he was looking intently at her as if he was about to lean in for a kiss. Despite all her misgivings, the idea of kissing him was appealing.

He shifted closer and Nicky tipped her head back. They were angled so perfectly, if she leaned forward, their lips would meet.

And oh, how she wanted that.

A light flashed near the exhibit entrance.

"I'm sorry folks, that area is closed tonight."

Was it Nicky's imagination, or had the security guard spoken more loudly than needed?

A murmur of softer conversation followed and she felt rather than heard Ty chuckling. He leaned closer, but shifted to the side until his lips brushed the edge of her ear.

"Why don't we slip out the way we came in? I'm guessing you'd like to avoid all of that." He waved his hand toward the growing sounds coming from the lobby.

He stood and led the way back to the stairwell and through the Egyptian exhibits, then paused before they stepped into the more open spaces outside the sculpture court where her grandfather's voice rose above the murmur of the crowd. Nicky cringed and considered her options.

"You checked a coat? Give me the ticket." Ty held his hand out and Nicky didn't hesitate to pull the little tab from the tiny drawstring purse on her wrist.

"Coat and a black canvas backpack."

Ty nodded then pointed back the way they'd come. "Meet you by the emperor."

Before she could say another word, he stepped out and swiftly crossed the room. She lost him when a group of people spilled out of the sculpture court and crossed to the lobby stairs.

Nicky shrank back into the darkness and watched for

another minute before turning and making her way to the giant statue of a Roman emperor near the stained-glass window. She wasn't worried about anyone finding her in the exhibit, but she was worried Ty might run into her grandfather and then what would she do?

He was back before her fears could get out of hand. He held her bag out and Nicky rummaged inside to find her foldable flats, then kicked out of her sandals with a sigh of relief.

"Should have known better," she muttered as she slid her feet into the delicious comfort of soft, and flat, shoes. She tossed her sandals into the bag, then took it and her coat from Ty.

"How'd you manage to avoid being commandeered into service again?"

"He was wrapped up in conversation with the board president," Ty replied. "I got lucky and ran into a lovely lady who is a long-time patron. He saw me engaged in lively conversation with a woman who donates substantially every year. Even your grandfather wouldn't interrupt that."

Laughter bubbled up and Nicky clapped a hand over her mouth, though it was unlikely for the sound to carry that far.

"Now that you're in better shoes, let's get out of here." He held open the stairwell door, again. "How are you getting home? I assume you didn't take the scooter. We can..." he stopped and pushed a hand through his hair. The simple gesture somehow made him more attractive—or maybe it just made him seem more human and less like some unattainable pretty boy.

"I walked," Nicky replied. "I'm fine walking home. It's only a few blocks. It's as safe as you can get in Baltimore."

She took the lead this time, coming out of the stairwell then turning down a darkened hall to the back doors and crossing her fingers the exit onto Peabody Mews was still how security personnel left to take their smoke breaks. Still, she hesitated before opening the door.

"It's not alarmed until the whole place is locked down." Ty pushed the bar and propped the door open with his toe, then held her coat out for her to slip into before shrugging into his own camel overcoat. Spring was right around the corner, but the nights were still chilly. Nicky stepped into the alley and headed toward Cathedral Street.

"At least let me walk with you." Ty fell into step next to her and Nicky shrugged. If he wanted to walk along with her, she had no problem there. At the corner, a steady stream of people crossed to the parking lot across the street, but they turned the other way and slipped into the alley behind the hotel. Nicky waved at the valet staff as they passed. At the end of the alley, she turned right and continued up the narrow street rather than risk being on Monument where it was possible, if not likely, her grandfather would drive past.

She stopped behind the School for the Arts and turned to Ty. "I'm just around the corner to the north. I'll be fine."

"And I'm to the south. How about I walk you to the corner and watch to be sure you get in safely?"

It was a reasonable idea. A good one, in fact. And it wasn't like she had any reason to fear him knowing where she lived. His suggestion had seemed sweet rather than creepy.

"Sure." The impulse to hug him was nearly overwhelming, and after the briefest hesitation, Nicky did just that. It was a quick thing—she stepped closer and embraced him. She meant for it to be a quick thing. No lingering. No putting her head on his chest, even though she wanted to.

His hands brushed against her back and a sense of warmth flooded her, sending tingles down her arms that prickled her skin with arousal. The pressure of his touch pulled her in and

Ty's head dipped down. The scent of him surrounded her. Nothing existed except his touch and the desire to fuse her lips to his.

Nicky rose up on her toes and did just that. The flash of heat was like a white-hot ball of desire rolling through her body. Forget tingles. This was electric currents setting all of her nerve endings on fire.

She broke the kiss and stepped back before it consumed her. Ty looked as surprised as she felt, but there was no sign of conflict on his face. Even the dimly lit alley, she could read his look—she wasn't the only one aroused. She needed to get control of herself and quickly, before doing something she might regret.

"Thank you," she said. "For walking me home. For being so understanding of... well... everything."

Ty cleared his throat and blinked, then smiled slowly. He took her hand as they walked out the narrow lane together, taking the half block in comfortable silence. At the corner, Ty squeezed her hand, then let her go.

"I should be thanking you," he said and leaned in to kiss her cheek. "You made my night. I'll stay here until I see you get in the door."

Nicky nodded and headed up the street. The big brownstone was only a few houses up and she turned back to wave at Ty. He lifted his hand before heading south.

She pushed open the heavy door and crept through the entry toward the stairs. It was possible her grandfather wasn't home yet, but she had no desire to find out and ruin what had turned into a surprisingly good evening.

NICKY—SATURDAY, APRIL 13

Thin morning light cast long shadows on the street as Nicky strolled toward home. She'd gotten up early and had coffee and a breakfast treat at Ceremony to avoid running into her grandfather. If she'd timed everything right, he'd be gone by the time she got back. She paused on the corner, watching as a shiny black car pulled up in front of the house.

Perfect timing.

Richard Mason still drove, but if he was going somewhere in the city he was just as likely to call a car service. Today, he had a brunch scheduled, so he'd be gone for at least a couple of hours, leaving Nicky the run of the house and she wanted to find her mother's photo albums.

She'd learned years ago it wasn't a good idea to ask about photos of her dad, and she was sure her recollections of him were way off. Her mother had loved the feel of what she called a "real picture" and spent hours putting them in old-fashioned scrapbooks carefully labeled with names and dates.

Nicky hadn't seen any around the house, not even on the bookshelves in Gramps' office. Which meant going up to the attic. Not something she was going to do with him home.

After her father stopped coming around, her mother and grandfather set about methodically wiping every trace of Charles Bissett's existence from their lives. Within a year, it was as if he had never existed—except in Nicky's childhood memories.

Her grandfather descended the steps and climbed into the car, but Nicky waited until they were well down the street before finishing the walk and letting herself in. She felt a little ridiculous, going to such lengths to avoid her grandfather.

Just like I avoided him last night.

She climbed the stairs, trying not to think about the clean, peppery nutmeg smell that surrounded Ty, and the fact that it got stronger when he leaned in close to her. Nicky sighed. He was perfect. On the surface.

Every experience she'd had with preppy men and Ivy League looking types followed the same path—they seemed ideal. But their beauty was only skin deep. Underneath the polished veneer, they were rotten in one way or another. She didn't imagine Ty would be any different, despite his claims of having no hidden agenda.

She needed to find another coffee shop. Seeing Ty all the time would be torturing herself in a whole new and, she was sure, unhealthy way. Dude was too damn good looking and nice for his own good.

In the attic, she found a box of photo albums tucked on a shelf under the eaves in the furthest corner. She hauled it down and settled on the dusty floor directly under the overhead light and hefted the first album her fingers fell on. The once smooth leather cover crackled under her touch.

Years in the un-airconditioned space had not been kind. The book protested as she opened the cover.

Pages upon pages—young Nicky holding a painting she'd done at school, all smiles. Nicky and her grandfather at the museum—no smiles there. Her childhood unfolding. She turned the page and there her father was at her seventh birthday party. His hair was a mess and his clothes were covered in stains from either clay or paint, but he and Nicky wore matching grins.

There was only one with him on her ninth birthday. She remembered that one. He hadn't shown up until after everyone else had left. Until just before Nicky's bedtime. Looking at the photo through adult eyes, her smile seemed forced. She was already in her pajamas, her face tear stained and her eyes puffy. The tears had started the moment the last guest left. Her daddy had missed her birthday.

That was the last she'd seen him. At first, she asked every week—is this my weekend with Daddy? Then it was once a month—when is my weekend with Daddy? Eventually, she stopped asking.

Nicky tossed the album back into the box and dug out an older one to find the same patterns. Whatever image she'd crafted in her mind, of her father being a kind and loving man who was always happy and laughing didn't match what she saw in pictures. She slammed the book closed and looked to the ceiling, as if she'd find answers there.

She didn't know what she'd expected to find—some hint about why he left wasn't likely to be in the photo albums. Though her memories of her father were rosy, the pictures painted a different story.

She pulled all the books out and arranged them in order, then leafed through them again. Every now and then, she found a picture that showed the man she remembered—

unruly hair and a wide smile, as if he was ready to burst into laughter. But her adult eyes saw things her memory had erased, or maybe never noticed as a child.

He was often absent in photos of important events. And sure, he was smiling in posed photos with her, but in candids and other shots he looked distracted. As if he was a million miles away. Every image of him had something slightly off. He'd be in jeans when everyone else was dressed up. Or his smile seemed too wide. His eyes rarely looked into the camera.

Again and again, she studied the pictures, looking for the man of her memories and finding instead a stranger.

Nicky dug out an album she'd made, trying to emulate her mother's meticulous record keeping, and an envelope of loose images tumbled. She caught her breath as she flipped them over.

Blake Roth, her first boyfriend. Captain of the lacrosse team. A senior bound for Harvard in the fall. She'd been smitten when he suddenly started paying attention to her and her art during winter break of her junior year. The preppy types didn't usually look twice at her back then. But Blake had been cute. And seemed sweet. And kind. Or so she'd thought.

He was her first kiss. And later, the last day of Spring Break, her first everything. It was sweaty and fumbly and nothing like she'd imagined it would be—pressed into a musty sofa in his basement. They hadn't even undressed. He'd pushed her skirt up around her waist, and the zipper from his jeans dug into her thigh the whole time. He asked if she came, and she lied, said she had. And for the first time wondered what would happen to them when he left for college.

She'd made no other plans because Blake. Everything in her life had changed to revolve around him. Her grandfather loved him. And that spilled over onto Nicky. The proof was in the photos. Her grandfather, smiling as he stood with her and Blake on prom night.

She'd been an honor student. Won awards in science and art. Consistently had top grades. But nothing made him prouder than her on the arm of a young man destined for Harvard and on to law school. If she wouldn't pursue a doctoral degree herself, at least she should marry a man with one.

She and Blake had not ended well. At his graduation party, she'd found him in the basement with one of the cheerleaders.

When Nicky asked what was going on, he'd replied, "What do you expect? Why would I keep dating a girl like you? You look wild, but you're not, and that's the only reason a guy like me would go for you. Easy, fun, freaky sex. Did you think we were gonna get married or something?"

Something in her broke that day. She'd fled the basement and the party, and spent the next week in her room, furiously painting the pain away.

Nicky put the photos back into the envelope, unwilling to continue with those memories. The door opened downstairs, and she hastily shoved everything back into the box.

Shit.

She'd lost track of time on her walk down memory lane. She had no idea how her grandfather would react to her digging, and she didn't want to find out. Worse, her little impromptu trip into the past hadn't answered any questions except to prove to Nicky that the image she had of her father was not accurate.

Heavy steps echoed on the narrow stairs, and for a moment, Nicky considered hiding. Just as quickly, she deemed the idea silly and picked herself up. No way would she be on the floor covered in dust when her grandfather came in. She looked up and Gramps stood half in shadow, half in light, his face unreadable.

"You left the downstairs door open." His voice was softer than she was used to hearing. "I should have gotten rid of all of this ages ago."

He moved into the room; his face painted in a scowl as his eyes fell on the box at her feet. But there was sadness in his voice. Or resignation. Either way, two emotions she never associated with her grandfather.

"Why?" Nicky nudged the box with her toe. "Why get rid of history?"

Gramps reached up and loosened his tie, a heavy sigh escaping him. "To save you pain." Spoken so softly that Nicky couldn't think to argue.

"Your parents divorced when you were six," Gramps said. "Your father, ah... He was not very good with time. Or commitments. Or keeping promises. There are only so many times you can watch a child's disappointment and hurt."

He nodded at the box. "Wouldn't it be kinder, easier, to keep happy childhood memories, and not the evidence that things were not as good as you remembered?"

Maybe his words were meant to be kind, but to Nicky they cut into her heart.

"I grew up thinking he was good and sweet and fun and kind," she whispered. "And you and my mother had pushed him away."

Gramps bent and scooped up the box, placing it firmly back on the shelf where she'd found it. "And where did you get that notion, I wonder?"

He turned back to her with a smile that was almost kind, and more than a little sad. A scream welled up inside her, but Nicky stuffed it down.

"Oh, I don't know," she muttered. "Maybe your constant

criticism. Maybe Mom's. Maybe the fact that neither of you ever said anything good about the man. Even when I was a child. And yet here you stand telling me that it's kinder for me to not see the evidence that my father was..."

She threw up her hands and let out a frustrated sigh. "You know what. It doesn't matter. It's not like I've been living my life thinking you were some ogre. Just that we do not get along. I used to blame that on me being young. Teens are tough, especially one who's lost both their parents."

Gramps stuffed his hands into his pockets and rocked on his heels. A move that told Nicky she was probably not going to like what he was about to say.

"You're not wrong," he said, and Nicky about fell over. Then he opened his mouth again. "I'm not going to claim I was perfect, or blameless. Only that I did what I could. What I believed to be best. But you have to take some responsibility for the decisions that have you where you are right now and stop blaming your childhood, or your mother, or me... or even your father. I blame him quite enough for both of us."

Nicky swallowed the lump in her throat and a little spark of hope formed. Maybe she and Gramps could find common ground. Maybe they could get along.

"And I see too much of him in you," Gramps said, and the spark of hope died. Snuffed out in one sentence. "You have the power to change that. Or you can continue as you are. Your choice."

And with that, he strode out of the attic, every bit the authoritarian that had always made Nicky chafe.

Damn that man.

TY—WEDNESDAY, APRIL 17

It had been five days since the retirement party, and Ty hadn't seen Nicky since. He'd never been the take-it-slow type, but while he was eager to take Nicky to bed, and reasonably sure she was similarly inclined—the kiss they'd shared had been brief, but hinted at so much more. He also sensed some hesitancy from her, and in the past, that would have been his cue to bounce, but with her? He'd wait. Ty hurried down the street, hoping to catch her at Ceremony Coffee.

A shock of rich purple hair caught his eye as he walked up. Nicky sat perched on a stool at the long window counter, a tablet and notebook in front of her and phone to her ear and looking none too happy.

He asked Gabe to hold everything except his coffee and slid onto the stool next to Nicky. She tossed her phone down, her face registering a mix of disgust and frustration. He wanted to reach out and snag her hand, stroke her fingers, and tell her it would be okay. She triggered some protective instinct in him. Not that he imagined she'd appreciate it.

Instead, he tipped his head to look at her notes. Her beautiful penmanship made even a to-do list look like a hand-lettered invitation.

"Job hunting?" Stating the obvious, but hey, whatever it took to get her to open up.

She scratched the last item off her list then looked at him with a sad smile.

"I'm doing okay with the hours at AVAM, my Etsy shop, and a few pickup classes here and there, but only because I'm living rent free."

She let out a long sigh. "I'm sorry. I don't know why I'm dumping on you like that."

"It's all good. So..." He chewed his lip, uncertain whether

to bring it up, but why the hell not? "I have a friend at the Baltimore Office of Promotion and Arts. They've got a couple things coming up that haven't been posted yet. I'd be happy to connect you. If you'd like."

"Really?"

Nicky's pale eyes bored into him, as if examining his motives. It wasn't as if he wasn't doing a bit of that himself. Ty found Nicky attractive and amazing to be around. Maybe if they had a little fling, he'd get over this weird obsession he seemed to have developed.

So much for no ulterior motives.

"Really," he replied. "Give me your email. I'll drop you a note later today with details about the positions, and you can let me know if they seem like a good fit. Then I'll get you and Alex introduced."

"Thank you. I appreciate that." She rummaged in her bag and turned back to him with a business card in hand. Ty slipped it into his pocket.

"I'm assuming the rent-free situation is not a long-term solution?" The look she shot him made him wish he could unspeak the words. "Yeah, message received. Sorry."

She broke into a strained looking smile. "I'm staying with my grandfather."

The words hung in the air as if they were a challenge. His experience with the man was mixed. On the one hand, Ty recognized the advantage he had lucked into when Mason took an interest in his career. On the other, people either loved or hated the man, and no matter what he was like on a personal level, an adult moving in with their grandparent had to be rough.

"I don't even want to think about how challenging that must be."

That drew a laugh from her—sparkling and bright. "Let's

just say it's not been ideal. So, thank you. Whether this works out or not, I appreciate you taking the chance."

Ty shrugged. He was saved from further response by a group of boisterous young girls, one of whom must have recognized Nicky.

"Hey Ms. Nicky! Great hair!" A chorus of agreement from the other girls, and a few polite exchanges later and Nicky turned back to the table, grabbed her coffee, and thanked him again. The smile she gave him was so bright and genuine it made him catch his breath. He waved a hand like it was nothing, and it had been nothing.

"The purple does look great, by the way. Though the turquoise was nice as well. How often do you change it up?"

Her smile broadened, and she ran fingers through the bright strands. "Oh, I've got bottles of color under my bathroom sink. This was my pick me up after a bad interview. Gimme a couple weeks. It'll be some other color. I can't do purple in fall—everyone'd think it was for the Ravens." She made a face, then poked at his orange and cream pocket square. "Who knows? Maybe I'll try orange, but then everyone would think I'm an Orioles fan."

Hey! He was an Orioles fan. The season had just started, and the pocket square was his subtle way of showing off. He opened his mouth to complain, but she was already at the door.

CHAPTER 8

The narrow motorcycle parking was right where Alex had said—tucked away and tight against the building. Nicky maneuvered the Vespa into the spot and shucked her helmet. In less than a week, she'd gone from struggling to find work to starting an eight-week, part-time trial as a Bright StARTS Art Workshop and Arts for Learning instructor. Thanks to Ty.

The work was right up her alley, and enough to rebuild her savings so she could get out of her grandfather's place. There was a light at the end of the tunnel.

With only a few days to prepare for the class and a curriculum goal of blending art and engineering, Nicky had settled on crafting tiny brushbots and having a race—the perfect project for middle schoolers.

She took in a deep breath, unstrapped the box of supplies from the scooter's rear seat and marched into the youth center. Outside the classroom, a frazzled-looking woman with short, colorful braids sat at a table, checking the last of the kids in. She looked relieved when Nicky walked up.

"Oh good, you're here! I'm Becca. The other two helpers are in the room, keeping order. Do you need anything to start?"

The obvious anxiety in the woman's tone put Nicky on edge, but she swallowed that down and gave a shrug.

"The curriculum was pretty sparse, so I checked with Alex before finalizing my plans. I've got the important supplies in here." She hefted the box. Damn thing was getting heavy. "Fifteen students, right?"

"That's right. This is an afternoon enrichment program, so whatever you've got planned I'm sure is fine. Can I help?"

Nicky shifted the box and inclined her head to the door. "You can grab the door."

Becca leapt up and Nicky stepped into chaos. Even with the presence of the other two volunteers, the chattering of the students reached near deafening levels. She greeted the volunteers—Chris and Leigh—and enlisted their help to pull one large table front and center where she let the box of supplies drop with a clunk.

The decibel level in the room dropped several points, but Nicky paid no attention to the students. Instead, she rummaged in the supply cupboard and pulled out anything that could be used to personalize the bots. By the time she had unpacked the large box and spread its contents out alongside the scavenged art supplies, the classroom was silent.

Nicky surveyed the table. Perfect. She tucked the small box of tools aside for the volunteers. Finally, she turned her attention to the students. Fifteen faces stared back at her, expressions ranging from amused to curious. *So far, so good.*

"Hi! I'm Nicky. Today, we're going to combine engineering and art. Who can tell me about STEM?"

The class erupted in answers, including some pretty funny ones, until Nicky pointed at a boy in the back.

"It's science, tech, engineering, and math."

Nicky gave him a thumbs up. "Exactly. What about STEAM?"

The responses were a little slower this time. A girl in the front raised her hand.

"The A stands for Art?"

"Bingo! I believe that art is an important element. Art helps to boost creativity—even in the sciences."

She stepped behind the table and held up a handful of toothbrushes. "Today, we're going to focus on engineering, with maybe a little art."

She had their attention, but it was clear the students were skeptical.

"Outta toothbrushes?" The girl in front pointed to the objects in question with obvious distaste.

"Yep. What we're making today are brushbots. Or bristlebots."

Nicky held up the example she'd made over the weekend —a tiny brushbot decorated with feathers and sequins. Then she connected the battery and sent the bot buzzing in circles across the floor.

One girl laughed. Another squealed and lifted her feet from the floor as if it were a bug. The rest craned their heads to get a better look at the thing as it spun and skittered around.

"Eyes up front please," Nicky called out and took a deep breath as fifteen pairs of eyes looked at her with a new level of attention. She retrieved her bot and disconnected the battery before placing it on the table.

"Your creations don't have to be fancy. They just have to move." She handed out the single sheet of instructions then got the volunteers to set up three cutting stations to trim the toothbrush heads. Later, they'd do the same with the wires.

If this went quickly, they'd have plenty of time to do a race. The older students seemed bored as they read the instructions and came forward to collect their building supplies.

The entire process went smoother than it had any right to, and soon the students were back at their tables, sticking motors to toothbrush heads and testing their bots. The constant buzz of excited voices as the students settled into personalizing their creations was music to Nicky's ears.

Even Lisa, the girl who had mocked making anything out of toothbrushes, decided this was pretty cool once she discovered she could glitter her project as much as she wanted.

Nicky loved every moment. The only thing she liked better than creating was helping someone else learn to explore their own creativity.

Nicky glanced at her watch—plenty of time to do a race. "Okay, what do you say we build a racetrack for these bots?"

It took a few minutes and cardboard from the box she'd brought to construct a side-by-side lane, allowing two bots to race against each other.

"We'll do this in heats, so..." Nicky wheeled over the dry erase board and listed each student's name down one side, then drew a grid. "Winners go against winners, and we go until we have the grand champion. Let's fine tune this track."

She grabbed her bot and turned it on. "Our pace car," she said, and sent the bot down the right-side lane. It circled more than anything, so they narrowed the lane until the bot skittered along, bouncing off the walls to the end. "Okay, now we make the other lane match and test it out."

"But there's a lot of luck there." A younger student had

his bot cupped gently in his hand as if he was holding a butterfly.

"Shawn is right. There is some luck here. How your bot moves is impacted by how much of the handle you cut off, how much tape and glue you used, where you put the motor, and how you decorated it. So many variables."

She held up her bot with feathers waving everywhere. "Even something as light as a feather can change the bot's behavior."

That seemed to satisfy Shawn and everyone, so they started the races. It came down to Lisa and Shawn and a tense hush fell as their race began, the only sound the gentle hum of two tiny motors as the students all watched, rapt.

Nicky never imagined brushbots could tie, but they did. Then they did another run, and both fizzled out right after being put on the track.

"Guess we have two grand champions." Luckily, she had multiple of the little blue '#1' flags she'd figured on sticking on the winning bot.

She handed out extra batteries, starting with Lisa and Shawn, and got the students to clean up the racetrack just as class time ended. She and the volunteers got the room back in order and Chris and Leigh took off. Becca lingered, taking her time wiping down the whiteboard.

"You're good, but I knew you would be," Becca said as she turned to Nicky. "Alex said he was really excited about this new teacher, and I've gotta tell you, we see a lot come and go in this program. The inner-city kids can be a challenge. I wasn't sure, but my cousin said you'd be just fine."

Nicky blinked. "Alex is your cousin?"

"No," Becca said with a laugh. "Sabrina. Anne is on the board here. Funny thing, they'd already suggested Alex should reach out to you, then... well..." She broke off, her eyes and smile wide. "You are every bit as good as Sabrina said."

"Thanks." Nicky made a mental note to thank Sabrina later. "This is what I studied for. Well, not this specifically, but art and education."

"Yeah, but I've never seen an art teacher do robots," Becca insisted.

"You could think of them as kinetic sculptures. Or the pairing of art and engineering. Whatever it takes to get students thinking creatively and looking at art with fresh eyes and maybe even thinking it's fun and accessible."

Becca flicked the lights out as they left the room, then turned to Nicky and shook her hand. "Well, mission accomplished, and welcome aboard."

The light at the end of the tunnel got a little brighter. It had been a good class and Nicky felt confident this would go well. With this work plus the hours at AVAM, she'd be back on top of things in no time.

TY

"We don't have the resources at this time," Sebastian Knox explained, as if that was all the justification needed for putting repatriation talks off for another year. "You are doing a remarkable job, but this project is not a priority."

Ty screwed on his best smile. "Thank you. I appreciate the compliment, but I believe we should do full and transparent research into our assets. This is an important topic, and..."

Mason's hand landed on Ty's shoulder, cutting him off.

"You have to admire the enthusiasm of the young." Mason laughed as he steered Ty away. "If you'll excuse us," he said over his shoulder to Sebastian. Mason let go of Ty once in the hall and gestured for him to follow to the director's office.

The door closed with a resounding thud and Mason whirled on him. "Why on earth would you speak to the board president like that?"

Ty barely kept himself from cringing at the anger in Mason's tone. The director sat in his chair with a heavy sigh and leaned across his desk.

"He's right. You are doing a remarkable job. You know this is paving the way for a solid career path..."

He trailed off and Ty stifled a groan. "I get it. Pushing back against Sebastian is not a good way to ensure that goes smoothly."

"No, it is not. There are opportunities on the horizon that you are more than capable of and qualified for, but you are very young."

Well, this is an HR nightmare.

"Right now, the board sees you as progressive," Mason said. "To some, that's a good thing."

The implication was clear, and Ty allowed himself a short laugh. Mason relaxed his posture, looking less like a man about to give a lecture to a wayward child and more like a peer.

"So, I need to temper myself. Is that what I'm hearing?"

"That would help. Looking like you have a stable life aside from work and school would help. Most of the board members are older. They have families. They're invested in the community."

Though Ty was sailing through his PhD program, carrying the weight of essentially two full-time positions, and had a model curriculum vitae, he was still under thirty and single—both points against him with the current board. Mason's interest and support would offset the negatives and meant a possible fast track to his dream job. Hitting that steppingstone was worth a hell of a lot of grief in Ty's book.

"I understand."

Mason leaned back in his chair, his eyes narrowed and he looked Ty over, as if appraising. "I was concerned to see you spending so much time with Moira at the retirement event."

What the fuck does Nicky have to do with anything? Mason's fingers tapped out a rhythm on the desk and his lips pressed together in a thin line as if an unpleasant thought occurred.

"Moira is talented."

That was a surprise. Ty was under the impression Mason hated everything Nicky stood for.

"Like her father, she doesn't apply herself. She sets her sights too low. Far too low."

Dread coiled in Ty's gut like a cold snake as he hoped this wasn't going where he feared it was.

"The right partner can help present an image of a young man who is serious and invested in furthering art and education."

This was looking worse and worse. Ty opened his mouth, but Mason held up a hand, silencing him.

"If Moira could be turned around, she would be ideal. Her connection to me could be an added benefit. As it stands, her less than mainstream approach to the world would be problematic to a conservative board."

Every fiber of Ty's being rebelled at the idea that anything about Nicky could be problematic to anyone in the art world. Worse, at Mason's implication she needed to change. On the heels of that, the audacity of suggesting that who he dated could, or even should, influence his career track.

That brought him up cold.

Because as fucked up as it was, that was the reality. No amount of HR nightmare would change things.

Ty had goals and kept his eyes on the prize—as he always had. It was how he'd gotten through a double major undergrad in three years and completed his graduate in equally short time. He was the youngest doctoral candidate in the Museum Studies program, and almost finished with that.

"What do you suggest, sir?" The words hurt to say. They ripped at his insides, but he'd worry about that later. That was why he'd eschewed relationships anyway—his career came first. Still, she was like a ray of sunshine on a cloudy day, and he liked it.

"I'm not about to tell you who to date, but you need to sell yourself as the right man for the job, not just inside this office, but outside of it as well."

He wasn't sure if Mason meant he should give up pursuing Nicky or work to bring her into line. Both possibilities made Ty's stomach churn. Changing Nicky would be like trying to battle a wildfire with a squirt gun filled with gasoline. He was just as likely to wind up getting burned. All to present a palatable appearance to the board.

If this was the shit Nicky had grown up with, no wonder she got grumpy about her grandfather. Holy crap.

"I think I understand." At least he hoped he did. Not that he was sure what he was going to do with that understanding.

"I'm glad we're on the same page. Not surprising. I saw the potential in you from the first time I met you."

That praise would have once made Ty's soul soar. Today, it echoed hollow and left a bitter taste in his mouth.

Eyes on the prize.

CHAPTER 9

It was a little early for afternoon coffee, but Nicky had free time between classes and it was a gorgeous day. She grabbed a drink and a selection of individually wrapped mini cookies then headed to the park to find a spot that wasn't in full sun.

Ty sat on a shaded bench, ankle on knee, a book balanced in one hand. She should ignore him if for no reason other than he worked for her grandfather. Never mind the fact that she'd kissed him. If that brief contact was anything to go by, the sex would be out of this world. But then she came back to his connection to the museum. No thank you. Still, she should thank him for the job reference.

Her feet decided for her and crossed the grass. Resigned, and determined to do the polite thing, Nicky tapped his foot and waited for him to look up.

"Mind if I join you?"

The smile that brightened his face was nothing short of beautiful. *Where did that come from?* She'd already decided this guy was trouble. Not what she needed at all. She plunked herself down on the opposite side of the bench.

"Thank you for…"

"Did you get a chance to interview…"

They both spoke at once. Ty trailed off. "You first."

Nicky felt the heat rising to her cheeks, though why any of this should embarrass her, she hadn't a clue.

"I just wanted to thank you for connecting me to your friend." Nicky opened the bag of cookies and offered them. "I started yesterday."

He snagged a treat with a shy smile. "Thank you, and you're welcome. That's what I was about to ask. That's impressively fast. Congratulations."

The heat in her cheeks intensified. There was no reason for her to react this way to the most basic of things from him. She smiled her acknowledgment and unwrapped a cookie of her own, not trusting her voice to say anything.

Because what she really wanted to know was why she couldn't get him out of her head, and why, even though she'd sworn off preppy types, she had an almost irresistible urge to find out if he was always so buttoned up. Something told her he wasn't.

That was a side of him she wanted to get to know.

"Something amusing?" Ty's words interrupted the decidedly non-family-friendly direction of her thoughts and Nicky bit her lip as she looked up into his face. His smile creased the corners of his eyes, their green mimicked the springtime trees. A shaft of sunlight pierced the shade, shattering that illusion and turning his eyes back to their usual pale shade.

Nicky struggled to form words. Any words. She grasped for anything remotely intelligent to say. Her eyes settled on the book in his lap, his finger still tucked between the pages, holding his place.

"Studying?" *Wow, nothing like stating the obvious.* She leaned in and read the title aloud.

"*Contested Holdings: Museum Collections in Political, Epistemic and Artistic Processes of Return.*" Nicky sat back and smiled. "Not exactly sunny spring day in the park kind of reading, is it? I mean, I'm sure it's riveting."

Brilliant. She was a better conversationalist than this. Ty's smile only widened into a soft laugh as he slid a bookmark into place and tucked the book into his bag.

"I'm pursuing my PhD."

"What was your graduate work?" No sense in being rude. "I'd be expecting an MBA or something like that for what you do. Or are you considering a change of field?"

"Master's in museum studies. This is more a next steps kind of thing."

Nicky opened her mouth to ask what he meant, then dots connected as if by magic. "You're looking to become a museum director."

His expression was all the confirmation she needed.

"Your grandfather knows. He picked up on it pretty quickly, and has been encouraging, in his odd way."

Yeah, Gramps was good at that—when it was something he thought was worthwhile, he could be encouraging as all get out. Though that encouragement came with strings, demands and expectations. Not her problem. Ty could figure that part out on his own. Probably already had.

"Look, I know you two aren't close."

Nicky bit her tongue. He seemed like he was trying to be nice. Maybe he was different. And maybe pigs could fly. She mustered a chuckle and shook her head.

"Big understatement. You were saying?"

His eyes narrowed again, then he broke into that disarming megawatt smile.

"The same thing I said at the retirement party." His voice was soft, pitched low, and it wrapped around Nicky like a soft blanket. "I enjoy the time we've spent together, and I'd like to get to know you more."

TY

Something deep and convoluted hid behind Nicky's slow smile and guarded eyes. Getting to know her was going to be one hell of a tightrope walk, but Ty wasn't about to give up. Before he could form his next thought, she turned toward him on the bench, pinning him with a serious look.

"You working at the museum. Directly with my grandfather. It's a little awkward."

Her fingers twisted in her lap and her eyes darted between his and the trees above them. He took a slow breath and weighed his possible responses.

"I can see how you would feel that way. Do you have questions? Or specific concerns? Or..." He spread his hands and leaned forward, hoping she would open up.

Her gaze flicked to his, then back to the trees. She nibbled at a cookie and Ty nearly came undone as her eyes fluttered closed and a hum of pleasure escaped her. Nicky was yanking him from one extreme to another—from confused to aroused and horny as fuck.

She finished the last bite of cookie, eyes closing again as she savored the moment. Ty couldn't help but wonder if she approached every sensual experience with such abandon.

"There is a difference between being liked and being respected. My grandfather is very well respected, and I'm sure some find him likable. Where do you fall on that spectrum?"

The bluntness of her question surprised him. The trouble was his feelings had been shifting as he worked more closely with the man.

"True, Richard Mason is very well respected. The work he has done for the museum is invaluable, but you know that. You are also correct that some find him likable..." He cleared his throat and looked her directly in the eye. If he'd misread her at all, he was about to strike out. Big time. "I am not one of them."

Had he not been looking right at her; he would have missed the widening of her eyes and the way her lips curved into a one-sided smile before everything fell into an expression of polished neutrality. She arched an eyebrow—a move he suspected she'd practiced in the mirror more than a time or two, it was so perfect.

"Care to elaborate?"

"It would be a mistake to assume that just because I work with or have to associate with someone for my job, that I count them as a friend."

Her eyes narrowed. "That's evasive."

"A bit." Ty looked down at his untouched cookie, still wrapped in its bakery paper, then brought his gaze back to hers. "I'm not sure where you are going with this. I am sure that I enjoy your company and would like to continue to enjoy it—beyond just work mornings at the coffee shop. I believe that interest is mutual, but if it's not, I'll back off."

Her narrowed eyes opened wide in surprise and her lips cracked into a broad smile. "You're either really good at saying the right things, or you're some sort of imaginary creature."

"So, we're both being evasive." He took a risk with that one. She could take it the wrong way, but the smile that sparkled in her eyes said she hadn't.

"I guess so. Still no ulterior motives?"

"Nothing hidden about this." *Well, maybe one thing.*

His cock had ignored his brain and snapped to full attention. Ty shifted on the bench, desperate to ease that particular sensation. Ideally, without her noticing.

"Hmm." She didn't look convinced. "Is it enough to know the interest is mutual?"

"Yeah. That'll work." *For now.*

They made an odd pair. It was a warm day, he'd ditched the suit jacket, rolled up his sleeves and loosened his tie. She was in a colorful sundress that looked like something straight out of the '50s. Pretty, delicate lines of floral tattoos with washes of color that looked as if someone had painted her skin decorated her shoulders. Three earrings in both ears, plus one on the upper part of her left ear.

What other ink did she have? What other piercings?

He looked like Wall Street.

She was the picture of where edgy and alternative met fairytales and fantasy. In a word, stunning.

"I should have taken you up on that offer of a ride home."

"Caught a bad ride share?" The twinkle in her eyes held his attention.

"No, that was..." He pushed a hand through his hair, suddenly unsure of himself. "That was a clumsy change of topic, and an even worse attempt at flirting."

The twinkle didn't change. She leaned forward, getting close enough the smell of her perfume carried on the breeze. Something sweet and floral. "Is that what that was? Flirting?"

Ty swallowed hard. She was so close, if he inclined his head, he could kiss her, and oh how he wanted to. Again. And preferably longer and more thoroughly than before. It would be easy to read the look on her face as an invitation, but he wasn't sure, so he restrained himself.

"Would you like to go out?" He swallowed again. "Maybe Saturday night?"

She blinked. Once. Twice. Her lips curled into a tight smile. She was going to say no. He'd overstepped his bounds and he'd have to apologize. He didn't want to make her uncomfortable.

"I have a class in the morning, and some errands in the afternoon, but yeah. I'd like that."

His eyes snapped to hers—bright blue and sparkling. He stumbled over what to say next. Suddenly feeling like he was sixteen again and uncertain how to impress the girl he was interested in.

"Yeah, okay." *Suave. Real smooth.* "Good. Cool. Uhh... I have your number. I mean if that doesn't work..."

She chuckled. "Saturday evening is fine."

What the hell was wrong with him? He wasn't normally tongue tied around women. "Dinner it is, then."

Her hand landed on his, squeezed, then retreated and that brief contact sent his blood rushing south. Again.

"Just text me a time, and I guess whether we're driving or walking or ride sharing, or what. I've got another class this afternoon so I have to go, but I'm glad I bumped into you today."

As if blown by the soft breeze, she was gone. He caught a flash of color through the trees as she headed down the street. Never mind the potential career fall out, he was excited at the prospect of a date.

He unwrapped his cookie—oatmeal. His favorite.

CHAPTER 10

Gramps stood in his office doorway, pipe clenched in his teeth, hands stuffed in his pockets. A pose that screamed displeasure. No, distaste. Nicky let the heavy front door close behind her as she froze in the entry.

"You set up your easel." No question. No asking why. Just a statement.

"We talked about this, Gramps. I've sold pieces in my Etsy shop and need to keep the inventory fresh. That's part of my income."

True, his face had been buried in a book when she'd mentioned it, and his responses had been monosyllabic at best.

"There's a perfectly good studio out back."

Was there resignation in his tone? Or exasperation? For the first time, Nicky saw her grandfather's age and wondered how his daughter's death had impacted him. There had to be something behind the gruff exterior and curmudgeonly ways.

"If you want to use that, you'd have to clean it up."

Nicky nearly screamed at him. She'd begged and pleaded to use the studio. Hell, to sleep in it. He had refused, with no explanation, and now he was offering it.

"It could work. But I'm hoping to find a place of my own. I'm not sure it makes sense to put in that effort if I'm going to be packing up and leaving soon."

Gramps plucked the pipe from his teeth and sighed. "It's spring. All the rentals in this area go quickly. I can't imagine you have the budget for something safe. Or that has room for your easel. Set up the studio. It has good light and an entrance in the alley. You can still use it, even if you move out."

The sting of tears prickled, and Nicky sniffed them away. Impulsively, she flung her arms around her grandfather. Never a man for hugs, he accepted the embrace awkwardly, roughly patting her shoulder.

"Thanks, Gramps." Nicky skipped up the hall stairs then turned back to him, but he had returned to his office. Once again, Richard Mason could be counted on to be a walking contradiction.

She changed into grubby clothes and made her way to the studio with a notebook. The familiar smells, overlaid with dust and time, transported her to childhood. Her happiest memories were in this room amidst the smell of wet clay. Here, she could laugh and be loud—there was always music playing. You didn't wear nice clothes—they would only get messy.

It had been here with her father that Nicky felt safe and loved. Outside of the studio, her young life had been filled harsh memories. In the house, she had to stay quiet and criticism was always waiting to pounce. Inside the house, she was too much, and not enough.

Nicky swiped at the tears trickling down her cheeks and surveyed the space from an adult perspective—an artist looking for their light.

If she got rid of the pottery wheel or at least moved it over, she could get the big table away from the window and have plenty of space to set up an easel. The shelves could be repurposed to hang drying pieces.

Her thoughts swirled—conflicted. She grabbed a broom and swiped at the cobwebs lurking in the corners. Cleaning always helped her focus. She could store the pottery gear in the alcove with the kiln. That would free up space. She cued up some music on her phone, shoved her sleeves up and got to work.

In minutes, she got lost in the rhythm of transforming the room. Nicky bagged the last bit of trash, pushed her hair from her face and looked around. Shelves on both sides, bare and dusted. A big open space in front of the window, where late afternoon sunlight cast a golden glow. This could work. She could find a loveseat somewhere. There were some sheet-covered pieces in her grandfather's attic.

She stood the broom in a corner, envisioning her easel filling up the space. Her back to the window. And all that gorgeous, magical light.

The golden tones gave way to red, and Nicky scrambled for her phone. Crap. Time had gotten away from her. She turned off the lights and hurried to the house, pounding up the stairs and straight to her room to shower. Ty was picking her up at seven.

A text from him greeted her as she emerged from the steaming hot spray.

> How does a tapas and wine bar in
> Hampden sound?

Wine sounded like perfection. She sent the text then went rummaging through her closet to decide what to wear. When confronted with a wardrobe full of art teacher funky and I'm-making-art messy, there weren't too many choices that said date night with Mr. Preppy. Black buttery soft palazzo pants and an off the shoulder top would have to do.

Her phone buzzed at seven on the dot with a text.

Should I come up?

Nicky cringed at the thought, fired off a fast negative response, gave her makeup a check, grabbed a light wrap and headed out the door, trying to ignore the feeling of butterflies in her stomach.

TY

The front door opened, and Ty's breath caught in his throat. Nicky came gliding down the steps, looking like a dark fairy— her long hair loose and flowing, the deep purple streak faded into a softer shade that shone in the early evening light. As she moved, her sleeves and pant legs fluttered in the breeze, making it look like she floated across the street.

He hopped out of the car and opened her door and got a bright smile in reward. A brief hint of her floral perfume teased his senses as she stepped closer. She paused and looked up at him—another perfect opportunity to kiss her. Before he could say anything, she lowered herself into the seat and the moment was lost.

He slid behind the wheel and took a deep breath before trying conversation. All his cool had gone out the window, and he felt like a tongue-tied teenager.

"How was your day?" He stifled the chuckle at the inane question.

"Class was good. And... well, the afternoon was confusing." She finished with a shrug and a crooked grin.

Sitting in the car with her was easy. Just like every morning in the coffee shop. Everything about being with her was simple and comfortable, and he wondered why he'd ever questioned the attraction. They passed the ride talking about a story they'd both seen on the local news station's social media that morning.

She turned her head as they pulled off the highway and a flash of pink from her upper ear caught his eye. She was a breath of fresh air. He found a place to park and turned to her. "Is it okay if I get your door?"

He'd been raised to do that, but his last girlfriend had called it sexist caveman behavior. He'd stopped doing it for her, and always felt like a jerk, but he'd learned his lesson. Ask first.

Her eyebrows arched up, but she nodded. The floral scent caught him again as she rose from the car. Floral and something deeper underneath—warm and rich, like sticky caramel and vanilla. Honeysuckle sweet, but with a bite of spice. He wanted to bury his face in her neck, then see if she tasted as sweet as she smelled.

His cock rose to attention at the idea of his lips on her skin and he shoved his hands in his pockets to hide the erection. *Like a damn teenage boy.* Inside, the restaurant was unusually quiet for a Saturday night. Nicky sank into her chair as if she needed a respite.

Somehow, he'd gone from thinking of her as not his type to wanting to wrap his arms around her waist and spend about an eternity covering every bit of visible ink with kisses. No, scratch that, not just the visible ink. He wanted to kiss all of it, no matter where it was.

Ty barely noticed the server coming up, but he hung on every curve of Nicky's lips as she asked about the different wine flights then settled on the same one he liked—deep, spicy reds, so dark they looked like blood in the glass. He ordered, then turned his attention back to Nicky.

She had her head bent over the menu, a finger tracing down the side of the page as if keeping her place. Her head popped up, blue eyes searing into his.

"How do you want to do this?" Her eyebrows arching up her forehead with the question.

"If you don't mind sharing, we could each pick a few to start."

She flashed a bright smile at him and slid her finger down the menu again.

"Okay, let's see..." Her bottom lip caught between her teeth and Ty wanted to kiss her, right then and there. Yeah, he really needed to rein himself in.

"I'm thinking the lamb meatballs, berbere carrots, and vegetarian samosas. Work for you?"

"You take forever to decide on a pastry in the morning. How did you pick three dishes so quickly?"

"I did eenie, meenie, miney, mo down the menu. Try it, it's fun."

He wasn't sure if she was joking, but she probably wasn't. It sounded like the kind of thing she'd do.

"Okay."

When the server came with their wine and took their orders, Ty pointed at three random items. As soon as she'd left, Nicky leaned forward, her expression suddenly serious.

"So, my grandfather is your boss, which means either he's horrified at the idea of us going out, or he thinks you can somehow make me toe his line. Which is it? I'm sure he said something to you after the retirement party."

Whether Mason had said something to her or she knew her grandfather that well, Nicky's certainty was clear. Ty could be evasive, but if he had any hope of seeing where things went with her, honesty felt like the best approach. He crossed his fingers she wouldn't go on the defensive.

"Apparently, I'm too young and too single for the board's taste. Mason seemed of two minds on whether my interest in you was a good thing."

A rapid-fire succession of expressions flashed over her face. Disbelief. Irritation. Anger. Frustration. Sadness. And then something he hadn't prepared for. Nicky threw back her head and laughed long and hard.

"Let me guess," she said as she caught her breath and wiped her eyes, "if only I were more respectable—in his eyes— we'd be perfect and the fact that you'd be dating the granddaughter of the Amazing Doctor Richard Mason would be your Golden Ticket to the Old Boys' Club?"

She'd come frighteningly close to Mason's implications, and it sounded even more ridiculous, outdated, and downright misogynistic than before.

"Yeah, that's about the size of it."

He dared a glance into her eyes. Still crinkled up as if she was holding back a laugh. Still twinkling at him and looking more amused than angry. So far, so good.

"So, tell me why you're here." She toyed with a wineglass, fingers tracking up and down the stem, delicately stroking. Ty wrenched his mind from the gutter.

"Nothing has changed. I enjoy your company and I'd like to get to know you better."

The server took that moment to arrive with their plates. They fell into an easy, comfortable rhythm, dishing everything out, tasting and commenting on each item. Nicky turned every first bite into an experience that had Ty aching for more.

Just like with the cookie in the park, she slowly savored

each fresh taste, her lips pursing in pleasure and her eyes closing as if she wanted to immerse herself completely in that moment. If she was this comfortable in a restaurant, what would she be like in private? Would she be as abandoned in bed?

"I like your company as well." Nicky's voice startled him out of the thoughts he'd been entertaining. "And for some unknowable reason, I'm inclined to take you at your word."

Her statement gave him an unexpected rush that sent his mind careening right back to the gutter.

He picked up a wineglass and held it up, waiting for her to do the same. When she lifted her own glass and joined him, he shot her a wink. "To friendship and getting to know each other, and wherever that may lead. See, no hidden agenda."

Her smile broadened, and she returned the wink before taking a sip of wine. Her eyes locked on his as she sat the glass down. Nicky held his gaze, leaned forward, and beckoned him closer with a crook of her finger.

"To wherever?" The cocked eyebrow and one-sided smirk she fixed him with gave him hope he wasn't the only one whose mind was jumping straight into the bedroom.

Ty reached across the table and captured her hand in his. He turned her palm up and stroked his fingers along the lines there, relishing the visible prickle of goosebumps that raised on her arm in response.

"I may enjoy being the driver, but you tell me where we're going, and when you'd like to stop."

Color flushed her face, but before he could open his mouth to apologize for going too far, her fingers closed on his and squeezed before retreating to curl around her wine glass again.

"Sounds like an interesting ride."

Damn if that didn't make him want to call for the check

and head straight home. Preferably with Nicky right beside him.

"I'm thinking dessert sounds good. I mean, that looks amazing." She nodded toward a nearby table that had just been served some towering chocolate thing covered in whipped cream.

That penetrated the fog of arousal in his brain. Hint taken. Time to reel things in, but now he knew beyond any doubt—she was interested, and just as attracted to him as he was to her. He had no problem being patient, and he suspected it would be more than worth the wait.

They stuck to safer topics for the rest of the night, the time passing so effortlessly that Ty was surprised to find himself parking across the street from the beautiful brownstone.

An internal war he hadn't felt since his teen years began. Should he kiss her or not? Their first kiss had been unexpected and he sure as hell wasn't complaining. After their brief but charged banter over dinner, he was certain she'd be okay with more. He was less certain of standing in view of his boss' house and kissing the man's granddaughter.

"I had a great time," Nicky said as he opened her car door. "Thank you. That was a needed break."

The swaying boughs of a tree blocked most of the streetlight, casting dappled shadows over her upturned face. Everything about her posture and expression said she wouldn't mind a kiss. There had been no discussion, no asking, last time and she had initiated it. He could assume, but he wouldn't. Ty took her hand then closed the door.

"My pleasure."

Nicky leaned against the car and raised an eyebrow. To hell with caution. He stepped closer and tipped his head down. "I'd really like to kiss you right now."

Her smile would have been answer enough, then she nodded and angled her face toward his. Ty braced his other hand on the roof of his car and leaned in. She wound her arms around his neck and her body brushed his. She was warm and soft and holy fuck never mind kissing her, he wanted his hands and mouth everywhere.

Instead, he bent his head and pressed a gentle kiss to her lips. She made a soft sound in her throat and shifted herself closer. Ty wanted to kiss her for hours. Hell, he wanted to be doing a lot more than kissing. Her hands tangled in his hair and her lips parted on a sigh.

The only thing that kept Ty from losing every shred of control was the knowledge they were standing in full view of his boss' house.

He lifted his head. "Should I walk you across the street, or…"

Nicky put a hand on his chest and laughed. "Let's not tempt fate. Text me so I know you made it home? I mean, I know you live close, but…" She shrugged and looked up at him from under lowered lashes.

"I uh…" Ty laughed and pushed a hand through his hair. "I live right down the street at 500 Park." Three blocks. They were only three blocks apart.

Nicky rolled her eyes. "So, we're neighbors. Still… text, please." With that, she let go of his hand and crossed the street. He stayed until she was up the stairs and the door clicked shut behind her.

In college, he'd have been asking if he could come up, even if it meant sneaking past parents. Or in this case, a grandparent. Just thinking of that had images of pinning her to the inside of her bedroom door and kissing her for about an hour dancing through his head. Both of them. His cock came to full attention again. He stuffed his hands in his pockets and got back in his car.

No. He'd given that shit up because it left him empty and unsatisfied. Something about Nicky tripped every single happy sexy button he had. A fact he had every intention of exploring. Thoroughly.

Shit, now he needed a shower. A cold one.

CHAPTER 11

"Thank you for inviting me. It's been years since I've visited this place." Ty's voice held a note of wonder and a heaping dose of reservation as they crossed the courtyard toward the entrance of the American Visionary Art Museum. Though Nicky expected it—people in Baltimore either loved or hated the AVAM—after their weekend date, she was eager for Ty to at least like the place. The midweek happy hour event seemed like the perfect opportunity to share part of her work with him.

"Do I want to ask why it's been so long?" Nicky arched an eyebrow at him. Ty stared up at the huge whirligig sculpture as they crossed the courtyard.

"Busy, mostly. School had me tied up in classes, internships, work. The usual."

Inside, figuring a glass of wine might smooth the way, Nicky quickly led him to the bar set up on the first floor.

Wine in hand, Ty cracked a bright smile at Nicky. "Well, do we start at the bottom and go up? Or..." He tipped his head back, staring at the Icarus sculpture hanging in the stairwell. "Has that always been there?" He pointed at the partially furled mirrored wings. Icarus, clearly falling, and yet the statue had such grace and beauty it looked peaceful.

"Since 2006. I suggest we start at the top and work our way back down. Especially since there are snacks on the top floor, and I'm starving."

They climbed the stairs slowly, as Ty kept stopping to view the rotating sculpture. "I do not recall seeing this before. It's stunning."

And with those words, Nicky's tension dialed down a couple notches. "The artist is Andrew Logan. He also did the Cosmic Egg out front and the Divine statue."

Ty chuckled. "Now those I remember. Along with some string sculptures, a giant bra ball, and ah... well..." He passed a hand over his face and gestured up the stairs. "Onward and upward, then?"

"Let me guess," Nicky said, leading the way. "You were in high school the last time you were here."

Ty mumbled something, and though Nicky didn't understand the words, she got the point. She was right.

"The Flatulence Post is in the basement," she said as they reached the top floor. Ty shook his head with a laugh.

"Yeah. That was the other thing I remembered. How'd you know?"

It was Nicky's turn to laugh. "Teenage boys are pretty predictable." On the top floor, Nicky spotted Sabrina and nearly grabbed Ty and rushed back to the lobby. The other woman had an uncanny ability to see things, and call them out, and Nicky wasn't ready for that when it came to Ty.

"So, this is what kept you from dinner with me and the wife on Saturday?" Sabrina sauntered up and stuck her hand out at Ty. "Sabrina Clements. Project manager and all-around creative wrangler."

Nicky held her breath, unsure how Ty would react to Sabrina. She didn't know why she should care what Ty thought—of the museum, of Sabrina, or anything really. They got along so well, and his kiss was sweet, but she kept waiting for the Joe Preppy side to emerge in all its stuffy, elitist glory. He worked for Richard Mason. There was no getting around that fact.

Sabrina's laughter pulled Nicky from her thoughts to see her coworker and Ty both with broad, genuine smiles on their faces, looking at Nicky like she'd missed something.

"The brie is amazing." Sabrina pointed over her shoulder at the cafe space. "Skip the mini crab cakes—they're a crime."

Ty made a scowly face. "How do you do bad crab cakes in Baltimore?"

Sabrina shrugged. "Somehow, the caterer managed it."

"Seriously, crab cakes and lacrosse are sacrosanct in this state," Nicky chimed in. "What's the third arm of the Maryland Holy Trinity?"

"The flag." Both Sabrina and Ty spoke at once, then looked at each other and laughed.

"You can keep him. He's okay."

Sabrina's phone beeped, and she glanced at the screen, then turned back to Nicky and Ty. "Duty calls." She pointed a finger at Nicky. "You are officially off the clock tonight, so enjoy this shindig and don't let anyone con you into working. As for you." She turned to Ty. "Pleasure to meet you. Enjoy your personally guided tour. Nicky has a way of communicating the stories behind our pieces here."

She dropped a wink at Nicky and took off at a brisk pace.

"Do you need to..." Ty began until Nicky waved a hand at him.

"Nope, I'm gonna do what I'm told for once." She grabbed Ty's elbow and tugged him toward the snacks. "I want cheese. Then I'll give you that tour."

In the crowded cafe space, Ty glided effortlessly through the crowd. It looked to Nicky like knots of people simply parted for him. They filled their plates, avoiding the crab cakes, and made their way to a small table near the windows.

"Wine on Wednesdays, huh? Not that different from our Thursday Nights. So, who attends these events? I mean, there's food and wine, but there are a lot of people for a weeknight. What's the demographic? Mostly donors and patrons?"

Nicky held up a finger as she swallowed her bite of the undeniably good brie. Of course, Ty would home in on those questions—this was what he did every day. She took a sip of wine and looked around before turning back to him.

"Things like this are mostly community driven. Members, patrons, donors—sure. But most of these folks are here because it's social and fun."

She waved her hand around the room. "Listen to the buzz. Look around."

Ty cocked his head, then followed her instruction. "I expect social chatter in a cafe."

"Yes, but hold on to what you see and hear up here as we go through the rest of the museum."

They chatted about their favorite live music spots—hers mostly in DC, his right here in Baltimore—while finishing their snacks, then grabbed more wine and continued to the exhibits. In the space where Reverend Wagner's Miracle at Midnight exhibition hung, Ty slowed down and stared at the big mural depicting the parting of the Red Sea.

"That's stunning." His words came out as a whisper.

"The artist is a controversial figure. Wagner had a spiritual awakening at age 50 that led him to turn away from what he called a life of sin and take up painting."

Ty moved to the information plaque, his eyes flicking back and forth as he read. He turned to the mural, then surprised Nicky by sitting on one of the benches, elbows on knees as he leaned forward, continuing to study the piece. After several minutes of silence, he sat back and looked at Nicky.

"This is the old familiar Bible story, but this depiction feels raw and personal. You're an artist, what's your take?"

"I see transformation. For Wagner, this was a spiritual journey and there's no escaping the Biblical references. But I don't think you need to view his work through the lens of Christianity to understand the nature of faith leading to freedom."

Ty looked back at the mural, his head tilting side to side as if contemplating different angles. "I don't disagree there. This is a journey out of bondage—literally and figuratively in this case. But I meant your take from an art perspective." He glanced at her with a quick smile. Nicky took a deep breath and braced herself for the conversation that could—would likely—kill anything between them if he was like the typical, more traditional art crowd.

"Everyone will have a different view. What I get out of it will not be the same as what you get. At its most basic, art is about communication. No matter what the technique or the skill level the artist possess. The question is—does the piece communicate something? Does it make you feel? Or think. Does it challenge you? Reward you? Soothe or excite?"

Ty nodded, his eyes fixed on her and a soft smile playing at the corners of his mouth.

"Tell me what you heard while you were sitting here staring at this piece," Nicky said.

Ty's brows scrunched into a frown. "What I heard?"

"You sat here for almost five minutes. You were silent. Contemplative. What did you hear around you?"

"People talking. Same as now."

"Close your eyes."

He did without question, his lids slipping down over his dazzling green eyes.

"Now," Nicky spoke softly, leaning in so he could hear her. "Tell me what you hear. Really listen."

Ty cocked his head, then turned slightly one way, then the other. "Someone is reading the artist's bio." His lips compressed into a line and a small scowl formed, as if he was concentrating very hard on something. His eyes popped open and stared into hers.

"At least two conversations about the meaning of god. Another about finding peace. And more than a few passing comments on the artist's life. Do I get a gold star, teacher?"

Nicky tugged on his sleeve, pulling him up to stand.

"Sure. I'm all about positive reinforcement. My point was you heard those conversations. And you'll hear them throughout the museum. This isn't a library. People talk here. And they talk about art."

Ty's eyes went wide as realization hit. "I get it. It becomes personal. Internalized. The atmosphere promotes discussion —and so people do more than sit and contemplate or admire. They think."

Nicky was impressed. He really seemed to understand.

"You asked my thoughts as an artist. I have an art education—I'm a trained artist. All the artists here are self-taught. And to people like my grandfather, that makes the works here less valuable. Worse, less valid."

Nicky took a deep breath and faced the mural. "I look at this and see the power it has to communicate, and that makes it good in my book. I don't care for this style, and there's no getting around the fact that the artist has talent, but not a lot of refined skills." She turned to Ty and found his eyes glued to her, a small smile firmly on his lips.

"Neither of those things changes the fact that this piece moves people. And that art is about."

She watched Ty's face for any sign of negativity. And she found none. Even mentioning her grandfather, his boss, didn't cause so much as a batted eye. Maybe Joe Preppy wasn't so bad after all. And then they came into the room that housed a sixteen-foot model ship made of toothpicks.

"The Titanic?" Ty pointed at the cracked open middle of the ship.

"The Lusitania. Sunk by a German U-boat in 1915."

"What conversations does this inspire?" Ty asked and Nicky bristled until she saw the laughter in his eyes. He wasn't condescending. He was being funny, and maybe a little flirtatious.

"Debate over how many toothpicks. And how many hours. And why."

Ty leaned down to read the info and Nicky could not take her eyes off the man's ass. He really was finely built.

"According to this, it's 193,000 toothpicks. And two and a half years. Okay, but why? What is he communicating?"

"I think that's part of the charm of this museum—not everything has to be serious. As for this piece? If the artist is to be believed, it's safer than climbing Everest."

Ty threw his head back and laughed. "Okay, you got me. I apologize. I've been underestimating this place for years."

She wasn't sure if he was being serious or a sarcastic jerk, but he sounded sincere. Then he draped an arm over her shoulders and turned her to the huge mural of the reclining woman.

"That is beautiful. Made up of much smaller images, I believe? Don't think I didn't see that look on your face."

Nicky shot a glance up at him, his eyes were glued to the wall. "What look would that be?"

Ty didn't take his gaze off the painting. In fact, he steered them closer and leaned in. "The one that said you were debating if I was being an asshole or not when I said I'd underestimated this place."

He straightened up and turned to look at her. "I wasn't trying to be, though I recognize it could have sounded that way."

Heat rose to Nicky's face. She had been thinking that very thing. "Jury's still out on that one." She gave him a big smile. If he could tease, so could she.

"Would you like to go out this weekend?" Ty raised his brows, and Nicky had to clamp her mouth shut to keep from gaping at him. He was unlike anyone she'd ever met, and she had no clue how to handle that. But she did know one thing for sure.

"Yes. I'd like that."

CHAPTER 12

The midday sun glared off the brightly painted door and Nicky shuffled from one foot to the other, oddly nervous, as she rang the bell at Sabrina's place. This wasn't her first time here. She'd met Anne and knew Becca from her classes with BOPA, though not her husband, Dru. She'd asked what she could bring to the cookout and Anne suggested beverages. After following up with Sabrina, Nicky had a bag full of canned sodas and the makings of two killer punch options for the grownups.

The door flung open, and Nicky stared into eyes so dark they were practically black that belonged to a small built man with delicate features and skin that could only be described as bronze.

"You must be Nicky." He stood back and gestured for her to come in. "I'm Dru."

He snagged bags of sodas from her and led the way to the kitchen. "There's a couple rugrats around here somewhere. Our kids, Dante and Layla."

Nicky deposited the punch makings on the counter and shook the man's hand.

"Sabrina is out back getting the grill going, and Anne is..." He paused and looked around as if expecting her to be in the room. "Uh... wherever the kids are. Which may mean watching a Disney movie in the guest room. C'mon back."

Nicky pointed the ingredients she was unpacking. "I'll be out in maybe fifteen."

Dru surveyed the growing pile on the counter and laughed. "If you're bringing this out, it'll be worth the wait. You've been here before, so you know where everything is. Nice to meet you."

He was gone with a wave and Nicky set to work chopping citrus, rinsing berries, and filling two giant plastic pitchers with punch. She cleaned up her mess and realized she couldn't carry everything at once.

"Need a hand?" Becca came in and gave Nicky a big hug. "Dru said there was no way you'd be able to handle the, and I quote, vats of booze you were making in here. What are these heavenly looking things?"

Nicky passed a pitcher to Becca. "I'll tell ya when we get outside."

Anne and two adorable children were just settling into a big swing on the back deck and Sabrina waved a spatula from the nearby grill. Dru was fishing drinks out of the cooler for the kids. It all looked so normal and sweet that Nicky felt a pang of what she'd missed growing up.

There were never backyard parties like this. Instead, it was dinners where she had to be quiet and on her best behavior. Even outdoor events meant dressing up. And here she was in black denim capris and a Hawaiian shirt tied at the waist.

"Adult beverages!" Nicky called out as she and Becca set their pitchers on a nearby table. "The purple looking one is berry-lemonade, and it's more like a mild sangria. Mix it with sparkling water if you want it even lighter."

"We know what Anne's drinking," Sabrina replied with a laugh. "But Dru said something about a vat of booze. That's wine."

"So, you want this one." Nicky held up the other pitcher. "Brunch Rum Punch seemed appropriate for a Sunday midday thing."

Becca made a show of holding Dru back as he nearly sprinted over to them. "You had him at rum."

Nicky laid out orange slices to garnish with and wiped her hands on a towel. "A lotta rum." She laughed and poured a glass, handing it to Dru. "Orange, pineapple, cranberry, and a splash of grenadine. Add sparkling water if you'd like..." She gave up explaining since Dru had already taken his glass and found a seat. Becca poured two lemonades and took one to Anne.

"Would you..." Sabrina stopped talking as Nicky handed her a glass of the rum punch.

"I've seen you drink; I know better than to put in seltzer."

Nicky pulled a chair around and soaked up the simple pleasure of being with friends.

"Enjoy the down time while you can." Sabrina added a couple hotdogs to the grill then fixed Nicky with that ever-patient gaze.

"Don't mind her. She gets like this every year," Anne chimed in. "Once Artscape planning is in full swing, free time is a rarity."

Everybody gave knowing nods at that, and Nicky was incredibly grateful when Becca leaned in and explained. "Anne and Sabrina are both on the Artscape planning committee. Dru is an emergency doctor, and he heads the medical coordination. The alternative art world is kind of an incestuous lot."

For the first time in what felt like forever, Nicky allowed herself to relax. No Gramps waiting to correct her. No Jeremy trying to mold her into his vision of the ideal partner. And barely a passing thought to her date with Joe Preppy later. Okay, maybe more than a passing thought.

"You gonna explain that dreamy look on your face?" Sabrina nudged Nicky with her foot.

Nicky shot her friend a smile and brought her attention back to the cookout. Sabrina had food piled high and Anne was shooing the kids to the table.

"I'm serious." Sabrina put the platter of food on the table and fixed Nicky with a penetrating stare. "I'm assuming it's Mr. Coffee Shop. You guys looked pretty cozy at Wine on Wednesday."

"I guess..." Nicky busied herself with the condiments and passing things to others at the table, trying not to look like she was avoiding the subject.

"Are you two dating?" Leave it to Anne to come right out with it.

Nicky couldn't avoid a direct question. The trouble was, she didn't have an answer. "We're... uhhh...Going out tonight." She took a quick sip of her drink and decided the best answer was brutal honesty. "It's a little, no, a lot early to call it dating."

Sabrina and Anne both threw back their heads in laughter. Dru leaned across the table and patted Nicky's hand. "I don't think most lesbians understand that concept."

Becca immediately smacked his shoulder. "You can't say things like that!"

Anne wiped tears from her eyes. "Maybe not outside this

group, but he's not wrong. So, spill. If it's not dating, then what is it?"

Nicky let out a slow breath. "We've gone out a time or two. Aside from the fact that he works for my grandfather, he seems great. I keep waiting for the other shoe to drop."

Sabrina's eyebrows arched into her hair line and Nicky shook her head. "You know… when something seems too good. I've done the preppy guy before—they always turn out to be jerks. Like serious jerks. And uptight—always uptight."

Becca tipped the last of her berry lemonade into her mouth, then leaned her elbows on the table. "How's he kiss?"

Nicky nearly choked on a swallow of burger. "They've been sweet."

His goodnight kisses had been soft and gentle, but had also felt like he was holding something back. That was a side to him she wanted to discover.

Sabrina rose and grabbed the pitchers to refill everyone's drinks. "Sweet? Girl, he's hot as fuck, and that's coming from a confirmed lesbian. I'm betting there's a lot more than sweet there."

Nicky rolled her eyes, racking her brain for a way to change the subject. She was saved by a minor meltdown between Dante and Layla. By the time their parents had sorted that out, the adult conversation had moved on.

Later, after Dru and Becca bundled their sugar-hyped kids into their car, Nicky found herself at the kitchen sink with Sabrina while Anne showered off the sunscreen. Something Nicky would have to do before seeing Ty later.

Sabrina dropped a tab in the dishwasher and bumped it closed with a slim hip.

"You're amazing. I hope Anne appreciates you."

Sabrina gave a salacious wink. "Oh, she does. Her first

marriage was to a man—some Pentecostal minister who thought sex was five minutes with the lights out." She stuck out her tongue and waggled it. Nicky rolled her eyes.

"I appreciate the help with clean up, but you've got plans tonight. Anne and I can handle the rest. No arguing with me. Shoo!"

Nicky practically floated back to her grandfather's. Spending a day where she didn't have to worry about someone judging her for her tattoos, or colorful hair, or denigrating her job had been a balm to her soul.

She loved working at both the American Visionary Art Museum and the classes at Baltimore Office of Promotion and Arts, but if she was being honest with herself, the BOPA job just reminded her how much she missed the classroom.

She let out a sigh as she unlocked the front door. No sense being sad about it. That ship had sailed, thanks to Jeremy. First things first, she needed to continue rebuilding her savings. And if that meant working two part-time jobs, so be it. She seemed to fit in better with the... Nicky gave an inward chuckle as Becca's words came back to her: the alternative arts crowd.

Mercifully, she made it through the house without running into her grandfather. She cranked on the shower, determined to shove all deep thinking aside and enjoy a night out with an attractive man. No sooner was she finished than her phone buzzed with an incoming text. Ty's name on the screen. She thumbed open her messages.

How was the cookout?

A simple question. Totally normal. But Nicky sat hard on the edge of the tub, her breath catching in her throat. It all felt too sudden. Too close. Somehow, without her even realizing it, Ty had become part of her routine. She was sorta seeing this guy. Not that either of them had said as much.

> Very chill. Good people. But I think I'm still stuffed.

Three little dots appeared, indicating he was typing, and Nicky forced herself to put the phone down and finish drying off before she looked at the message.

> I had a late lunch with my PhD advisor, not all that hungry myself. Maybe something other than dinner?

Her stomach tightened as every thought in her head took a decidedly adult turn.

> What'd you have in mind...

She hit send and immediately wished she could take it back. That sounded too suggestive. Like she was hinting at something, but hadn't she been thinking that? Dammit, she needed to figure out what this was between them.

> No agenda. Keep it simple. Walk down Charles and see what grabs our attention?

Who knew he could be spontaneous. Or maybe it was his way of keeping it casual with no expectations. She didn't have the brain for those thoughts.

> Gimme 15 minutes.

She sent the text and threw open her closet. Casual, he said. She suspected her version of casual and his were two very different things. She settled on a pair of leggings and, after checking the weather and seeing the temperature had dropped, tossed on a tank top and hoodie. Nicky debated skipping makeup, but that seemed too casual. Eyeliner, brows, lips. Hair in a ponytail. That's what he was getting. If he didn't like it—tough.

TY

It was eighteen minutes before she came out the door, but who was counting. Even dressed down, she looked so damn good. Just seeing her made him smile.

"This may be too casual for a drink." She gestured at her outfit.

"Nah, you're fine." He wasn't in his usual either. He'd thrown on worn jeans and a t-shirt under an old button down. "There're a couple of places in The Marketplace, or we can head up Charles and hit Mick O'Shea's."

"Not The Marketplace—too loud and busy."

He caught her hand, holding it loosely, giving her space to pull away. When she didn't, he stepped closer and pulled up a map on his phone, tilting it so she could see the screen.

"What do you think? The Irish pub?" He pointed out Mick O'Shea's, a little over half a mile away. She shrugged, and he led them across the street and down Park Avenue. Halfway down the block, the idea of a pub felt wrong. He wanted quiet. He wanted space to get to know Nicky. Ty stopped quickly enough she bumped into him.

"I don't want you to think I'm being pushy or expecting anything." He kicked himself mentally. *Way to set things up, asshole.* Now she'd be nervous and on guard. The wary look on her face was evidence enough. "We could go to my place. I've got a couple of good bottles of red. I might have beer. We can order out if we want food. Your call."

She dropped his hand. Well, shit. He'd stuck his foot in it. He opened his mouth to apologize but shut it with a snap when she stepped off the curb and gave him a c'mon gesture with her head.

"You live at 500 Park, right?" She pointed down the street and he could only nod. Her hand slid into his again and they finished the walk, chatting about little things—schedules, work events, the Chinese restaurant that used to be on the corner they just passed. It all felt so natural, like they'd done this hundreds of times.

At his apartment, she admired the small space, made appreciative sounds about the photography on his walls—all Zach's work, who had developed a love of photography back in high school—and said yes to a bottle of Côtes du Rhône. She settled into the sofa, and not all the way against one side, but closer to the middle. Ty took that as a good sign.

He handed her a glass and sat, leaving half a cushion between them. He didn't want to presume. She let out a quiet sigh and settled back in her seat as if letting go of the weight of the world.

"I know I've had a busy weekend, but now I'm wondering about yours."

Nicky turned her head and flashed a small smile. "It's been a week of a lot of on time if that makes any sense. I'm an extrovert, but even I reach a too-much point. The idea of a bar..." She trailed off and shook her head. "This is much better."

"Yeah, been there. The whole weekend got turned on end. Thank you for being so understanding about that." He didn't add the fact that even though they saw each other every day during the week, he was hungry for her company again.

She sipped her wine and tipped her head back against the cushions. Even in leggings and a hoodie, with minimal makeup, she was striking. He was fucked. That's all there was to it.

"Work shit happens. I live by my calendar, but you learn to be flexible."

Ty would never have imagined this ethereal creature was a planner who kept a schedule. Stranger things had happened, he supposed.

She nudged his knee with hers and tipped her head to the side, eyeing him through lowered lashes. "What are we doing here?"

The question caught him off guard. "I'm not sure I understand the question."

She didn't move, didn't shift her head. The only change was a slight curve of her lips. "This..." She waved a hand between them, vaguely pointing at his jeans and her leggings. "We've done the first date thing. The first kiss thing, couple kisses, I guess. Had lunch a few times, and I don't know if you wanna call Wine on Wednesday a date. It sort of feels like the beginning of dating. So, what is this?"

Their few kisses had caused him more than a few sleepless nights. He'd been hesitant to take things further, unable to admit to wanting more for fear of scaring her off, and that was so not like him.

He sat his glass on the table and plucked hers from her hand before sitting it next to his. "I have no expectations. I'd like to think we're friends and I'd say we're clearly attracted to each other. What we do with that attraction and where it goes from here is a topic for discussion."

He caught her fingers in his and held them loosely, gently stroking his thumb over the back of her hand. He slid his thumb around her wrist, relishing the little gasp of air from her.

"Damned unexpected." She breathed the words as his thumb traced under the cuff of her hoodie. Her skin was so soft, so silky, and warm. She hadn't moved. Her head rested against the couch cushions and a soft humming sound escaped her lips. He could lose himself in her.

"If you're thinking of kissing me, now would be a good time." She had to be reading his mind. That half smile quirked at her lips again. He slid his hand up, over her shoulder, until he cupped the back of her head. Her eyelids fluttered open and there was no mistaking the hunger in that gaze.

The faintest touch on his hand pulled his attention away from her mouth. He had one hand in her hair and the other resting on her thigh. Her fingers twined around his, gently pulling his hand across her body, until there was barely room between them for breath.

Nicky's tongue slid out, across her lower lip, and back in before her teeth bit down, pulling on one side of her lip. Ty was entranced with her mouth. He leaned closer, breathing her in—caramel, vanilla, sweet honeysuckle, and orange blossom.

He hitched in a shuddering breath before closing the tiny distance between them. The moment his lips touched hers, he knew he was an absolute goner. The kisses they'd shared before had the taste of uncertainty. Like they were testing the waters and feeling each other out. Tonight, she was all silken softness and yielded to the press of his mouth, granting his tongue access.

Her hand tightened around his while her other hand wrapped his body, pressing her palm against his back. His fingers clenched into her hair, and she gasped, arching against him, and sending him into raging hard on zone.

He traced his lips along her jaw, relishing how she tipped her head back to give him a better angle. When her hand left his and firmly gripped his belt loops, he smiled and pulled her closer to him. Her legs parted, allowing him to press one thigh between hers.

He fastened his lips at the base of her throat and licked. She gave a soft moan. He let his teeth graze her skin, and the moan rose in volume while her body tensed. A little nip and her hands clutched into his hair, holding him in place while her head threw back and gasps of pleasure filled the air.

He sucked a little, then bit more firmly. The soft gasps and moans turned into keening, but she pulled his head up and fixed him with a gaze filled with passion and laughter.

"No leaving marks." Her voice was husky and soft. He had no doubt if he suggested it, he could carry her to his bed right now. He wanted to hear more of those little gasps and moans. As wonderful as that sounded, he wasn't sure her desire went beyond the raging chemistry between them. He needed it to be more and for it to be only him who could scratch that itch.

"Noted." Kissing her was a delight—it overwhelmed his senses, eclipsing everything else. His world was only her and her intoxicating scent and taste.

He wanted his tongue over her entire body. Wanted his face between her legs where he could taste her and find if this honeyed sweetness was all over.

She shifted slightly and his hand was on the zipper of her hoodie. He flicked his eyes to hers, silently seeking the okay to go ahead.

"Yes." The word came out on a breath, and he tugged at the zipper. Her hoodie fell open revealing a flimsy tank top and no bra. He wrapped both hands at her waist and held her tight to him as he rolled onto his back, pulling her on top.

She swung a leg over his thighs and settled into his lap,

straddling him and his hands were filled with the perfect round globes of her ass. Her fingers coiled into the hair at the base of his neck just before she kissed him. Molten heat radiated through his jeans and the scent of caramel enveloped him.

Making out had never felt like this before. She was pure fire, surrounding him, infusing him. Her lips left his and her teeth fastened onto his earlobe, and it was his turn to shudder. He slid his hands up her back, firmly, squeezing and pressing along the way, then back down to her waist. His fingers toyed with the hem of her tank top.

Her hands closed over his wrists, and she pulled back. Something had changed. The heat was still in her gaze but tempered. Ty swallowed hard. He'd found her limit tonight. Then she was smiling and kissing him again and the kisses were different. Still just as sweet, but no longer laced with an almost overwhelming ache for more.

He lost himself in the pure bliss of kissing her as their bodies rocked together. The sense of the fire still there and smoldering beneath the surface, ready to flare up, but under control, for now.

Kisses turned into snuggles, her head tucked against his shoulder. His arms cradled her body against his, holding her in a way that was far more intimate, far more intense than any of his previous sexual partners. Then she was sitting in the corner of the couch, her feet under his leg, as they sipped their wine and shared stories about life. They'd both grown up in the city, attending different private schools. While he'd once dreamed of leaving the city, he'd found himself invested during college, and now he couldn't imagine living anywhere else.

Nicky, however, had imagined leaving as soon as she was done with college. Maybe moving to San Francisco or New

York. "The dreams of a naïve child. Now?" She gave a small smile. "I feel like I belong here, I guess."

A second glass of wine turned into a third, along with a food delivery. Before Ty realized it, hours had passed, and Nicky looked like she was drifting. Ty waited until she deposited her empty glass on the table, then slid her into his lap. She curled into him, and he was struck with how good and how right she felt.

"I've gotta get some sleep." She mumbled the words against his neck, and what he wouldn't give to tuck her into his bed, then curl up alongside her. Instead, he cupped her ass and rose, lifting her with him, then gently letting her legs slide down until she was standing in front of him.

"I'll walk you home." He dropped a soft kiss on her lips. The smile and nod she gave him were so sweet they tore at his heart. That was a thought he didn't want to dwell on.

They walked back to her grandfather's place in silence, her hand clasped in his. She rose on her tiptoes to kiss him at the foot of the brownstone's steps.

"We seem to have gone from desire, past motivation and straight to action," she said, then chuckled. "Please note that is not a complaint. But the question remains, what is this?"

Ty wrapped his arms around her waist and claimed her lips with another kiss before answering. "Good question." She gave a little pout, and he nearly came undone. "I am not interested in friends with benefits, and I don't make out like that with just friends. Beyond that, do we need a name for it?"

The play of expressions ranging over her face fascinated him. It was like watching a series of emojis in real life. The soft smile faded into a brief scowl, then a pout, before turning back into a playful grin.

"I don't do anything with benefits, either. I'm okay leaving it ambiguous. For now." She pecked him on the cheek and practically skipped up the steps. She blew a kiss at him as she slipped through the door, then leaned back out. "But expect to revisit this topic. Text me when you get home. This is Baltimore."

With that she was back inside, and Ty stood on the sidewalk wondering how in the hell he'd gone from nope, not happening, to this. More importantly, he realized, just as Nicky had said, he wasn't complaining.

NICKY—THURSDAY, MAY 9

"You said a mural class?" Ty's eyebrows shot up his forehead. Not that Nicky could blame him. The art in his world was hung on walls, not painted on them. "You're teaching..."

"Not teaching. Attending. Not my area of expertise. I met Shea through BOPA, and she was asking for help in her intro classes."

He parked the car in the nearly empty lot and opened her door.

"This kind of class, it's good to have multiple assistants. Shea suggested I attend a session first, see if I feel comfortable with it, and I agree. I can do large format, but murals are their own thing. Now c'mon. I wanna get there early so you can meet her."

She grabbed Ty's hand and hurried toward the building she never thought she would enter again. The Copycat—a former warehouse that had become questionably legal living spaces, but primarily served as artist's loft. It was also the site of her couch surfing days post Jeremy breakup. And where Shea Dominguez held her classes.

A stocky woman Nicky semi recognized stood near the door and let them in as soon as she spotted Nicky. And the smell of the place hit them. Paint. Sawdust. Countless different foods. And cannabis. Lots and lots of that.

"Whoa." Ty blew a breath out and blinked. "That's…"

"It's a lot, yeah." Nicky followed the brightly printed arrows through the halls. "Artist's lofts. You get used to it."

A final turn and the hall opened into a large, all white space where the smell of fresh paint overwhelmed everything else. In the middle of it all, laying out the tools of her trade, was a tall woman with hair so black it shone in the bright lights, a broad streak of pure white shot through one side.

"Nicky!" Shea's rich voice echoed as she called out. "Who's the handsome devil you brought along?" Shea gave Ty a thorough once over then stuck out her hand.

"Ty Lake. Nicky's told me about your work. It's a pleasure to meet you."

Shea gave a little bow, then grabbed Nicky's hand and dragged them both to the assortment of tools.

"Nicky will know all of this stuff." Shea pointed at the array. "Do you paint? Or draw?"

"I'm afraid not. I'm more of an admirer of art. I do understand the basics about the tools and theory. I'll confess, I'm not familiar with murals, but the class sounded like fun."

Nicky could have kissed him for that one. What he'd actually been was vaguely confused, but entirely game to go along. Shea gave him another long look, from the tips of his Chucks to the faded gray Henley. She pointed at the black leather watchband on his wrist. "Maybe take that off."

Ty muttered something that sounded like a curse and quickly stripped the watch, stuffing it in his jeans pocket.

"Is he always so polite?" Shea arched a brow at Nicky. The smile on her face said it was a tease. Still, Nicky swallowed hard, unsure how Ty would handle the good-natured ribbing.

"If you knew my parents, you'd understand." Ty gave them both a lopsided grin and raised his hands in a what are ya gonna do gesture. "Dad's a southerner through and through, and Mom grew up in a family where polite was practically a religion."

Shea threw back her head and laughed. And with that, Nicky relaxed. Seeing Ty at ease in an unfamiliar environment that would have had her grandfather bristling felt like a weight coming off her shoulders.

"So, that's a lot of white wall." Ty turned around, gesturing at the whole room. "We're not painting all that today?"

Shea shook her head, and Nicky could almost see the switch happen—from mild flirtation to teacher mode.

"This is a basics class. Today we'll talk planning, tools, and scaling, then do some painting." She pulled a small remote from her jeans and pushed a button. The wall in front of them lit up with a huge abstract design. Ty made an appreciative noise.

"So, you're not doing the grid method?" Nicky walked to the wall and ran her fingers along the bright curves of the design cast by the projector.

"We'll talk about it. But I've found beginners want to get to painting quickly. So, I get them there. If they like it, and want to go deeper, I teach other methods of scaling. This way, we'll actually be painting in the second half of the class."

Before she could continue, a small group of chattering college-age students came streaming into the room. Shea sent Ty and Nicky to an end section of the wall, clicked the projector off, then moved to greet the newcomers.

"Why do I feel like there's a reason she put us on the end?" Ty had leaned in, his lips close to Nicky's ear and his breath tickled her neck. Nicky breathed in, the subtle scent of him came through, even with all the other smells in the place.

She scanned the room. More students had come in and Shea was busy getting everyone arranged down the wall. Nicky turned back to Ty and giggled. She'd said wear clothes he didn't care about getting messy in. She'd been too busy admiring his forearms and ass to think about the fact that he still looked polished.

"You're less likely to get paint on you from other people if you're on the end." She plucked at his sleeve, then looked down her own outfit—a pair of old Levi's so battered and paint stained it was hard to tell what color they used to be (black, of course) and an oversize t-shirt that she'd picked up at a thrift store. She had a drawer full of them for just this purpose.

"I usually paint barefoot." Shea's voice carried as she addressed the whole room. "But here we need to keep our shoes on. Hello everyone, my name is Shea Dominguez and..."

Ty's arm slid around Nicky's waist, and the teacher's words faded from her consciousness. He wrapped both arms around her, settling her against his chest as if it was the most natural thing in the world. And damn, it felt good.

Nicky stole a glance up. Ty's attention was focused entirely on Shea. His eyes followed her, and his head cocked slightly to the side. A position Nicky recognized from years in the classroom—he was alert, attentive. And yet, his hands sat clasped at her waist and Nicky couldn't recall ever feeling so comfortable or at ease in a man's embrace.

She tuned in to Shea's voice, listening as the older woman went through the basics of murals, and what they'd be doing today. The projector whirred to life again, but what painted the wall this time was a picture of one of Shea's more famous pieces on the side of a children's hospital in Bogotá.

Ty shifted and Nicky felt like she was falling back, then she came to an abrupt halt, and it was like she was resting against a wall of hard muscle. A quick look over her shoulder explained it—Ty had propped his back against a pillar, planting his feet wide apart, with her standing between them. She could definitely get used to this.

"Okay, let's see the project we're gonna work on, then we'll talk tools." Shea's finger flicked the remote and the class gave a collective ooo as the colorful mural lit up the wall.

Nicky had to hand it to their teacher. The mural was bright and filled with swirls of color, but all of it was broad lines and simple patterns. Easy for beginners to paint, but still attractive. Nicky couldn't imagine how many layers of paint were already on this wall. And how many more Shea would add.

Later, when they were dismissed for break, Nicky reluctantly pulled herself out of Ty's arms. Nothing about the way they'd been standing felt ambiguous to her, but she resolved to enjoy it without overthinking. Being with Ty felt good. Simple as that. She didn't need a label to enjoy that. She turned to him, still leaning against the wall, and his expression caught her off guard. There was nothing ambiguous about the look on his face, either.

His eyes crinkled at the corners and his mouth sat in a half smile as he caught her gaze and held it. He reached out and caught her hand, twining his fingers through hers as they grabbed water bottles from the cooler. His lips parted and Nicky's world narrowed to the man in front of her.

And then Shea was back and calling for everyone to collect brushes and paint cans.

"Since we're just doing the big blocks, why don't I do the

edging," Nicky suggested. "Then you can do the big fill in stuff. Would that work?"

The look of relief on Ty's face bordered on comedic as he sighed, and a broad smile replaced the tight-lipped concern that had etched itself around his mouth.

"Great!" He breathed another sigh. "I am really not artistically inclined, and I don't want to make a mess of this."

"That's part of the process." She dipped her brush into the bright blue that would make up the majority of their section. "It's all good."

She quickly lined the largest area, running the edge of her brush right up against the swirls of other colors and blocking out a big section for Ty to fill in.

His first strokes, he didn't have enough paint on the brush. Then he overloaded and the bright blue paint dripped, splattering as it hit the floor. Nicky dropped a paper towel on the mess, then demonstrated how to load his brush properly.

After that, it was smooth sailing as they both worked their section. She ducked under him. He reached above her or slid around behind her. As if they were dancing a dance they'd done hundreds of times. Fluid and easy.

Their laughter bounced off the wall in front of them and then they were done. All the blue filled in. Nicky dropped their brushes into a bucket, stuck her hands on her hips and surveyed their handiwork. Not bad for a guy who claimed he didn't have an artistic bent.

Ty scooped up the discarded paper towels just as Shea called for everyone to wrap things up. A squeal of laughter echoed from behind Ty, followed by a loud clang and blue paint arced into the air. Ty whirled, then half hopped, and half skipped away from the splatter as the group of college girls apologized.

"That one played lacrosse." Shea gestured in Ty's direction. "Probably a middie."

Nicky managed to not roll her eyes. She must be the only Marylander who didn't have a damn near religious opinion on lacrosse. Ty once again surprised her by helping the girls clean up the blue paint now covering a large section of floor.

Shea turned back to Nicky. "Becca said you're great in a classroom and know your way around paintbrushes. I like to have an assistant because I can't be everywhere at once. So, what do you think?"

Nicky pulled her eyes away from Ty—who was bent over, tying a giant trash bag closed.

"I'm in. I love your approach, and the class is informative and fun."

A smile broke across Shea's features. "Great. If you two don't mind hanging around, we can talk after everyone leaves."

Ty stepped in next to Nicky and slid an arm loosely around her waist as if it was the most natural thing in the world. "I'm afraid I've got a work event tonight."

It took a moment for that to register with Nicky. Oh yeah. The Thursday night cocktail party at the Walters. Of course, he'd have to be there.

"I can stay for a bit, but I'll have to watch the time. I left a change of clothes in my office, so I can push as late as possible. If you don't mind me using your sink." He held up hands still smeared with blue.

Shea made a sweeping gesture toward the work sink along the far wall. "There's orange goop in a tub that will take most of that right off."

Ty's phone pinged loudly before he could take two steps and he fished it out of his pocket and kept walking. Then came to a sudden stop and turned back to them.

"I'm going to have to run. Mark, the Director of Development, was supposed to handle the setup for tonight's event, but his wife just went into labor. I need to get there early, or Dr. Ma..." He broke off and gave Nicky a pained look.

"I can catch a rideshare home." They'd already discussed that he wasn't available for dinner. But this was cutting into their time. It shouldn't sting. But it did. A little.

Ty's fingers squeezed on her hip and his eyes drilled into hers. "You sure?"

Nicky shook off the odd feeling. "I'll be fine, I promise. Now go on. Shoo. Being late is not an option."

His laughter wiped away the last of whatever weirdness had settled over her. Then he put a bow on that when he leaned in and kissed her gently.

"Call me later?" Ty didn't move until she nodded her response. And Nicky tried not to stare at his ass as he walked away. She failed.

Once he was out of sight, she swallowed any discomfort and turned back to Shea. "Okay, how can I help?"

TY

The fresh air outside the Copycat was a welcome relief after the paint and pot fumes of earlier. Ty cast another glance at his watch as he jogged back to his car. He felt like a dick leaving Nicky to fend for herself, but she was right. Being late was not an option. He didn't have time to go home and shower, never mind anything else. It was a good thing he'd left clothes at the office.

Ty practically threw himself into his seat and tore off, buckling his seatbelt as he pulled out of the parking space. The city driving gods were on his side and he hit every green light making his way across town. He parked and hurried to his office, pelting up the first flight of stairs two at a time. He needed to change and clean up before...

"Mark said you'd be handling things tonight. Seems the baby is finally on the way." Richard Mason stood at the top of the next flight, smiling pleasantly. Well, that was a good sign. Except the smile faded the closer Ty got to the top.

"What on earth..." Mason's voice trailed off as he waved a hand at Ty.

"I was on my way to clean up when I got Mark's message. I came straight here instead. I've got a suit in my office. I'll only be a few minutes."

Ty bypassed his office and headed down the hall to the bathroom, only registering mild surprise when Mason followed.

"You're covered in paint."

Covered wasn't quite the right word. There was a spot or two on his shoes, sure. The Chucks would never be the same. He had smears of blue on his forearms, and some still around his fingernails. He was pretty sure that was it.

"I'm sorry. I didn't expect to need to be here for another half hour. I'd have had plenty of time to go home and shower. Give me a minute..."

Ty didn't want to slam the bathroom door in the Museum Director's face, so he gave an apologetic smile and closed the door gently. Then turned the latch, just to be sure. He cranked the water as hot as he could stand and got to work.

"I assume this was something with Moira." Mason's voice carried through the heavy wood door with ease.

"Yes." Mason had cautioned him about Nicky. Ty suppressed a laugh. The memory of her trim curves resting against his chest caused an involuntary twitch below the belt and he stuffed that thought aside for later. He'd enjoyed the class. Enjoyed being with Nicky and seeing the world through her eyes for a while.

He dried his now paint-free hands and drew in a deep breath before opening the door. No surprise, Mason stood against the opposite wall, his arms over his chest.

"Tyler." The word came out like a sigh, in the tone of a disappointed parent. Ty had the good sense to stop in his tracks and listen.

"I suppose I have to take some of the blame here. I did say I couldn't advise you who to date."

Ty looked down at the blue spots on his shoes. Vibrant color on the gray background. That was what Nicky felt like to him—a bright spot in a drab world. Mason's voice droned on and Ty only half paid attention. It wasn't anything surprising. Until it was.

"I've seen what happens when a promising career gets derailed by empty charms." Mason's voice held a tinge of sadness. Ty wasn't sure he wanted to hear where Mason was going with this, but he was equally sure he had to. At least for his career. How that would impact his growing relationship with Nicky... well, that was between him and Nicky.

"Moira is far too much like her father. Charming and an all-around compelling individual who seems to draw people to them like flies to honey." Mason closed his eyes, as if memories from the past were clouding his vision of today.

"Like her father, Moira doesn't think. She lacks ambition or drive. She lives in an idealistic fantasy, which would be fine if she would at least allow others to guide her." Mason shrugged and lifted his head, his ice-blue eyes settling on Ty. Eyes the same shade as Nicky's, but while hers called up images of tropical seas or the finest of gemstones, Mason's were glacial. Cold and hard.

"Respectfully, sir, your granddaughter is an amazing artist, and everyone she works with seems to love her." Ty wasn't sure about the wisdom of contradicting Mason, but the man's view of his own grandchild was seriously skewed.

"Also like her father," Mason continued as if Ty hadn't spoken, "Moira doesn't know what is best for her. When she fails—as she always does—she drags others down with her. I wouldn't want to see that happen to someone with so much potential. All I'm suggesting is you examine your choices."

There was the unspoken threat. If Nicky wouldn't toe her grandfather's line, Ty should drop her like a hot potato. Well, too late for that. Ty cleared his throat, buying time to wrap his head around a response that would get Mason off his back tonight.

"I appreciate your concern. Just as I appreciate the interest you've shown in my career." That seemed to hit the right note. Mason's sour expression faded just a little. Ty glanced at his watch, then back up at the Museum Director. "You can be sure that my priority is the museum, and my role within it."

Career first. That had been Ty's motto for years. He saw no reason for it to change now, even if it meant dancing around the plans of a major control freak.

"Give me ten minutes to get changed, and I'll be in top shape." Ty mentally crossed his fingers and held his breath. Only when Mason chuckled and patted his shoulder did Ty dare breathe again.

"That's the spirit I've come to expect from you. Don't give it another thought. Take your time, I'll see you when you get over there."

He squeezed Ty's shoulder and turned for the stairs. Ty waited until he heard the downstairs door click shut before bolting for his office and locking the door behind him.

What in the hell had he gotten himself into? There was no way in hell Nicky would ever change, especially not for her grandfather. There was even less chance of Ty asking, or encouraging her to change. If Mason was going to tie his career prospects to Nicky's choices, Ty was in for the balancing act of his life. Shit.

He yanked the Henley over his head and pulled his dress shirt off the hanger. For now, he'd just have to do a better job of keeping things separate. Which shouldn't be that tough since Nicky so clearly wanted nothing to do with her grandfather.

Ty walked through the museum doors exactly ten minutes after Mason had left. To his credit, there wasn't a speck of blue paint visible anywhere. Though visible was the key word. He'd noticed a few missed bits on his forearms as he pulled on his shirt. Oh well. They were covered, and that's what mattered.

He spotted Mason near the information desk and took a deep breath, screwing a pleasant smile on his face. Time to focus on the career and not Nicky and the way she felt so good in his arms. Or how easily they'd worked together. Or the way she smelled like some intoxicating mix of candy and flowers.

None of those thoughts were helping him focus on work. Mason's words echoed in Ty's head—examine your choices. He needed to pay attention to the opportunities Mason represented. He needed to complete his PhD.

Ty made his way across the lobby to join the Museum Director. Somewhere, a quiet voice inside whispered: what he needed was Nicky.

CHAPTER 14

Nicky hurried up the steps to the BOPA offices, juggling her bag and the drink carrier filled with coffees. Safe bet the buzzing of her phone was yet another message from Becca. Who would just have to wait. As soon as she got inside and to the elevator, Nicky fished out her phone and thumbed the screen. Sure enough, it had been Becca.

Are you here yet?

Nicky pocketed the phone as the doors opened. The largest free arts festival in the country was two months away and the guy who had been organizing the children's programming had dropped the ball. Big time. Luckily, the rest of the event was already planned.

"Oh, my god. You got coffee. You're a saint. You freaking out yet?" Becca grabbed the drinks as Nicky came in. Nicky held back a groan when she saw the pile of papers on the worktable.

"I have to apologize. You were supposed to be support staff for this event. Congratulations, you've just been promoted. Since Chad has left us, you're the new Kidscape coordinator."

Nicky grimaced and made her way to the sprawling mess covering the table. "First, what the hell? Why? Did he quit or do something colossally stupid? Second, he didn't believe in digital files or something?" She flipped open a folder—a mix of contracts, scribbled notes, and spreadsheet printouts.

"He quit and didn't give a reason. This was everything we could find in his desk. I'll help you go through and make sense of it all. There are some emails as well, we'll get you set up with access today. Are you okay with some extra hours?"

Nicky was more than okay with it. She was making ends meet now, but more would not hurt. Especially when it came time to move out of her grandfather's place.

"I'm sorry it's so disorganized, I found out last night and haven't had the chance to dig into this," Becca said.

"I hate to say it, but maybe it's a good thing he bailed." Nicky sorted through the stack of papers and a picture began to emerge. And not a good one. She fought down the rising tide of panic at the disorganized mess she was looking at. Nine weeks. With most of the big stuff done, she could do this. It would mean some long days and giving up weekends, but it was doable.

It took the two of them the rest of the day to sort through the emails and files. In the end, it wasn't as bad as Nicky feared. Most of the setup was done. It was only a month of unanswered emails and follow-ups.

Becca dropped the last of the folders into the file drawer

and stretched her back. "I'm impressed. I thought for sure this would be a bigger headache."

Nicky closed the now tidy and organized email. "Yeah, I didn't know if I wanted to scream, cry, or punch somebody."

"Chad seems a good candidate. This deserves cocktails. And hey, it's Friday. I'll text Sabrina, too. I know Anne's working late."

It took less than half an hour to finish up and make their way to Don't Know Tavern where Sabrina had already staked out a high top and three stools. Nicky ordered a drink and slid onto a stool, enjoying what might be her last bit of relaxation for the next couple months.

After the third round of drinks, Sabrina leaned back and flashed a wicked grin. "Anne says you should bring your boyfriend when you come to dinner tomorrow night."

Nicky paused with her drink halfway to her lips. Not at the idea of dinner with Sabrina and her wife, but at bringing Ty. "Uh... We aren't... I mean, that's not..."

She tried to find the right words. That type of activity was Dating—with a capital D. Sure, she might be too preoccupied with finding out if he was as good in bed as he was at kissing, but... They sure as shit hadn't talked about meeting friends yet.

"I'm not sure that's the kind of relationship we have. But I promise I'll ask him. On that note, though, I do need to go."

Nicky was thankful she had taken the bus to work today because alcohol on an empty stomach left her a little tipsy. Definitely a night for a rideshare home. As soon as she was inside the door, she pulled out her phone and had her thumb over Ty's name. She'd just seen him this morning, and she missed talking to him. And who was she kidding? She wanted more of his kisses. And she needed to ask him about dinner with Sabrina and Anne. Before she could make up her mind whether to call him or not, her phone buzzed with an incoming text.

> I know it's late and a Friday night. But I'd like to see you if you're free and interested.

Nicky didn't think twice, she told him to come on over, but meet her at the gate in the alley. Then she looked at the text as if someone else had sent it, hoping that maybe he wouldn't see it right away. No such luck, the message showed as read. Then three little dots appeared indicating he was writing back.

> On my way.

Nicky tossed the phone on the bed and rushed to the bathroom to brush her teeth. She needed something to do. Something to take her mind off the fact she was slightly buzzed and more than a little worked up.

Her work clothes felt all wrong. Nicky whipped everything off and pulled on a pair of soft jeans and an even softer pullover just as her phone buzzed with a text from Ty. She hauled in a deep breath and ran down the steps, out the back door and unlatched the gate. She dragged him into the studio without a word.

And then he was there, inside with her and his arms were around her waist, his hands pressing against her hips. His lips warm and firm on hers.

"I missed you." His voice was a soft purr and Nicky chuckled.

"You saw me this morning."

He turned them until her back was against the closed door.

"True." Ty's breath ruffled her hair as he dipped his head

and kissed her again. Slowly, so slowly Nicky thought she would die. "But not like this."

One hand trailed down her thigh and she curled her leg up and around him. A moan escaped Ty's throat and Nicky wanted more of that. She arched against him, grinding against the hard bulge in his jeans. She didn't normally rush into sex, but right now, all she could think of was how much she wanted to get him out of his clothes.

His lips grazed her neck and even semi-coherent thoughts about whether she had towels in the tiny studio bathroom sailed out of her head. Ty consumed every bit of her brain.

The spicy, peppery, nutmeg scent of him. The feel of his beard, coarse against her skin. His kisses, soft and yet demanding. And his hands... oh god his hands. His fingers blazed a trail along the skin above her waistband. A gentle tug and she nodded, then Ty whisked her top over her head before stripping off his own.

Her breath caught as he pulled the shirt off—washboard abs and a chest that looked chiseled from marble. A dusting of soft hair... her fingers traced the line down his middle, stopping just above the button of his jeans where the little bit of hair got darker, heavier.

She wanted to feel him. Taste him. And she wasn't sure she'd ever felt such an overwhelming desire for a man. Her teeth sank into her bottom lip at the thought of him naked. Then Ty's mouth was on hers again and all she knew was want.

Ty's strong fingers dug into her hips as he pulled her forward, away from the door and toward the small couch she'd found and stuck in one corner. His lips never left hers as he slowly walked them that way.

He dropped into the cushions and pulled her into his lap, straddle his hips—and she was perfectly fine with that. She was even more fine with it when his fingers hooked behind her bra, and he arched an eyebrow at her in question.

"Yes, please." The words rushed from her lips, and before the echo of them left the room, her bra joined their shirts on the floor.

And his lips, those amazing soft, demanding lips, caressed her breasts. His tongue lavished her nipples. Gently. Maddeningly. She ground against him, winding her hands into his hair, as if by keeping him tight against her, she could control his movements.

His hands closed around her ribs, holding her away from him, and Nicky pouted, but the sight of his upturned face, lips wet, eyes dark with desire turned the pout into a groan. He caught her gaze and held it; eyes boring into hers as he leaned back into her. His lips closed on her nipple, and she felt like she could fly off the couch at the sensations whirling through her.

The roughness of his beard on soft skin. His lips and tongue, warm and wet against her. And his teeth. Oh god his teeth—gently grazing her nipples. Then harder until she gasped and squealed, writhing in his lap as a rush of warmth flooded her. Ty didn't stop. He kept going, holding her against him as he moved to her other breast.

Nicky couldn't take it. She wanted him. Needed to feel him. Now. "Ty, please." It came out as a pant, pleading and soft. She tangled her hands back into his hair and tugged until he focused his eyes on hers. "I..."

"I um...I'm not complaining here, but I called to see if you wanted to grab a late dinner. I'm not prepared... It's been a while, and... Shit, I'm fucking this up. You're fucking irresistible, but I don't have a condom."

Dammit. Neither did she. It wasn't like she'd been thinking of having sex. She was on the pill; the thought of skipping protection danced at the edges of her brain. The throbbing hard on pulsing in Ty's jeans certainly seemed to agree that protection was overrated. But...

A soft chuckle pulled her attention back to his face. That oh so handsome face, made even more so by the warm smile on his lips and the light of passion in his eyes.

"I can almost hear the thoughts. I know, tempting, but we haven't had that talk yet. I'm fine waiting."

"What did you say about dinner?" Nicky had a hard time focusing on words. Ty's thumbs caressed her sides, stroking under her breasts.

"Later. I want dessert first."

For a moment, Nicky forgot how to think. The look of raw hunger in his eyes was unmistakable. She was more than happy to oblige. No condom? Fine. That's what a blowjob was for. She wiggled in his lap, preparing to slide to the floor, but Ty's fingers clenched on her thighs.

"Not me," he murmured. "You, beautiful. You're dessert." He shifted on the couch, somehow rolling and twisting until she was laid back into the deep cushions.

"What about you?" She managed to form the words. Managed to get them out of her mouth, even though her brain was so fogged with desire that it seemed the only thing she wanted to say was 'fuck me now.'

"Oh, I'll get mine. Eventually. May I?" He pointed at her jeans and Nicky moved to unbutton them, but he gently pushed her hands away.

His touch was deft, quick, and in seconds, her jeans were on the floor and Ty's fingers were sliding along the waistband of her panties. His thumb stroked lower, making her jump.

"You're wet." The words were worship and praise from his lips. Then he lowered his head to plant kisses along her belly, his tongue tracing the ring at her navel before traveling down to the tops of her thighs. He moved, and then her legs were on his shoulders, her feet resting on his back. And the tickle of Ty's beard was rough against her inner thighs.

He kissed every bit of exposed skin, always skipping over her panties. She wanted... oh... what she wanted... But she'd never been good at asking. She moaned and arched, trying to bring the parts she wanted touched closer to his mouth. The gentle stroke of his thumb sent shivers that wracked her entire body with need.

"I want to go down on you." Ty's voice was ragged and deep. "I want to taste you on my tongue. You smell so sweet, so amazing. Let me make you come."

All it took was a nod and a whispered "yes" from her. Then his fingers dipped into her panties, gliding, stroking, until she thought she was going to explode. When his lips and tongue followed the path of his fingers, Nicky did just that. Every bit of tension she'd been holding released in a long, shaking convulsion that left her panting and exhausted. And looking at him in absolute wonder.

The smile on his face was nothing short of beautiful and told more than any words ever could—he'd enjoyed that.

"I was right, you do taste sweet." The smile changed; soft happiness replaced with a wicked grin. "Let me know when you're ready for more."

Nicky stretched and smiled. She had a promise to keep and now seemed as good a time as any. "I'm gonna need a minute. But uh...what do you think about dinner tomorrow night?"

Ty's brow furrowed. "I think you need a round two. Hell, maybe even a round three if your brain can still go there, but I'm free tomorrow night. What did you have in mind?"

"More on that later. Right now, what I need is this." She

slid forward on the couch, wrapped her arms around his neck and kissed him.

"Round two it is," Ty murmured against her as he laid her back on the couch cushions.

TY—SATURDAY, MAY 11

A tiny drill sergeant supervised as Ty loaded the dishwasher. His first reaction to meeting Anne was relief that she was not another Sabrina—tall and intimidating as fuck at times. Anne was barely five feet tall, adorable, and looked like the sweetest kindergarten teacher ever. She was still intimidating as fuck.

Or maybe that was just him. Nicky had been uncharacteristically nervous about this dinner. These women were important to her, and Nicky was becoming important to him. He was certain that was going to be a problem before too long, but he couldn't muster the energy to care too much.

He deposited the plates on the counter and barely resisted the urge to grab Nicky's ass—highlighted so perfectly by the apron she'd put on to do dishes.

"Down boy." Sabrina flicked his elbow with a dish towel. Ty flashed her his most charming smile then feigned an innocent look.

"So, why isn't there more collaboration in the art world?" Anne leaned back against the counter and picked up the conversation they'd started over dinner. One that brought up questions Ty didn't have answers for.

"No different from any other industry or art," Sabrina replied. "There's always a divide between those with means or education, and those without."

Nicky let out a laugh that shook her whole body. She certainly had the education, and yet she fell firmly on one side of the art divide, and he on the other. Sort of. He wasn't her grandfather. At least he hoped not.

"I think that's oversimplifying," Anne said. "It's reductive."

Nicky handed Sabrina the last of the hand washing and turned around. Her features set in a small frown. "I think that divide exists and is at the core of the elitism in the art world," she said. "But I don't think it's that simple."

Anne poured coffees and they moved into the living room. Ty had just sat down, Nicky's hand resting warm on his thigh, when a cat blacker than he thought possible made its way into his lap, curled up and started purring.

"Huh." Sabrina looked taken aback for a moment, then a broad grin broke on her face. "Looks like you've been accepted."

Ty scratched the cat behind the ears and was rewarded with an escalation in the purring. Somehow that pulled his brain back to the little gasps and moans that came out of Nicky just the night before. Shit, he needed to get his mind off that right now.

"Okay," he said, more to try to bring his mind back to the conversation and not think of Nicky's kisses. "If Sabrina's approach is reductive and too simple, then what feeds that divide? Because I see it all the time, and the Walters is a free museum."

Anne smiled as if he'd said something important. "In a way, that free set up contributes to the elitism."

Wait? What? He'd spent too many years working with donors to let that go without question, but before he could open his mouth, Anne was shaking her head.

"I know, I know. But hear me out. You've got this terrific resource and it's open to the public. Which is awesome. And it should be. But you've also got a budget that comes primarily from donors. And donors have expectations…"

Something clicked in Ty's brain. An almost audible thing that jolted him out of the comfortable place where he saw himself.

"Because they have the means, and usually the education, or at least experience, they feel…" He didn't want to say it. Even though he knew it to be true—hell, all he had to do was look around at any fundraiser he attended. Shit. "Entitled."

Sabrina and Anne both nodded, but it was Nicky's reaction that was his undoing. Her eyes went wide as she stared at him, her lips slowly stretching into a broad smile and a look of wonder in her eyes.

"Nailed it. If it was just about background, or education, or money, my grandfather wouldn't have a problem with me and what I do. But it's not just those things."

There it was in a simple sentence. The conflict Ty faced— because Richard Mason's objections about his own grandchild had nothing to do with her being an artist, and everything to do with how he perceived her behavior and choices.

"It's about value," he said, so softly he wasn't sure everyone heard. But three sets of eyes turned to him. "Or rather, perceived value."

Hadn't he been guilty of that himself? The way he looked at the works at the American Visionary Art Museum said he had. Or at least, the way he used to look at them. His views had changed the moment Nicky had shown him a different perspective.

"That still doesn't answer the question of why there's such a divide," Anne said. "Artscape is a wildly successful festival. It's free, accessible to everyone, and features art and artists of all varieties. And still gets sneered at by many."

Ty couldn't deny that. While most of the museum staff he

knew loved the festival, far too many saw it as commercial pandering. Two words that didn't belong in the same breath as art as far as they were concerned. Richard Mason fell firmly into that category.

"I don't know that you can answer the why," Ty said. "I think it's too individual."

Nicky's fingers tightened on his thigh, and she leaned forward. "So true. I feel like it's an expression of their own biases. It's learned behavior."

What did that say about him? He liked to think he was more open-minded than Dr. Mason but was he really. Even if he was, that would be a difficult mindset to hold onto when surrounded by the opposite.

"Where do you fall?" Sabrina's dark eyes drilled into his. As if she knew he was already going down that path.

Ty cleared his throat and laced his fingers through Nicky's. "Anyone in my position would like to claim they're as unbiased as possible. Entirely altruistic and focused on supporting the art world."

He swallowed hard. This was his career he was talking about here. For the first time ever, he wasn't one hundred percent certain he was going about it in the right way.

"If they did, they'd be lying." The words fell from his mouth like stones. Crashing into the floor and shattering. Taking some of his complacency and certainty with them. "Where am I?" He held Sabrina's gaze for a moment, then turned to Nicky. The warm welcome in her eyes gave him the encouragement he needed. Ty took a deep breath and blew it out slowly, never taking his eyes off Nicky's.

"I'm evolving."

Her smile stayed firm, and he dared a glance back at Sabrina. His answer seemed to have satisfied her. She sat back and smiled anyway. Then she steepled her fingers under her chin and that smile started reminding Ty of a cat about to pounce on its prey. The trouble was, he felt like the prey.

"And what about you two?" Sabrina asked. She waved a hand between them as if that explained everything. "Nicky keeps saying it's too early to call it dating. In fact, she said it last weekend, and again yesterday, but this doesn't look like too early to me."

Beside him, Nicky stiffened, her eyes wide and a little gasp escaped her lips. Last weekend... That would have been right before their couch make-out session at his apartment. The one that had caused him to take a very cold shower. Then give up and take a very long, very hot shower to take care of things as thoughts of Nicky ran through his mind. Last night, well...

Ty reeled himself back to the present and took Nicky's hand then gave it a squeeze. "I'd call this dating."

Sabrina nodded her approval, but Ty only cared for Nicky's response. Her eyes went wider still, and a deep blush crept up her cheeks. He had a split second of worry he'd said the wrong thing before a smile lit up her face.

"Works for me," she whispered, and Ty wanted nothing more than to smother her in kisses.

CHAPTER 15

A life-size projection of Gustav Klimt's The Kiss, and the inspiration for today's mosaic class, filled the wall. Nicky tore her eyes away from the bright golds of the image. Why had she chosen that piece for this class? It was a perfect inspiration piece, but it inspired not-safe-for-work thoughts about Ty.

It felt like an eternity. And it felt like only a moment. In the past week, they'd gone out multiple times, seen each other every day, that kiss, and oh yeah, the toe-curling experience on her studio couch Friday night. Then the dinner with Sabrina and Anne. It was a whirlwind.

"Which do you think is better?" A woman's voice pulled Nicky from her thoughts, and she turned to see an elderly woman holding two different tile pieces—a deep, opaque red and a brighter, translucent orange-red.

"You chose the vase, right?" Nicky glanced at the table where the woman's daughter still sat, sorting through the bin of tiles. The Mother's Day event was mostly mothers and daughters, though there were a few sons in the mix.

The woman nodded and Nicky led her back to their worktable to review their other color choices. Shades of clear glass, ranging from the palest butter yellow to a rich honey color nestled with a small selection of opaque cobalt. A striking and beautiful combination. Nicky tapped the orange.

"I'd go with the translucent. It will catch more light. Let the blue be the only opaque color, maybe." Nicky laid the orange piece on the table then rearranged the others until the daughter sucked in a surprised breath as the warmer shades created an ombre effect. "Try it out on the light table if you'd like."

Nicky moved around the class, checking with each pair, making color suggestions, helping with getting the random shaped pieces to line up right and just chatting with the students. They had a choice between a vase, a tray that could also be used as a trivet, or a small wall hanging. Using The Kiss as inspiration, the students chose their tile pieces and created their own design.

She loved interactive classes like this one—where the focus was on allowing people to create. No right or wrong. No rules of what the art had to mean or communicate. Just free flowing expressions of beauty for the sake of making something pretty.

Something people like her grandfather didn't seem to understand. And then there was Ty, who had gotten past her objections to dating yet another preppy type. He seemed interested in exploring a world outside the elitist art bubble her grandfather lived in. Looking at Ty, he appeared every bit the buttoned-up type.

Behind closed doors was a whole different story. There was nothing reserved about the way he kissed. Or the way…

Nicky pulled her mind back to the classroom. Pining over a guy was not in her vocabulary. Or at least, never had been. There was just something about Ty—from the first time she'd seen him, she couldn't get him out of her head.

So much for bringing her focus back to the room. She'd have to text him once she was done. Meanwhile, she had a class to lead.

"Now that you've got your colors and basic pattern, it's time to think about laying the tiles out on your chosen piece—but do not use the adhesive yet," Nicky said. She switched the image on the wall to her own sample mosaics. "My samples are on the front table if you need to get a closer look."

She spoke as she walked the room again, making sure everyone had the tools they'd need. When she made it back to the front, she clapped her hands together, smiled brightly and braced herself for the questions to start. "Okay! Let's make some pretties."

Within seconds, she was fielding questions. Do we have enough tiles? How do we make these all fit? These pieces are too big. These pieces are too small.

It took a full twenty minutes before the inevitable happened.

"Oh crap!"

Nicky turned to the source of the voice off to one side near the front of the room. A mother and son stood hunched over their tray while he frantically tried to pull tiles up from the adhesive already spread on the surface. Nicky took a slow breath and kicked her patience into high gear. She'd said it umpteen times already—don't lay the adhesive down yet.

As she approached the pair, the frustration rolled off them in waves. The teenage son's shoulders hunched up to his ears and the mother practically wringing her hands. Nicky moved in quickly.

"These stupid tiles won't move!" The young man shoved at the tray.

Nicky caught it before it slid off the table and faced him squarely with her best smile in place. "It's not a problem," she kept her tone bright and casual. "Happens all the time. Folks get excited to design things and that glue just doesn't have the courtesy to not set up."

As she spoke, his shoulders crept down a notch or two. "Gregory, I've got extra trays up at the front, why don't you go grab one?"

That took his shoulders almost back to normal. As soon as he turned his back, Nicky faced his mother.

"I went to get more tiles and he'd already put on the adhesive, I'm sorry..." The woman's hand wringing intensified. Nicky scanned the table, they still had plenty of tiles, but it would be a close call. Before she could say anything, Gregory was back with a new tray and Nicky scooped it from his hands then pocketed the bottle of adhesive.

"If you two will get started practicing your layout— without adhesive—I'll grab you some more tiles. Looks like it was the pretty jade green ones and some of the translucent rose?"

That brought a shaky smile and nod from the mom and an eye roll from the son. Nicky would lay odds this whole thing was the mom's idea. Probably trying to recapture the childish gifts most kids brought home from grade school.

She grabbed more tiles for them, finished checking on the rest of the class then got set up for the next steps. The adhesive step was always a bit harrowing. In order to have a piece participants could take home right away, she used a quick set adhesive, which—as Gregory and his mother had discovered—

did not allow for time to rearrange once you laid the tiles down.

Surprisingly, there were no more mishaps and even Gregory got into it once it came time to set their tiles—a beautiful jade background with rose and gold pieces set so they created a ribbon of flowers. The design was striking and the execution this time flawless. And Gregory was beaming.

Only after she got all the participants out and the classroom cleaned up did Nicky allow herself to relax. Classes like this were fun, but also draining in a way that a traditional art class was not. And being distracted the whole time by thoughts of a certain sexy Joe Preppy didn't help.

Friday night. Holy crap. Oral was not something most men excelled at in her experience. But Ty... oh, he more than excelled. The man was pure magic. Still, she'd wanted more. She'd wanted him.

She fumbled her phone from her pocket and checked the hours of the CVS nearest home. Cool. Still open. She'd stop in and pick up a box of condoms. She wasn't about to get caught unprepared again.

TY—SUNDAY, MAY 12

Condoms. Where the fuck...

Ty found them in the aisle with the tampons and pads. Right next to the baby products. He supposed it was a logical arrangement. He tossed a box into his cart and headed for the registers. He and Nicky had been spending more and more time together and he was in an absolute haze of desire. He couldn't get enough of her.

He kept trying to tell himself this was just lust. Expected after over six months of nothing. No amount of logic from his brain was getting through and this was unlike any lust he'd ever experienced. He'd enjoyed every second of making Nicky orgasm. Repeatedly. That was two days ago, and he had high hopes of getting her into his bed soon. Hence the condoms.

"Did you want your milk in a bag?"

Ty shook his head.

Back home, groceries put away, he stuffed the condoms into his nightstand drawer and swallowed hard. Sex shouldn't be this big of a deal. It never used to be. Hell, he'd been right there with Deke and Zach. Find a girl who was interested, slap on a condom, good to go. No questions asked. Even his casual relationships were barely more than that.

Until Nicky. From the first moment he'd seen her, she'd captivated him in a way he'd never experienced.

His phone buzzed, pulling him from those thoughts. Shit. He still needed to shower and change from his Mother's Day afternoon tea clothes. He thumbed open his phone to find a text from Nicky.

> Hey, I just got home from a long day and need to decompress. You up for company?

Ty resisted the urge to tell her to just come on over. They'd order out and spend the night in bed.

> Absolutely. Sorry for the long day. What are you in the mood for?

He hit send and stripped down for the shower. He was just about to get in when his phone buzzed again.

> Not bad, I'm just people-d out. I hate to be boring, but can we maybe get takeout? I need down time.

His cock twitched in response as soon as he read her message.

> Sounds great. Give me maybe twenty minutes and I can meet you to walk you over.

He hit send and jumped in the shower, so he didn't see her reply until he got out.

> Haha, it's still daylight. I just need to change, and I'll be at your door in 15.

He was still in his towel when the doorbell rang. Not bothering to dress, he flung the door open and couldn't resist smiling when her eyes went wide in appreciation.

"I'm sorry, do I need to give you more time?" She slid past him into the room, the scent of honeysuckle trailing with her, and Ty was momentarily tongue tied. She was in some slim fitting bright purple jeans that showed off long legs and her trim build. The colorful streak in her hair was pure silver today, matching her top and the silver boots she had on.

Ty closed the door and found his voice. "No, sorry. I didn't see your message until just before you got here. I'll get dressed."

Nicky shrugged, a smile slowly curving her lips and lighting her eyes. "Why?"

Oh, that was a pleasant surprise.

"Besides, I need to return a favor."

All sense of restraint departed at her words. Ty groaned as she came into his arms, her fingers cool against his bare skin. Her kisses were sweet and honeyed, and hungry.

"Is it okay if I..." She glanced down at his towel and Ty nearly lost it at the clear desire printed on her face.

"Babe, you can do whatever you'd like," he replied as he

backed them into the room. When they reached the couch, she gently guided him to sit, then sank to her knees in front of him.

A firm tug and the towel came undone. Nicky's eyes went wide again, and he braced himself for her reaction. He wasn't a small man by any standard, and he was uncut.

Her fingers slid over him, softly, gently, teasing at the head just poking out from the foreskin. Then she wrapped her hand around him, smoothly sliding and releasing as if she knew exactly what he liked.

Half hard grew to fully hard in about two strokes and she was practically purring as she licked from the base of his shaft up to the head and back down. Then she slid his cock between her lips and Ty nearly came as her tongue swirled over the head. Watching Nicky suck his cock as if it was the most amazing thing she'd ever had in her life was mind blowing.

Her hands did remarkable things, and she took her time, bringing him to the edge of an orgasm and then stopping. When she changed her angle and took nearly all of him down her throat, Ty lost it. He managed to croak out a warning that he was going to come a split second before he did.

Nicky didn't miss a stroke and kept going until the last spasm ratcheted through him. Then she sat back, her eyes watery and her lips swollen and red. And she smiled.

"I'm gonna get a glass of water," she said as she pushed herself up to stand.

Something nagged in Ty's mind—he should get up. He should take care of her needs. She was the guest here. His entire body felt like gelatin and moving was not on his radar. Somewhere it dimly registered why she needed water—she'd swallowed.

Before he could wrap his head around that, she was back,

pressing a glass of water into his hands and cradling one herself. "What sounds good for dinner?"

Ty took a sip then set the glass aside. He stood, leaving the towel on the couch, and pulled her up with him.

"Are you that hungry?" When she shook her head, he lifted her, wrapped her legs around his waist and headed for his bedroom. "I've had you for dessert. Tonight, you're the main course."

In the bedroom, she squirmed out of his arms and stripped. He sank to his knees in front of her, intent on giving her the same kind of pleasure she'd just given him, but she tugged at his shoulders and pulled him up, shaking her head.

"I want you."

He was about to protest, he needed time to recover. Then her hands were stroking, and he was hard again, his cock throbbing and begging for attention.

"Are you sure..." he began.

"I've got condoms in my purse." Nicky moved to go back into the living room, but Ty caught her wrist and gently pulled her back to the bed before fishing the package of condoms from his nightstand.

"Great minds think alike," he said. Nicky took a foil packet from his fingers, opened it, and rolled the condom down over his length.

"I want you, now," she whispered into his ear.

Ty curled an arm around her and laid her back on the bed. Her legs wrapped his waist, and her heat beckoned him. His cock slid against her—slick and wet, already wanting and waiting for him. She wriggled, lifting her hips, and tightening her legs and Ty pressed the head of his cock into her.

And there it was. Her mouth opened in a wide O, her head threw back and a little hiss escaped her. He started to pull out, but her fingers clenched into his ass, and she pulled him closer. Fuck she was tight and every experience in his life screamed at him that he needed to use his tongue, his fingers, to get her ready for him.

Nicky shifted, lifting her legs higher and wider. "Don't stop." The words breathed out of her as Ty pressed his way forward, feeling her body opening around him. And then he was there. Fully inside her. His balls resting against her. His cock wrapped in warm softness. And her face registered pure bliss.

"Ty, please..." The pleading note in her voice sent a jolt straight to his cock and she sighed in pleasure at the twitch. He braced himself and stroked, slowly, gently. The way he'd always had to the first minute or two of sex. "Fuck me."

There was no pleading in her voice. That was pure command and Ty's body responded before his brain could catch up. He hooked his arms under her legs and pushed deeper. Then again. The gasps coming from her driving him to go harder, faster, until their bodies slammed together, and she was crying out his name.

He rolled, pulling her with him and without losing a stroke, she tucked her knees under her and adjusted her angle.

"Ride me, baby. Get yourself off on my cock. I wanna watch you come."

Her fingers dug into his chest as she ground against him. He'd thought her beautiful before, but her face in ecstasy was a whole new level. Her eyes locked on his and he lost himself in pools of blue. Nicky's every gasp echoed in the empty spaces of his life, filling them with her. Nothing but her.

He rested his hands on her hips, rolling with her as she took her pleasure from him. Her thighs trembled and she tightened around him as her body tensed, arching back, and shaking, then a rush of wetness surrounded him just before she collapsed against his chest. He stroked her back, letting her catch her breath.

"Ready for more?"

She raised her head, her eyes glazed and happy looking. And she nodded.

"On your hands and knees." He issued the command and waited to see what she would do.

Without a question, Nicky slid off him and assumed the position, her delectable ass poking up in the air as if waiting to be fucked. Oh god how he wanted that. One day. But not now. Right now, all he wanted was to see his cock buried in her while his hands wrapped that tiny waist.

He got on his knees behind her and pushed in, trying to go slow, but Nicky had other ideas and ground back against him hard. She arched her ass higher and tossed her head back and Ty's passion-hazed brain had an epiphany of sorts. Nicky liked it a bit rough.

Well, he was more than happy to deliver on that front, but there would have to be some serious conversation before he was willing to go too far down that path.

He tangled a hand into her hair, not pulling, just holding, and she squeezed around him. He pulled, gently, and Nicky quivered. The clenching of her muscles and the sweet moans coming from her mouth had him on the edge of losing control.

"Fuck me, Ty."

Those words destroyed every shred of his control. Ty leaned into her, pounding her body into the mattress until sweat dripped from them both and she grabbed the pillow to muffle her cries of pleasure. He came again with a roar, his fingers digging into her hips so hard they left bruised indents, and still, he kept coming, as if it would never stop.

When he finally eased himself from her, Nicky lay flat on

the mattress, her hair mussed and tangled, her fingers still clenched into his pillows. He disposed of the condom and came back to bed, pulling her into his arms. Her body trembled and he stroked the hair from her face.

"Are you okay?" He wasn't sure. She was so quiet. They had talked sex, but not the borderline rough play they'd just had.

Her hands reached up, captured his face, and pulled him down to her for a kiss. The sweetness soaked into him, her breath filled him, and he felt himself shatter into tiny pieces, then come back together around her. Oh, he was so entirely fucked. If he hadn't already been a goner after the fun they'd had earlier in the week, he definitely was now.

"That was amazing. And I'm fine. I uh... guess we have some more talking to do, huh?"

Ty barely resisted saying 'ya think.' From what he could tell, Nicky had a kinky side. Well, hell. So did he. That was a beast he didn't let out too often; he'd had too many partners freak out over it, or not able to handle it. And here was Nicky, wrapping her body around him and reassuring him that she was just fine, thank you very much.

She tipped her head back and gave him a sly grin.

"Now I'm hungry." She disentangled herself and disappeared. Moments later, she came back in, phone in hand. "How about sushi? And then round two? Or would it be three? I guess it would be three for you."

She picked up the pack of condoms on the nightstand. "Hmm. Two more."

Ty slid an arm around her waist and pulled her back into the bed with him. "Sushi sounds great. And it's early. Plenty of time for whatever rounds you want."

"Good thing I brought my own condoms, huh?" The wicked grin that spread on her face had his cock jumping back to attention despite the fact that he'd just had the most intense orgasm he'd had in years, maybe in his entire life. It didn't help when her tongue snaked out and wet her bottom lip when she noticed it.

"Food first," he said firmly. "After, you can have all of me you'd like."

Nicky bounced onto the bed, thumbed her phone on, and shot him a wink. "Good. Because I'm greedy."

NICKY—TUESDAY, MAY 14

A dull ache throbbed between Nicky's legs as she straddled her scooter. She and Ty had spent all of Sunday night in bed, though very little involved sleeping. She'd woken him up once in the night, and he'd woken her in the morning. Two days later and she was still sore, but she wasn't about to complain. Who knew Joe Preppy was beyond great in bed and was secretly kinky? She liked. Maybe too much.

It was too soon for her to be feeling this way. They'd only known each other a month and a half. He was all wrong for her in so many ways. Except... he wasn't. And she was guilty of judging a book by its cover—assuming he'd be the same as every other buttoned up suit she'd ever known.

She parked the scooter next to Sabrina's truck and strolled into the community center gymnasium. Today she was representing BOPA at an information fair for local organizations to highlight their summer programs.

She found Sabrina already setting up the AVAM table in

the cavernous space. Right on the other side of Sabrina's table was a team from The Walters. Shit. Ty had mentioned this, and she'd been in such a fog it hadn't registered. She scanned the group for anyone she knew. Not that she expected her grandfather to be at a high school summer activities fair. Though she was pretty sure the slim woman who delivered a box of information pamphlets to the museum's table was his assistant.

She shuddered and turned back to setting up the BOPA displays—colorful signage highlighting summer events like Artscape and a new series of classes and activities. A shrill whistle caught Nicky's attention just in time to catch the water bottle Sabrina lobbed at her.

"Stay hydrated," Sabrina said with a laugh. "You've done one of these before?"

"Similar—the school's elective fair plus community information events."

The room hummed with activity, voices echoing off the wood floors and hard walls. An electronic buzz somehow cut through the cacophony in the auditorium and Nicky grabbed for her phone, thumbing up her message app.

> You at the info fair today?

Nicky sent a quick yes and stuffed the phone away to finish her table set up before the doors opened for students.

"Hey, um...."

She glanced up at a pretty woman in a dove gray blouse and matching slacks. A colorful scarf—probably hand painted —draped her shoulders. She looked like a carbon copy of Gramps' assistant, and everything about her screamed poise and polish. Not a hair out of place. And a Walters name tag that said her name was Jessica.

"Sorry to bother you. We don't seem to have any tape and figured you probably did."

Nicky flashed a smile. "Yeah, sure. Hang on." She pulled out her supply box. Guaranteed to have a stapler, scissors, multiple types of tape, glue, a hole punch, and a host of anything Nicky had discovered came in handy over years of hosting student events and classes.

"What kind?"

The other woman scrunched her nose. "I don't know. Just tape."

Nicky took a deep breath. "To tape paper together? Or a tablecloth to the table? Or for the banner?"

Jessica's scrunched nose gave way to giggles. And not the nice kind. "One of the grommets on our banner tore. I'm not here to do an art project."

She snatched the roll of blue duct tape Nicky held out—blue to match the color of their banner—and without a word of thanks, marched back to the Walters' table.

"Wow," Sabrina commented. "She was a charmer."

Nicky glanced up to see Jessica had handed the tape off to a young man in a Walters polo shirt. Probably an intern.

"Out of curiosity, how is Mr. Coffee Shop?" Sabrina poked Nicky's thigh, pulling her attention away from the Walters' staff. "I assume you two went out over the weekend."

"He's..." Nicky cleared her throat, searching for words for just how amazing he was. "He's..."

Her words died on her lips as the auditorium door opened and Ty strolled in. Slim fitting dark pants made his legs look a mile long, and Nicky had to squash the memory of how firm his ass was under her hands. Shirt sleeves cuffed up and showing off toned forearms had her brain recalling how easily he lifted her, and the bulge of muscles as he held himself over her.

He lifted a hand and waved at Jessica, then swerved and headed straight toward Nicky. His lips curled into a smile, but the smolder in his eyes said his brain was right alongside hers.

"Hey, Sabrina." Ty gave a nod and leaned into Nicky, his beard brushing her ear as he spoke. "Hello, gorgeous." He slid into the chair next to her, his hand skimming her knee, squeezing briefly before retreating to his own space.

"I've got a really packed week and won't have time for lunches. Might not even be at the coffee shop. Can we make plans for Friday night?"

Nicky blinked, trying to make the jump back to normal conversation when her thoughts were still on them in the bedroom. Finally, his words made sense, then the questions came.

"Sure. Gramps pushing you?"

His mouth turned into a thin line for a moment before adopting that lopsided grin she liked so much. "Dumped the board meeting on me this morning, and it didn't feel right to text about the change in routine. That feels like a face-to-face thing."

Her heart fluttered, sending butterflies bouncing around her chest. Thinking of her, wanting to talk in person—those weren't the actions of someone who didn't care. And where the fuck did that come from? And the sudden thought—why was he here? Was this a work visit, or for her?

"I've gotta check in with the team. At least seem like I had a job-related reason to come here." Well, that answered that question. Maybe he was reading her mind. "By the way, Jessica is a snot, but she is good at her job."

Nicky rolled her eyes. "I've already discovered the snot part. Text or call later and we'll figure it out."

He leaned in again, one hand resting on the back of her chair, and all Nicky wanted to do was curl herself into him and get lost in his warmth and peppery scent. Friday seemed too long to wait.

"Late nights can be an option," she said and was rewarded with an almost instant purr of satisfaction from Ty—a deep rumble in her ear that sent shivers down her spine.

"I was about to suggest the same." His voice intensified the shivers until her entire body tensed as if waiting for his next move. His hand slipped into her hair, fingers caressing the back of her neck a moment before withdrawing.

When he stood, a hard outline in his pants made it clear he wanted more. Ty cleared his throat and took a moment to collect himself.

"Oh, and would you get my tape back from Jessica, please?" Nicky assumed her most innocent expression and batted her eyelashes at him.

"Can do, beautiful." With a final tug on his pants, he headed toward the Walters' table. She kept her eyes on his retreating form until he stopped to talk to Jessica.

Nicky tried to get back to work, but the table was set up and none of the little tasks remaining could hold her attention when he was right there. She told herself it was nothing but lust. The problem was lust had never camped out in the pit of her stomach like this. She could ignore lust if she had to. She couldn't ignore Ty.

He dropped the roll of tape on her table with a wink and a mouthed "see you Friday" as he went back out, and Nicky's heart rate skyrocketed.

"Is six weeks too fast to..." Nicky stopped herself, unwilling to give voice to her feelings. Her chest tightened, and the room was suddenly too warm, but her feet and hands went cold. Breathing felt like sucking air through a straw.

A slow smile spread across Sabrina's face. "I am not the right person to ask if you're looking for a negative answer.

Anne and I moved in together after only two weeks. That was fifteen years ago. When you know, you know."

Sabrina's words did nothing to ease the tightness in Nicky's chest. She pushed out of her chair and headed for the side door—away from the main entrance and the parking lot where Ty was likely just getting into his car. If she saw him right now, she'd have a very hard time controlling whatever emotions were threatening to boil over. She needed fresh air and a moment to breathe.

Nicky burst through the door into a day that had turned humid with a sky so bright it was nearly white, making her wish she'd grabbed her sunglasses. She leaned against the building where a sliver of shade offered some protection from the sun and sucked in air, trying to calm the cyclone of thoughts whirling through her head.

She couldn't be in love with Ty. Sure, he was nice, and sweet, and amazing in bed, but she had no clue how their worlds would align. She'd started out thinking he wasn't her type, but she couldn't name a single way he was wrong for her —aside from looking like Joe Preppy and working at the Walters. And if that didn't make her the shallowest person on Earth, she didn't know what did.

The squeal of the door opening pulled Nicky's attention out of the heavy clouds building at the edge of the sky. Sabrina ambled over and leaned her tall frame against the wall next to her.

"We've got about fifteen minutes before the doors open. You wanna tell me what this is about?"

Nicky gulped air. She'd never been this nervous before. Hell, she'd had boyfriends she loved. Well, thought she loved, and never felt like this. Everything in her world felt off kilter.

"Why does he have to work at the Walters? With my asshole of a grandfather."

Putting it into words felt good. It gave Nicky a sense of her feet coming back to the ground. Though, by the look on Sabrina's face, it was clear she had no idea what Nicky's grandfather had to do with Ty.

"My first serious boyfriend was..." Nicky shook her head and sighed. "He was a classic prep schoolboy. All American all the way. I'm sure he's married and has a trophy Stepford wife, and..." She stopped herself and hauled in a long, slow breath. Sabrina hadn't moved, and her expression hadn't changed.

"All my life, I've had... well, that boyfriend was a jerk in so many ways. And predictable. And in hindsight, a really bad lay." Nicky laughed. Her high school boyfriend had seemed experienced, sure of himself, but he'd been all fumbles. Years later, she was certain it was his first time as well. Despite how much he bragged about the girls he'd slept with and talked about expecting Nicky to be wild in bed.

"I don't have a good track history with the buttoned up corporate types. Grandfather. First boyfriend. Last boyfriend."

Sabrina scrunched up her face, a sure sign she was stifling a grin. "Have you tried a relationship with an artsy type?"

Laughter bubbled up, but Nicky stomped it down, fearing it would never stop.

"A musician, and he was just as bad—in different ways. A couple of casual relationships that were very short. I guess I'm a fan of stability."

Shit.

She thumped her head against the building behind her. "I think I've fallen head over heels for Ty. And that scares the crap out of me." At least the crushing sense of the world pressing in on her had eased up.

"You wanna talk about that?" Sabrina raised an eyebrow.

Nicky bit her lip. She needed to get over this shit and deal.

Ty was amazing in so many ways. And yet, he was another buttoned-up suit. Sure to disappoint in the long run.

"Ty's focused on his career, which is great. Except his career is tied directly to my grandfather who seems to think I need fixing."

Nicky paused. Those weren't the root of the problem, "I think Ty likes the boost to his career. And I'm terrified he's going to be just like every other buttoned up, uptight man in my life."

But he wasn't. At every turn, Ty had proven he absolutely was not like every other Joe Preppy. And that might be the scariest thing of all.

"Sorry. I had a... a moment there. I'll be okay. I need to get back inside and finish setting up."

She pushed away from the building and headed in before Sabrina could question further. Truth was, Nicky didn't want to think too hard about her sudden realization. She sure as hell didn't want to talk about it. Talking about it would mean examining her feelings, and why they scared her so much.

TY—FRIDAY, MAY 17

"Our European exhibits have been a staple of the museum for years." Murmurs of assent greeted Sebastian's words and Ty gritted his teeth. He'd spent all week preparing for this board meeting. It had already gone nearly two hours over, and things were not running smoothly.

"The role of museums is changing," Ty countered. "If we want to expand our membership and stay relevant in years to come, we need to focus on a more global vision."

The room exploded with voices as everyone seemed determined to show how their viewpoint was superior. All that meant is they were once again at an impasse and this meeting would go nowhere—half the board wanted to feature a series of traditional art from around the globe, while the other half agreed with Sebastian and wanted to expand on European artwork.

Why on earth Mason had saddled Ty with the responsibility of leading this meeting, Ty hadn't a clue. It sure as shit didn't help his growing distaste for the man.

"I think," Ty began, but his voice was lost in the surrounding chatter. Every person here was a professional and yet they were behaving... *Shit*. They were acting like the determined, assertive people they were. He sighed, straightened, and cleared his throat, loudly. To no avail. Sebastian's voice rose above the rest, going on about tradition.

Ty rose and slammed his hand onto the table. The noise startled the room into silence and all eyes turned to him.

"Clearly, this is a sensitive topic," Ty said before anyone, like Sebastian, could start in. "It's also a very important one that impacts budgeting and planning for years to come, and I think it's apparent we will not agree today."

A few murmurs of assent and nods all around gave him hope they could at least table the discussion for now and he could get the hell out of the overly stuffy boardroom filled with too many egos.

The murmurs grew as the discussions resumed, as if Ty hadn't said a thing until one rose above it all. "I move we adjourn!"

Once again, everyone stopped talking and looked toward the source of the motion. Dr. Lillian Fletcher, a retired orthopedic surgeon, stood, her hands pressed into the table as she scanned the room.

"I, for one, have dinner plans this evening," she said, her voice returning to its more typical well-modulated tones. "And I agree with Tyler. We are not getting anywhere today. I move we adjourn and table this for our next meeting. We might be wise to schedule a longer than usual session for the ensuing discussion."

Sebastian rose as if to object, but Lizabeth, sitting off to one side taking notes, chimed in. "There's a motion on the floor."

Sebastian sank back into his seat as another member seconded the motion and the vote was called. From there, it was a matter of minutes before everyone was filing out of the boardroom. All except Sebastian, who came up and laid his hand on Ty's shoulder.

"This may be a sensitive subject," Sebastian said, his voice low as if he feared being overheard, even though they were alone. "Your behavior at a recent event was ah..." He paused as if he couldn't decide what to say next. Finally, he cleared his throat, dropped the hand from Ty's shoulder and looked him straight in face, his expression hovering between serious and smug. "Let's just say, observed to be less than professional."

Ty wasn't sure which event Sebastian could be referring to, or why he wasn't hearing this from Mason, rather than the President of the Board.

"I'm not sure how to respond to that. Could you elaborate?"

Sebastian pressed his thin lips together. "The summer programs fair." He blurted the words out as if they explained everything, and Ty supposed maybe they did. He had gone there to see Nicky. Anything museum related had been an excuse.

"I believe you are seeing Dr. Mason's granddaughter. That's a double-edged sword, and if you have your sights set on moving up the ladder here, you'd be wise to consider that."

Without another word, he walked out the door. Ty gave him a slow ten count before he headed to his office, hoping to avoid running into any other board members and getting roped into conversations. He needed to breathe without worrying how someone might take it the wrong way.

Once settled in his office with the door closed and locked for good measure Ty yanked his tie from his neck and loosened his collar. He thumbed open his phone and saw several texts from Nicky. Shit. Thinking of her had been the only thing keeping him from exploding when the board divided right down the middle on the new exhibit proposal.

He'd dropped her a text when he realized the meeting was going to go long, but then he'd silenced his phone and now there was a string of messages.

> Oh, that sounds fun. Thanks for the heads
> up. Keep me posted.

A series of question marks about thirty minutes later. And another thirty minutes after that. Then about half an hour ago a longer text.

> I'm guessing you're buried. Tell ya what, I'll
> make plans for tonight. Text me when you
> know what's going on.

The tension in his shoulders loosened, a bit. Instead of flying off the handle—and she'd have been within her rights to be upset—she'd taken charge. He leaned back in his chair and took the first easy breath he'd had in hours. He'd hoped to get home before his date with Nicky, but... Ty sighed and hit reply.

> Just finished. About to leave the office.

He hit send, and before he could gather his things, his phone pinged with an incoming message.

I'll pick you up. Meet me out front.

Ty sent a thumbs up, decided to leave everything at the office rather than try to navigate Nicky's scooter with a messenger bag, and was out his office door feeling better than he had all day.

He cut through the museum, waving at the security desk as he passed, and stepped out into the golden afternoon light, and immediately regretted his decision. He should have told Nicky to pick him up in back. Or that he'd get her. Or something. Instead, he was face to face with her grandfather as he stood surrounded by Lizabeth and the very board members Ty would like to chuck into the streets.

"Tyler," Mason greeted him. "Lizabeth was telling me the meeting was rather contentious. I'm disappointed."

Ty ground his teeth and forced his expression into some semblance of neutral. Or at least he hoped that was what he conveyed. He had no clue what game Mason was playing, but he was feeling like a pawn rather than a valued team member. And that was not a good feeling.

Mason had insisted Ty lead the meeting. He had to know where the split was. Just as he had to know Ty would always support forward growth and continued evolution.

Mason pulled away from the group, effortlessly guiding Ty to follow along until they were a few steps removed.

"Don't lose sight of your goals. I know it's a challenge right now, but..."

His words were cut off by the beeping of a horn. At the curb, Nicky sat straddle her scooter.

"Hiya, Gramps!" She flashed a big smile at Mason then turned to Ty. "Heads up!"

She flung what looked like a bright red bowling ball at

him. Only the thing he caught was too light to be a bowling ball. Nicky nodded at the back of her scooter.

"You didn't have a helmet last time. You ready?"

Sebastian's earlier comments rang in Ty's head, as did Mason's expectations. This was his career on the line. He took a deep breath, turned to his boss and did the only thing he could do under the circumstances—keep his plans with Nicky.

"I apologize. The meeting went over and I'm afraid we have dinner reservations. While things did not go as smoothly as I'd have liked, I don't feel it was a total failure. And it's good to know the lay of the land."

Ty tipped his head toward Nicky, who sat straddle her scooter, that gorgeous smile lighting up her face. "For now, I have a promise to keep. I would love to take this conversation up on Monday."

He didn't wait for Mason's reply. Instead, he slid the helmet on, tightened the chin strap, and got on the scooter behind Nicky, resting his hands lightly on her hips. She pulled away from the curb, waving over her shoulder and shouting "See ya, Gramps!"

"Where are we going?" he shouted the words over the engine whine as she turned south onto Saint Paul.

"Does it matter?" she called back before turning her attention to navigating between the cars on the packed street.

Ty decided in that moment it didn't matter one bit. Sebastian may be president of the board, but his comments about Nicky were unprofessional at best. Never mind his overbearing behavior during the meeting. Mason... Had he always been such a pompous, controlling ass, or was this a new facet of his personality? Or maybe Ty had missed it in the past.

At a stoplight, Nicky rested her hand on his thigh and his heart skipped a beat. The feeling of her hips against his legs and his arms around her waist had him thinking of skipping whatever plans she'd made and going straight back to his place.

She wheeled into the parking garage near the Harbor East theater and as soon as they were parked; she was off the bike, her helmet in her hand and her arms around him. Ty had barely gotten his own helmet off, but he knew an invitation to kiss when it was presented. Kissing Nicky was always a pleasure.

Every time he was with her, things felt right. She felt right. When her lips touched his, he forgot every bit of the stress and drama of the day. Nicky stepped back and gave him a quizzical look, one eyebrow raised slightly, and her lips curled into a half smile.

"That must have been an interesting thought. You were like a live wire and suddenly you relaxed."

Ty cracked a grin and laughed, trying to cover—he wasn't sure why that thought had hit him so deep or so hard, but it had. On the surface, everything about her was wrong—Mason's mixed messages about his own grandchild, and Sebastian's cryptic warnings continued to echo in his head. But when they got together, she made sense. And she never asked him to be anything but himself.

"So... uh... what's dinner?" He got the words out despite the fact that his lips wanted to go back to kissing her. To never stop kissing her. Or maybe to stop only to tell her how much he... He clamped his mouth shut lest the words slip out somehow.

Nicky hooked her arm through her helmet and grabbed his hand. "Do you trust me?"

Ty chuffed a short laugh. Of course he did. Maybe far more than he should. Though her grandfather claimed she was wild and unpredictable, irresponsible even, Nicky was actually methodical and cautious. The fact she'd remembered to bring an extra helmet for him was a perfect example of that.

"Omakase?" Ty read the sign over an unassuming door—out of place in the upscale Harbor East neighborhood.

"Just opened. Sushi... but with a twist. You list your allergens or things you specifically won't eat, and then trust the chef."

The host greeted them at the door and led them to seats at the bar before giving them the list of fish for the night. Ty peeked over at Nicky's paper, but she didn't mark anything as a 'no'. He scanned his list, trying to recall what sushi he did and didn't like. Nicky's finger slid down his page and tapped on one line.

"Sea urchin. It's a love it or hate it kind of thing."

He marked it as a no. He'd had it once and found it too overpowering. She rattled through the rest of the fish listed. In the end, the sea urchin was his only no.

By the end of the meal, the stress of his day had faded into the background and Ty found himself laughing and truly relaxed. He snagged Nicky's hand, pulled her close and kissed her cheek.

"You're amazing," he whispered in her ear.

Nicky sat back with a quizzical smile on her face. "Rough day?"

"Kind of, but not anything I want to rehash." She didn't need his Richard Mason troubles dumped on top of her already heaping pile of reasons to dislike the man. "I think... No, I know that's one of the things I enjoy about time with you. It doesn't matter what we do, or what we talk about. You make things easy."

She rolled her eyes, but he caught the smile and pink flush that crept up her cheeks. She tossed her napkin onto the bar and gave him a piercing look. "You ready for a movie?"

After the movie, back at his place with Nicky straddle his lap on the couch, her clothes disheveled and her lips swollen from kisses, he captured her face in his hands, holding her cool blue gaze as their breath mingled. They were so opposite in so many ways and dating her while her grandfather continued his chokehold on the museum could be career suicide in more ways than one.

But in this moment, with the heat of her soaking into him and her gorgeous eyes staring into his soul, he didn't care. All that mattered right now was how quickly he could get her out of her clothes and writhing under him.

CHAPTER 17

Squeals and giggles punctuated the air, making Nicky jump back just in time to avoid a face full of paint covered sponge. Instead, it hit her square in the chest with a loud splat as the bright red paint spattered everywhere. Nicky managed to catch the sponge before it hit the floor and made an even bigger mess.

She shot an evil glare at the child's mother, to find the woman was actually congratulating her preschool age son on the powerful throw. So much for her plans for a simple change of clothes before meeting Ty and his friend Deke for an early happy hour. Now she'd need more than a quick shower—she was pretty sure she had paint in her hair.

Nicky sank her teeth into her tongue. Class was almost over, and it wasn't the kid's fault. Not really. His mother had been a pill from the start. First it was fussing that her son should be allowed to participate, even though he was under the age limit by six months. Because what else was she to do with him while attending the class with his older sister.

It had gone downhill from there.

Nicky whisked her smock off before the paint could drip on anything else—and how had the kid managed to get the sponge so full of paint? Another quick glance at the kid and Mom answered that—he was upending an entire cup of paint onto a new sponge.

Nicky whirled into action, gently pulling the cup from the child's messy hands. "Oh, I'm sorry, but we need to keep the paint in the cup. Thank you." She plopped a pile of paper towels in front of the mother. "Class is almost over. I'm about to call for cleanup."

She didn't wait for a response before getting everyone's attention. "It's time to put your paint sponges down and hang up your masterpiece!"

Volunteers swooped into action, guiding parent-child teams to hang their artwork on the drying wall. A few of the parents had clearly done this before as they grabbed paper towels and started mopping up their child's mess.

The paint thrower was still smacking his hands into the puddle of paint on the table, the pile of paper towels left untouched by his mother. Nicky squatted next to the pair and addressed the mom. "Would you like me to take his art to hang up while you get him to the restroom so he can wash his hands?"

The kid needed to wash more than his hands, but Nicky was holding onto the last shreds of her patience with this woman. A wet hand landed on her thigh as the kid scrambled into her lap and planted his other hand smack on the side of her face. Great.

"Are you all done?" The woman scooped her child up, ignored Nicky, and carried him and his dripping wet paper to the drying wall where she fussed about not being able to hang his work next to his sister's. And kept fussing until Nicky came over and strung a new line for their work.

When all the kids and their parents had gone outside for lunch, Nicky was still looking at one incredibly messy paint station.

"We have the registration list, right?" she asked Brigette, who'd been handling check-in and who had called her when the woman pitched her first angry tirade.

"Oh yeah. And this would not be the first time we banned a parent." Brigette handed Nicky a fresh roll of paper towels. "Not that I think a glorified Kleenex is gonna help much. You're kinda covered."

Nicky didn't care about her clothes. She didn't wear nice things to a paint event for four- to six-year-olds. She did care that her team had to shoulder a greater burden than they should have because she'd been dealing with that family. And that she had paint in her ears. How, she didn't want to think about. And she still had a mess to deal with since that woman hadn't bothered to clean up after her own child.

"Good." She snagged the roll of towels and bent under the cabinet for a mop bucket. "I think this is a bigger job than towels alone can handle. Go grab lunch, I've got this."

The entire team, all four of them, looked at her like she was speaking nonsense, and Nicky could have burst into tears of gratitude. Together they wiped the art station, and the floors, and the bathroom, and got all the spattered paint off the walls and windows. The kid did have a remarkably strong arm—and the sponge had been really full of paint. They were finishing up when it was time for the families to come in, collect their artwork and leave.

Nicky treated her crew to lunch after everyone had gone, then sent a quick text to Ty to let him know she'd be late before climbing onto her scooter and zooming home. She maneuvered through the back gate, stowed her helmet in the studio and gave a passing thought to showering there rather than risk running into her grandfather, but that was not a good plan.

The hot water in the studio was questionable at best and this was the first time she'd be meeting someone from Ty's life. She didn't want to risk missing any paint. She shook herself before memories of Jeremy intruded. Nope. She wasn't going there. Nicky heaved a sigh and crossed the yard, hoping against hope her grandfather wasn't home.

She wasn't expecting to find him inside the kitchen door, scowling. As if this day needed to get more fucked up. The disdain on his face was nearly palpable as he took in her paint smeared appearance.

"I'm sure I don't want to know. Do you have a moment?"

Tempting though it was to flat out say no, it wouldn't make any difference and Nicky wanted to get upstairs, showered, and changed. And fast. It was easier to be blunt.

"I really don't have more than a moment. We had a little paint mishap during class, and I have plans." She let the statement hang and avoided, barely, looking at her watch.

Her grandfather let out a heavy sigh, as if what he was about to say was difficult for him. She was pretty sure it wasn't. "Since you're so pressed for time, I'll get right to it. You are doing Tyler a disservice."

Nicky's mouth dropped open. Was her grandfather really trying to insert himself into her love life?

"He is a fine young man on the edge of his career taking off. And you..." He spread his hands as if to say, 'look at yourself'. No amount of arguing that she had a good job that she was proud of would change the fact that right now, she looked like she'd spent her Wednesday afternoon rolling around in finger-paints.

"I'm not sure I want to have this discussion, or what business it is of yours," Nicky replied.

"Moira, if you even half lived up to your potential, you and Tyler could be something wonderful and good. Instead, you seem hell-bent on single-handedly ruining his career. If you can't see that, you are either blind or selfish."

He turned away, hand rubbing his forehead as if the whole thing gave him a massive headache. He was certainly giving her one.

"That stunt you pulled after the board meeting on Friday?" He turned back to her, his arms flying into the air in a show of exasperation. Another familiar move. "Have you any idea the damage that could cause? You should at least act like a respectable woman and do your part to support him."

Incandescent rage flooded her. "So, let me get this straight. You think I'm not good enough? That something about me will ruin Ty's career opportunities? And that I should... I don't know... somehow transform myself into the perfect not-for-profit wife?"

Her grandfather spread his hands wide and gave a sad-looking smile. "Your words, Moira, not mine. Perhaps it's your conscience telling you what you already know. That was one of the biggest troubles your parents faced—your mother needed more from Charles than he could give. He never fit into her world. Worse, he never really tried, and your mother stupidly allowed that to go on for far too long."

Nicky crossed the room in two steps and flung open the hall door before turning back to her grandfather. "Who I see is none of your business, which makes the rest of the conversation completely pointless."

He opened his mouth as if to speak but shut it as Nicky glared at him before marching through the door. She'd spent her youth being bullied by her grandfather; she wasn't about to let him pick up where he'd left off.

"You know," he said, pushing through the doorway as she hit the stairs. "It was the relationship with your father that ultimately killed your mother. She had so much potential but threw it all down the drain in the hope of changing Charles. And you are so much like him."

"Good to know what you really think of me." Nicky spat the words at him and resisted the urge to rush back down, shove him into the kitchen then slam the door in his face. Instead, she turned and pounded up the stairs to her room.

Nothing that came out of his mouth surprised her. It was just a new facet of the same old problem—she didn't live up to her grandfather's expectations and his solution to that was to tear her down so he could rebuild her in his image.

"The truth often hurts, Moira." His parting words carried, reverberating against the walls and chasing her down the hall.

TY—FRIDAY, MAY 24

"Can this morning go any slower?"

Ty rubbed his eyes. He needed a coffee like nobody's business. Nicky had been exceptionally charming at dinner with Deke, then after, she'd suggested going back to Ty's place. Sleeping was not on her agenda. She'd been demanding, almost frantic, but refused to talk about what was bothering her. If she needed to use him for stress relief, fine. He'd just like to be in on the reasons.

"Tyler, do you have a minute?"

Richard Mason stood in Ty's office doorway; his brows knit into a deep frown.

"Of course," Ty replied and nodded at the open chair in front of his desk. The other man closed the door and sat.

"Something I believe you should hear directly from me. David Clyde has accepted a director's position at The Smithsonian."

Ty forced his expression to remain neutral even though the news came as a complete shock. The current assistant director had hired him. He'd been one of the reasons Ty had come to the Walters, but he couldn't imagine what David's leaving had to do with him. Ty swallowed hard and summoned a smile.

"I'll have to congratulate him—privately. I assume that's not yet public knowledge. Whoever you find to replace him will have some big shoes to fill."

Mason nodded and tapped his finger on the chair arm. "Indeed."

The finger tapping stopped, and the director pointed at Ty. "I'm putting your name before the Board for the position. They'd have to vote on it, of course. You'd be the youngest Assistant Director this museum has ever had, but I believe that's a good thing."

Every breath of air sucked from the room as Ty tried to process that news. This was his dream, handed to him on a silver platter. He'd never imagined it coming this quickly.

"You'd need to finish the PhD, of course." Mason sat back, loosely folding his hands over his waist. "I wanted to have this conversation with you before taking it to the Board. I can tell you right now, the vote will most likely go through. Not unanimously, but it should pass."

That piece of information wasn't surprising, but it still stung. Despite the contentious board meeting last week, Ty thought he had a good relationship with all the voting board members. Though there were a few sticks in the mud who didn't care for his more modern approach. Sebastian came to mind, but most would follow the guidance of Mason as the director of the museum.

"I'm honored. You of all people know I'd say yes, still I am curious about the objections you expect."

The other man shook his head. "That's a delicate subject. Between the two of us and these four walls, right or wrong, the board will look at far more than your curriculum vitae." He offered a smile that radiated smug satisfaction. "I'd like to think I've been good for this institution and that even my detractors could admit that. As such, my advice and opinions carry weight. Good and bad."

Ty scowled, hoping this wasn't going where he suspected it was. "I'm going to need more specifics. In my experience, everyone here respects you. Even if they disagree." That last was a risk, but whatever Mason was aiming at, Ty was sure he didn't want to hear it. Though he needed to.

"You already know the board is almost evenly split. People like Sebastian, and if I'm being honest, myself, who believe if it isn't broken, don't fix it."

That age-old argument again. "On the other side of that coin are those who feel it's time to grow and change to move forward."

"Precisely. The concerns I expect to see are less about professional ability and more about vision, politics, and, since we're being honest, image. David and I usually saw things eye to eye, and he was in all ways above reproach."

Mason leaned forward, elbows on the desk. "You, on the other hand..." His words trailed off and Ty didn't bother to stifle the laugh that came unbidden.

"Do not always see things the same way. I like to think of myself as a bridge between those two sides. I respect the past, and what works, but I also recognize the need for careful and considered evolution."

"And if that was my only concern, we wouldn't be having this conversation." Mason sat back, folded his long hands together and hung his head. "I was not thrilled when you and Moira started seeing each other. Then I hoped perhaps you could be a positive influence on her."

Ty should have seen it coming. Nicky's continued failure to change and become the woman Mason thought she should be flew in the face of everything her grandfather stood for. A fact that would make Ty look too risky to the more conservative board members.

The more progressive board members would cease seeing Ty as a bridge and instead see someone standing on the opposite side. Because of his association with Mason and Nicky's relationship to the man.

Shit.

"There are two sides to this equation." Mason's shoulders raised on a deep sigh as he looked back up and held Ty's gaze. "As much as we would all like to say the art world is the art world and we should all be working together. I have no shame in admitting I believe one needs proper background and education to truly appreciate art. This museum is a place of quiet contemplation and decorum."

And there was the problem. Nicky worked in a world that was wild and untamed—where the definitions of art were very different. She might have an education from a stellar university, but she was hardly the image of the typical patron of the arts and would have to fundamentally change who she was to fit into Mason's vision of this world.

Ty swallowed past the lump in his throat. He could never, would never, ask that of her. Not that he believed she would agree to change. She had to know this. How could she not, considering who she'd grown up around?

Ty pulled his attention back to the conversation.

"I'm not officially telling you this. When it comes to the vote, biases will come into play whether we like to admit it or not. Some members have a particular idea about the direction the museum should go and what image they want to project. And as the assistant director, you are part of that image."

Ty pulled in a slow breath. "I see... so, what is your advice?"

"Trust the majority of the board will overcome the rest. Be aware of what events you attend outside of work functions and I strongly urge you to come to those alone. I would suggest you consider being particularly cautious—keep your relationship quiet until after the vote. It's not like anyone can ask who you're dating."

Ty suppressed a bitter chuckle. "Surprising advice from you. I get it. It's a lot to think about. Thank you."

"If you see this as a long-term relationship, it's a good opportunity to encourage her to tone things down."

Bile rose as Ty's stomach clenched over the very idea.

"Tone down Nicky?" Mason gave him a blank look and Ty tried again. "Moira." The name didn't feel right on his tongue. "Your granddaughter. Have you tried to tone her down?"

The other man's eyes narrowed, and his features arranged themselves into a look of confusion. Eyebrows scrunched together and raised, lips in a half smile. "For many years, yes."

"Then you know the idea of controlling her is preposterous. It would be like trying to dim the sun." Ty heaved a sigh, his shoulders sagging under the weight of everything. He needed to play politics, whether he liked it or not. "I appreciate your advice, and I will take it to heart."

That seemed to satisfy Mason. He smiled, pushed himself up and gave Ty a questioning glance. "I suspect I know the answer..."

"You know I'd take the position if it's offered."

Mason offered his hand and Ty shook. "I thought as much. The rest..." He paused, took in a deep breath, and shrugged. "Politics. You're going to be playing them in one way or another for the rest of your career."

He headed out, leaving Ty stewing over the dilemma. It didn't matter if the vote was unanimous or not. If he got the position, then he got the position. He wasn't about to stop seeing Nicky over it, though now he was wondering where she was on all of this. Especially after last night, when she wouldn't talk to him about what had gotten her into her tense state. Maybe it would be a good idea to keep things more private.

That didn't sit right. He'd just invited her to his family barbecue on Monday. He wanted her there. Wanted her to meet his parents. That was a fucking first.

Now he was questioning everything. Her interest. His career. Mason's intentions.

Fuck. Things he didn't need to be worrying about.

CHAPTER 18

A hundred and fifty bucks in postage. Yikes. Still, Nicky couldn't complain. If she had more months like this, she wouldn't be sweating affording a place of her own. She had to get through till she found out if she had a position in the Fall semester. She could stick it out with her grandfather a bit longer.

Since she'd transformed her father's old pottery studio into her art space she'd been able to add several new items to her Etsy shop which translated into a spike in sales. If she hurried, she could swing by the art supply shop and still be home in time to lay down the first outlines of a new painting she had in mind. Then dinner with Ty.

Her body warmed at the thought. As if summoned, a text from Ty popped up.

Got time for a quick coffee this afternoon?

Nicky scowled at her screen. Odd request, since they were going out tonight.

> Sure. Should I go straight there, or after the art store? Gimme about an hour for that. What's up?

She straddled her scooter and waited, foot tapping impatiently for his reply.

> Just work shit. Let's talk in person. See you after the art store.

Well, that didn't sound good. So many possibilities rattled around in her head she barely paid any attention to the drive over to Blick. By the time she parked and got into the store, she was fairly certain whatever was up had to do with Ty's work—and that meant her grandfather. Gramps had been remarkably quiet since their Wednesday blow up.

He might be a big enough control freak to say something to Ty. He was definitely a big enough control freak to make Ty work so hard he never had time for her.

She grabbed fresh paints, picked out a new brush, and a sketchpad and headed for the checkout, trying to quiet her spinning brain.

No luck.

She fired off a text to let Ty know she was on her way and stuffed everything into her messenger bag. Whatever ulterior motives her grandfather had, she didn't like it.

But had he really discouraged her from seeing Ty? Or had he encouraged her to change into what he believed Ty needed? Which happened to match the direction her grandfather had been pushing Nicky all her life.

Mercifully she found a parking space near Ceremony. All the convoluted thoughts about Ty and her grandfather were making her head hurt and she needed caffeine in the worst of ways. A quick glance around as she came in showed no Ty yet, so Nicky ordered a coffee and settled in to wait at a table in the back, as far away from any other customers as she could get.

She didn't have to wait long. Ty bypassed the counter and headed straight to Nicky; his face set in hard lines. Things were not looking good.

"Hey." Ty breathed the word, and his face relaxed a stitch or two. He leaned in and gave Nicky a lingering kiss and her own tension melted a bit. "Sorry for that cryptic message. I didn't want to be a dick, but it's a work thing and... I mean... I know how... The thing is..."

Nicky reached out and took his hand, squeezed, then tugged until he looked at her. "You work for my grandfather—his fingers in your life mean strings attached. Lots of them."

Ty pulled in a slow breath and his shoulders slid down about an inch. Seeing him visibly relax made Nicky breathe a little easier herself. Ty took another deep breath and squeezed her hand back.

"Nailed it in one." He gave her that lopsided grin she loved so much. "He's insisting I attend a dinner tonight, despite the fact that I told him I already had plans."

That could be just about anything. "Who else will be there? There's so much to consider with him."

Ty gave a shrug and Nicky would've bet anything Gramps hadn't told him much. Typical.

"He said it was a casual get together. People he wanted me to get to know outside of museum business." His voice was tight with conflict. Hell, she knew her grandfather's games, and he still got her all wrapped up in knots. Ty had to be a mess.

"Well, you have to go, there's no doubt about that." Ty's expression bounced between relief and frustration. A mixture she understood. All too well. "You know this is a test, right? Will you cancel plans at his beck and call?"

"Yeah, I figured." Ty ran a hand through his hair. This was his career. His dream. And the man who could make it or break it was her grandfather. That alone was a complicated path. Her relationship with Ty made things infinitely more complex.

"You know I hate doing this, and I wish you could come along. But I also…"

Nicky shook her head; trying to guess what Richard Mason had in mind was a guaranteed route to anguish. Every time. The man thrived when everyone around him was miserable.

"What's changed at work?" It had to be something. He seemed far too uptight for it to be just the dinner.

"Politics. A whole lot of politics all tied to whether I want to go anywhere in this museum."

Nicky restrained herself from some smartass comment. That much was obvious if you knew her grandfather. And oh, hey, she did. Classic Richard Mason all the way. You want something? Everything has a price. Well, there was one piece of advice he had given that she agreed with—she could support Ty. That went without question.

"I'd be there with you in a heartbeat if it was the right choice." She made a face, then gave him a smile that he returned. Good. Progress. "But it's not."

Ty flashed his megawatt grin and Nicky about melted in her seat. Sure, she was frustrated, but not at him. She knew the source of this shit, and his name was Richard Mason.

"Can we do something Saturday night instead? I'll make it up to you."

The look on his face made it very clear what form the making it up would take, and she had zero complaints about that. The man was truly amazing in bed. Or out of it for that matter.

"You're on. Are we still doing the thing on Monday?"

Ty's smile didn't fade or falter. He raised her fingers to his lips and kissed her knuckles. "Yep. You. Me. My family's annual Memorial Day barbecue. Mom and Dad spend the morning at Arlington—both of my grandfathers were career military—the afternoon is all about food and family."

His face turned serious, the smile fading and a look of concern crossing his features. "Look, I've rarely brought people home, and never to this. You're going to get a lot of attention, and a lot of questions."

Nicky fought back an eye roll. "You're not the first Joe Preppy I've dated. I know how to act around parents. I can even look relatively conservative."

"Be your charming self," Ty replied. "On that, I really have to get back to work. Thank you for understanding."

The kiss he gave her had Nicky wishing they weren't in a public place. She'd send him back to the office with something a little more memorable.

Instead, she finished her coffee and made her way home. With an entire evening now free, she could change into her painting clothes and really work on filling up her Etsy shop. And probably have a lot better time than Ty, having to stay all buttoned up and well behaved for hours on end.

Maybe she would take some spicy pics to send him while he was at dinner. A large canvas and some body paint and she'd have some sexy pictures plus a great abstract art piece.

Yeah, this could work.

TY—SATURDAY, MAY 25

Richard Mason and half the board—all the sticks in the mud, of course—sat gathered around the table. Ty groaned inwardly as he took his seat. His brain whirled with possibilities. He didn't believe Mason would invite him to this dinner to fire him. There had to be some other reason for insisting he attend.

The chatter was all social—families, kids, day jobs—nothing remotely work related. He spent enough hours at the museum, and the inevitable social events and didn't begrudge a minute of it. He did not want to spend his few free hours with this same group. He gave up a night with Nicky for this. Conversations turned to global politics with the salads and finally got around to art world news by the entrees.

Unsurprisingly, Ty found himself the most liberal leaning person at the table, but while they all had their disagreements about museum politics, the dinner conversation was at least lively and enjoyable.

Maybe that was Mason's intent. Pull together the loudest voices of dissension, those board members who seemed anti-progress, or at least anti-change, and... Ty scoffed at himself. What? Let them find common ground that could sway their opinions? No. Far more likely this was meant to sway Ty's viewpoint.

By the time coffee and after-dinner drinks arrived, Ty was thinking this was strictly a social event and he might emerge from the night unscathed. Which didn't make him feel any better about the fact that he could have been at home with Nicky wrapped in nothing more than a sheet and her warmth.

"I'm sure you've heard the news," Sebastian Knox said as he leaned closer to Ty. "About our Assistant Director moving on."

So much for it being just a social event. With the announcement, the board would consider candidates for the position. Seemed like this was his first unofficial interview. Well, second, if he included Mason's unexpected conversation yesterday. The man worked fast.

"Nothing official." Ty tried to decide how honest he could be. How honest he needed to be.

"Many feel it's a prime opportunity to bring in a fresh outlook." Sebastian dropped two sugars into his coffee and stirred, never taking his eyes off Ty. "I don't disagree. Does that surprise you?"

It did. Very much, but this was all about politics. No wonder Nicky could be so hard to read sometimes—she'd grown up around this crap. As expressive as she was, her ability to put on a neutral face was near sorcery.

"I've got to be honest; it is surprising. I've always thought of you as a traditionalist."

Clearly the right word choice. The other man practically preened.

"Perhaps so. However, I am also a man who believes in balance." Sebastian fixed Ty with a clear gaze. "A young man like yourself, with a strong background, excellent education, and progressive ideology looks very good for the museum."

That was high praise coming from Sebastian. There had to be a but in there somewhere. A shoe waiting to drop.

"I am interested in evolution, not revolution. Change does not happen overnight. This is why balance is important."

Ty had no clue where the board president was going with this commentary, but it was intriguing. Ty had always proposed an evolutionary process—small, incremental changes.

"A museum is like a large ship," Ty replied. "It's not possible to make rapid course shifts."

Sebastian nodded, a slow smile spreading over his face. "Well said. I believe we understand each other."

He rose, shook Ty's hand, and moved down the table to join a different conversation, leaving Ty baffled, without a clue what understanding they'd come to. He didn't have long to contemplate that before Mason himself took the abandoned seat.

"That was exactly why I wanted you here tonight." Mason sipped a brandy as he surveyed the others, now deep in conversation, led primarily by Sebastian Knox. Ty imagined Sebastian regurgitating the conversation they'd just had.

"Was that so I could come to understand their point of view, or impress on them my respect for a... ah... balanced approach?" Ty managed to keep the sarcasm from his voice. For the first time, he wondered if every museum was like this, or if this was unique to Mason. He suspected the truth was somewhere in the middle.

Mason placed a large hand on Ty's shoulder and leaned in close. "A bit of both. It's no secret my opinions land closer to Sebastian's than yours. But I also see great potential in you."

Ty knew a prod when he heard it, but he waited a beat, allowing his eyes to drift to the board members. It wasn't like they were huddled at the far end of the table. If he listened, he could pick up bits and pieces of their conversation.

"...so young..."

"...ambitious..."

"...could be problematic..."

"...right direction..."

On it went. Good and bad. Ty turned his focus back to Mason and gave his best smile.

"I appreciate your interest and support. Working with you has been a privilege, and there's no doubt, a boost to my career."

Ah, the tap dance. He'd honed those skills working with donors and potential donors. Learning what someone wanted to get out of their gift to the museum—it was rarely as simple as a tax write off or wanting to support the arts—and echoing those feelings back to them was a talent he had developed early on.

Nicky struggled with her grandfather not because they were so opposite in their views on art, but because she was the embodiment of everything Richard Mason saw as inferior. Worse, she had the unmitigated temerity to take pride in breaking the mold.

Mason's reasons weren't too difficult to figure out. The man had enough ego that he couldn't handle the idea of something, or in this case someone, that came from him was less than perfect. It reflected badly on him. Add in a giant control streak and it all made sense.

Mason clapped Ty on the shoulder again. "I'm looking forward to seeing where you go with everything." He signed the check with a flourish, rose from the table, bid everyone a goodnight, and made his way toward the restaurant door.

As if that were the magic cue, one by one, the others followed suit until Ty and Sebastian were alone at the table. The older man stood and gave Ty a long, appraising look.

"I believe you are about to discover how difficult life's choices can be," Sebastian said, his smile a little sad. "And that sometimes, none of your options are entirely satisfying."

With that, he left. Ty sat for a moment, trying to digest what Sebastian was implying. He wasn't in a rush to get out the door and run into anyone lingering in the parking lot. Too many conflicting feelings swirled around like bees in his head.

He still wasn't entirely sure why Mason had insisted he attend tonight. Sebastian's parting shot dug into his brain. All Ty could imagine was Nicky. Sebastian had been among those standing out front when Nicky had picked him up on her scooter.

At the time, he'd not realized the potential fallout. Well, he'd considered it. Briefly. He rubbed his hands over his face. This was all too big of a mess. He pushed out of the seat. He stopped at the door to scan the parking lot for lingering board members. When he was sure it was safe, he stepped out into the clear, cool night.

Whether Sebastian was talking about Nicky and his job or not, Ty already felt the pressure of that. Even without considering she was Richard Mason's granddaughter and all the politics that meant, there was no getting around it—Nicky would never fit in among the more conservative crowd.

He slid into the driver's seat and pounded his hand against the wheel. No, that thinking was wrong. If Nicky weren't related to Mason, this would all be a non-issue. Or at least, less of an issue. She had been fine at the retirement party. She was charming, intelligent, witty as fuck, and people took an instant liking to her.

To everyone except Mason, this was absolutely all about who she was, not how she looked or where she worked. He started the car and glanced at the time. Half past ten. Not too late to call Nicky. To see her. They hadn't made plans for tonight, but that could change. He had his phone in his hand, finger hovering over her name.

No. His head was a mess right now. She'd spot it in an instant and rightly assume it was over her—what else could it be when it involved Ty, his job, and her grandfather. He'd text her when he got home. Say he was tired, and he'd see her tomorrow. She'd understand.

That didn't calm the desire to touch her, to feel her warmth and softness against his skin. Sebastian had said something about none of the options being satisfying. At the moment, Ty understood the truth of that statement.

All he wanted in the world right now was Nicky but going to her would raise questions and discussions he wasn't ready for. If he continued down the path he was on, if he was offered the Assistant Director position, he'd be walking this tightrope for the rest of his career—or at least until Mason retired and all board members who sided with him were gone as well.

Minimum five years. More likely ten.

Ten years of keeping his personal life entirely separate from his professional one. Ten years of balancing the politics of Nicky and the museum. Of rarely, if ever, having his partner beside him at work events.

Years of dreading the day that Mason went too far and said something hurtful to or about her in front of Ty. How could he protect her from the toxic relationship with her grandfather when he worked for the man?

He pounded the steering wheel again and scrubbed a hand over his face. He didn't have any answers—not even shitty ones.

All he had were fears and questions. And an aching need for a certain quirky woman who never failed to make him smile.

CHAPTER 19

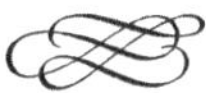

The early morning light felt like it was searing her eyes as Nicky stretched out as much as she could on the small studio sofa. It was too damn early to be up. She'd crashed as the sky started to lighten in the east. She glanced at her phone, mercifully plugged in—not quite eight. Nicky groaned. A little over two hours of sleep. Yuck.

The large canvas she'd worked half the night on hung over the bookshelves—a full print of her body in gorgeous sunset shades, behind it, a vague shape in contrasting blues and greens, like water.

Her phone buzzed and Nicky thumbed it open to see a text from Sabrina.

> Finishing up my run. In your area. Wanna join me for coffee?

> Just woke up. Get takeout and meet me at the studio in back?

A thumbs up came from Sabrina and Nicky forced herself to get up and at least brush her teeth. Ten minutes later and feeling vaguely human, she let Sabrina in and practically snatched the coffee from her friend's hands.

"Holy shit that is hot!" Sabrina stood in front of the new canvas. "I love the contrast in the couple."

Nicky's eyes snapped to the painting. Couple? She hadn't painted a couple. But now, standing on the opposite side of the room, she saw it. Clear as day. The way the blues flared outward right about her head height—shoulders. Broad ones. And the tendril of greens that snaked over the woman's orange hip was a hand—protective. The pose spoke of passion and belonging. Trust and comfort.

It was abstract, but undeniably there.

"Inspired by Mr. Coffee Shop?" Sabrina still gazed at the nearly six-foot-tall canvas.

Nicky flopped back to the sofa, cradling her coffee cup. "Not intentionally, but looking at it now?" Nicky stared at the piece, and she knew. She'd painted herself and Ty, and the painting told the truth about her feelings.

"I had a vague idea." She was unwilling to dig too deeply into her own revelation yet. "It started with the body impression and the colors. Sort of fire and water. Got some amazing selfies from it, too."

Sabrina threw a lascivious glance over her shoulder at Nicky.

"Yeah, I know…" Nicky pulled up the pictures and handed her phone off to the other woman.

A low whistle escaped Sabrina's lips as she scrolled. "Wow. Have you sent any of these to Ty yet?"

Nicky shook her head. "I was up really late painting. Hell, I barely cleaned myself up. I must've fallen asleep editing the pics. I'd just woken up when you texted."

Once Nicky started talking, it was like words spilled out of her without thinking. "I've got a date with Ty tonight and his family barbecue tomorrow, and he's never taken a date to that before, and I don't know what I'm going to wear, and..."

Nicky stopped to breathe, surprised at everything that had come pouring out. Sabrina's eyebrows rose. "Oooo. Meeting the family. That's big league. Serious relationship stuff. So, what's the problem?"

Sabrina gave her a wide-eyed innocent look that sent Nicky into a fit of laughter that bordered on hysterics. She needed a nap.

"Yeah," she breathed the word out. "It was his idea to begin with, and he keeps telling me it'll be fine. But he's been... shit... I don't know. I feel like an idiot worrying about it all."

Sabrina leaned forward, elbows on her knees. "Sounds like nerves."

"Mine or his? He's been distant all week. He said it was work stuff. Lots on his mind. And my grandfather cornered me after a horrible class and basically told me to either let Ty go or transform myself into some trophy wife—for his own good. Or for his career good."

Nicky barely stopped her fingers from crushing the cup in her hands. She'd hoped painting would help burn off some of the nervous energy. She needed something all-consuming for body and mind. First though, she needed more sleep.

"Your grandfather really is an ass. You know that, right?"

"Yeah." It came out as a whisper. "Look, you wanna grab breakfast? Now that I'm semi-awake, I'm kinda hungry."

They wound up getting sandwiches to go from a corner shop, then Sabrina helped Nicky clean up the mess from the night before. By the time they were done, Nicky could barely keep her eyes open, and Sabrina headed off with the admonishment to get some rest.

Which Nicky intended to do. But first...

She pulled up her message app, snapped a picture of the new painting and sent it off to Ty with two words.

> New piece.

She was in the main house just coming out of the shower when his response came in.

> WOW! That is spectacular! Truly. That's you, isn't it?

A smiling devil face emoji followed, and heat spread out from her belly. She selected one of the sexy pics and sent it next. No explanation needed. She crawled into bed for some much-needed sleep.

Her alarm woke her hours later and she found a string of texts from Ty.

> I'm speechless. You're amazing.

That one came in minutes after she'd hit send. The second came a few minutes later.

> You know I'm going to have to check for paint later. Right?

An hour after that, a third message.

> I can't stop thinking about you. Heading out to play ball with Deke. I'll call later.

Then a series of emoji texts, including some clearly meant to be naughty. That had Nicky giggling.

Her phone lit up with Ty's number.

"Hey," Nicky greeted as she picked up the call.

"Yeah, hey yourself. I damn near dropped my phone when I saw that pic. Wow."

The heat she always felt with him rushed right back in.

"Sorry, not sorry. What are we doing tonight?"

The silence on the other end crackled with energy. And Nicky realized why painting hadn't satisfied that all-consuming need.

She loved Ty, but more importantly, she needed him.

She silently wished he would somehow know. Just understand.

"What about take out and a night in?" Ty's voice was smoky, rich, and sticky sounding. Nicky wanted to crawl into his words and be surrounded by them, consumed by them. Her grandfather's warnings tried to insert themselves, telling Nicky she wasn't right, she'd only harm Ty and his career. She silenced that voice and the nagging that she was setting herself up for heartache.

"Lemme clean up. I'll be there in twenty?"

"Sounds good. See you soon."

She forced herself to take her time. Matching bra and panties. A floaty sundress. She knocked on his door exactly twenty minutes after they'd hung up.

The door opened to Ty in low slung linen pants and no shirt. Without a word, he reached for her hand and pulled her into his apartment. His lips pressed against hers as his hands wrapped her hips and hunger flared even higher. She pouted when he pulled back from her.

"I ordered Chinese. We've got about an hour. I think that's plenty of time for a little pre-dinner appetizer."

And here was the Ty she had grown to adore. Open, funny, affectionate. Maybe his distance had just been work.

Made worse by her own insecurities courtesy the conversation with her grandfather.

When Ty pulled her back against him, all her doubts fled. She didn't care what her grandfather thought. Any reservation she'd ever had disappeared the moment Ty touched her. There was nothing uncertain in his touch, or his kisses.

She tried not to think about the fact that they were alone in his apartment—not out where others could see, or judge. She pushed those thoughts aside and lost herself in Ty's kisses and the familiar pepper and nutmeg smell of him as he scooped her up, carried her into the bedroom and laid her on his bed.

Ty pushed a lock of her hair out of her face and chuckled. "This past week has been surreal, but this... you... are always perfect. You're my peace."

Nicky shifted against him, loving the instant response from his body. Ty slid her dress up her body, slowly revealing her legs, then hips, and everything. It was short work, untying his pants and sliding them down his thighs. They moved in a smooth, unhurried rhythm.

This was what she needed, and she suspected he did as well. They both had stresses they needed to forget, and sex was the one thing that could wipe them all away.

His fingers traced over the vines running down her back. Everything should be as easy as they were together. Outside of other influences—they were perfect. They shared humor and movie tastes. Liked the same foods and music. Had perfectly complementary kinks and desires.

Ty lowered his head, nuzzled her neck and Nicky's world stood still. Nothing else mattered—not work, or her grandfather, or meeting his family, or anything else. Just Ty, holding her in his arms. Every day should start like this, pressed naked against this amazing man who could make her forget anything negative in the world.

She pushed against him, and he settled back into the pillows. In one swift move, she was straddle him, her fingers reaching into the nightstand, then rolling a condom down his length. Ty's hands sank into her hair just before his dick slid home. She rolled her hips, grinding on him, her eyes locked on his and a low moan of pleasure escaped her lips.

Ty slid one hand down her body until his thumb rested against her clit. His other hand fisted in her hair, pulled her close to him. Her moans turned to gasps as his thumb circled. This. This was what she needed.

Ty somehow filling every part of her so there was no room for even thoughts of anything else.

"Take what you need." His words were a growl. A command she could not refuse and didn't want to. "That's it, baby."

Nicky rocked against him, rolling her hips, and grinding as the tension built. Until her entire body shook, and she arched her back. Her fingers digging into his chest as she came.

Before the last tremors faded, he rolled them over, wrapping her legs around his waist as he pushed deeper. So perfectly in tune with her needs.

She clung to his shoulders, his muscles tensing and bunching as he moved above her. She wanted it all from him. Everything he had to give.

"Harder, please!" Nicky barely recognized her own voice —half plea, half command, and the chuckle that came from Ty sent her soaring. His next stroke was hard and deep. Sharp enough the sound of flesh slapping echoed in the room.

"Like that?" His words came out gritty and rough. And Nicky nearly came apart.

"Yes!" His touch changed again. No more gentle caresses.

This was Ty demanding everything of her. And she gave. Willingly.

Calling out his name. Nails digging into his back. Head thrown back and nearly crying from the intensity of it all. Ty's body slammed into her, leaving her gasping, and begging for more. And somehow, he met that need. She thought he'd taken her as high as she could go, but then...

Oh, then...

Ty hooked her legs over his elbows and levered himself into a different angle. His body grinding into her as she came again. Just when she thought she would shatter if he kept going, that one more stroke would break her, he pulled her legs to his shoulders, fisted his hands into her hair, and ground her name out through his teeth.

This was bliss. This was perfection. This was where she belonged always and forever—in his arms. Ty pressed his forehead against hers, his body still tight and rigid.

"My Nicky." The words whispered against her, and Nicky clutched onto them, tucking them into her heart. Ty eased her legs down and curled her into his arms, holding her as she trembled against him, clutching at his chest. He pulled a blanket around them and held her tight against his body. His lips caressing her ear as his touches went from rough demand to the softest, gentlest stroking imaginable.

"Shhh," he whispered into her hair. "It's okay. I've got you. I'll always have you."

TY

Nicky tipped her head back and the look of raw vulnerability on her face hit Ty like a punch to the gut. God, he loved this woman. Loved everything about her. He wasn't ready to admit that out loud. He cradled her face in his hands and kissed her, gently covering her lips, her cheeks, her nose, her eyelids, everything with tiny kisses.

"You know, you have a beautiful pu…"

Her lips pressed against his, cutting him off and when she pulled back, the look of vulnerable kitten had been replaced with her more normal playful expression.

"Yeah, well…" she shrugged as she slid out of his grasp and stood. "As peens go, yours is pretty spectacular."

His phone buzzed. "Perfect timing. Dinner's here." He rose, disposed of the condom, and threw on his pants while Nicky made a mad dash into the living room for her sundress and phone.

He retrieved the bag of food from his front door. The Chinese takeout smelled amazing, but he wasn't hungry at the moment. Nicky sat curled on the couch, her expression unreadable.

"So, I have a question about the barbecue." She tucked her feet under her, tight and closed off. A marked change from moments ago. The return to polished neutrality set his teeth on edge.

"It's a family barbecue. What questions?"

A hint of something flashed on her face. Irritation? It was gone too fast for Ty to figure it out. Now she was looking down, engrossed in something on her phone. Ty tried again.

"Okay, clearly you've got something going on. So, let's have it." He set the food down and joined her on the couch. Ty slid a hand up her arm then cupped her chin, slowly bringing her face back up to his. That flash hadn't been irritation. It was uncertainty. Nicky looked worried—her eyes wide, mouth pressed tight shut. All he wanted to do was hold her and make the world right.

"No judging. Promise?" Nicky poked his chest until he nodded his agreement. "We didn't do barbecues. The thing at

Sabrina and Anne's was the first time I've ever been to a cookout type event. I have no idea what to wear."

Ty nearly burst out laughing. In fact, he deserved a damn award for holding that in. She was so adorable. So earnest. He'd never seen Nicky give a single care to what anyone thought of her. This was the woman who wore bright yellow Doc Martens to a job interview, and she was stressing what to wear to a family cookout?

"Casual. Just keep it casual."

She rolled her eyes at him. "I'm serious Ty!"

So was he. Before he could say anything, she flopped back into the couch cushions and the sight of her perfect breasts pressing against the thin fabric of her dress made him want to peel her clothes off her and lick every single bit of skin. Somehow, he didn't think that was what she needed right now.

"Casual as in my art crowd casual?" She twisted to face him and arched an eyebrow. "Or my grandfather's art crowd casual? Last time a guy told me casual for a fall family trip to an orchard, I showed up in jeans and a sweater."

She let out a sigh, and Ty was confused. "That sounds about right for apple picking. What else would you wear?"

"Judging by the other women, the choices were a denim jacket over a long summer dress plus ankle boots and lacy socks or knee boots, skinny jeans and a cream or brown turtleneck topped with a quilted vest."

Oh yeah. That look. "Han Solo season," Ty replied and was rewarded with genuine laughter from Nicky. "I do see your point."

He leaned into the cushions next to her and wrapped an arm over her shoulders, pulling gently until she turned toward him.

"Whatever you wear is going to be fine, but since you're stressing it... I'll be in shorts and a button up."

Nicky scrunched her nose up, but her smile was broad. "Joe Preppy, all the way."

It came out as a joke, but Ty suspected that was the crux of her problem. That and the fact that he worked for her grandfather.

"My parents go to the cemetery first, so Dad is in uniform, and Mom wears a dress. They change when they get home though. Mom's usually in um... what do women call those pants that stop like just below the knee?"

"Capris?"

"No, not the tight ones. Things that look like a skirt, but not."

"Those are culottes or gauchos."

"Yeah," he replied. "Mom's usually in something like those and a plain top."

Nicky rolled onto him, resting her head on his shoulder. Ty tightened his arm around her and waited.

"Are you worried about my tattoos showing?"

"Nope."

His parents would be thrilled he brought a woman home. They'd love Nicky.

"Babe, you always look amazing." He whispered the words into her ear and felt her little chuckle.

"Even when I'm covered in paint?" She wiggled against him, and his cock twitched, reminding him of the incredibly hot picture she'd sent of her wearing paint and nothing else.

"What are you going to do with that piece?" He had half a mind to ask her to let him buy it. Though he wasn't sure how much of that was because it was Nicky's body.

"I don't know yet. Maybe put it in my shop, but it's big."

That painting didn't need to be in an Etsy shop. It needed

to be in a gallery space. With a hefty price tag. She'd created something simple, but utterly remarkable.

"I'm thinking maybe denim capris and an off the shoulder peasant blouse type thing," Nicky said, her words pulling his mind back to the barbecue and away from how delicious she'd looked and how much he wished he could have seen that in person.

"That sounds good." He bit his tongue to keep from asking about accessories. Nicky tended to the quirky or edgy. The few times he'd seen her dressed for events at her work, things could get a little whacky. Even at the retirement party, when she'd been the picture of glamor and elegance, she'd had a few not-so-conservative touches. Not that any of that would be a problem with his folks.

A low chuckle interrupted his thoughts as Nicky reached over, her fingers snaking into his hair and tipping his head down to face her.

"I can hear the wheels turning in your brain, you know." Her eyes flicked to his lips, then back to his. "Ballet flats, in case you're worried. For now, I need dinner. And round two. Not necessarily in that order. You up for that?"

Her hand slid between them, into his pants and closed over his cock, making it very clear which she wanted first. A desire he was more than happy to oblige. The blood flow headed south pushed all concerns from his head. It was his parents. They weren't that uptight.

Then Nicky slid down his body and wrapped her lips around his growing hard on and that was the end of his thinking.

Later... much later... Nicky sat bundled up in his robe, munching on cold noodles and looking like...

"What's going through your brain now?" Nicky passed him a crab wonton then licked a bit of sauce from her fingers.

She was looking like forever. That was what was going through his brain. He didn't think she ready to hear that. Hell, he wasn't ready to think that, much less say it. "Just enjoying how damn good you look in my robe."

There. That was close enough. Judging by the blush that crept up her neck and into her cheeks, it was the right thing to say. Maybe round three was in order.

His phone chose that moment to vibrate, 'Mom' popped up on the screen and he caught something about tomorrow in the message preview.

"Sorry," he said to Nicky. "Let me check this." He turned the phone to her so she could see it was his mother, then thumbed open the text message.

> Your aunt and uncle are joining us tomorrow.

> Thanks for the heads up.

Okay. That wasn't too bad.

> Along with your cousins and spouses. I thought you should know.

Ty's stomach dropped to his toes. That took the backyard barbecue from a quiet day with his folks to a party of ten. His cousins had been baffled at his pursuit of museum studies— Don had even questioned Ty's sexuality when he'd learned his major. The thought of cancelling lasted about two seconds before being stomped out. His mother would guilt trip him to death and Nicky... he didn't think she'd take it well.

> And you're just telling me this now?

Nicky nudged his leg. "You've got that something's fucked up look on your face."

He had to tell her. Had to warn her, and he had to do it in a way that didn't make her worry—about herself or him. Not that he was sure he could do that.

"My mom." *No shit. Keep it simple. That's the best bet.* "Her sister and brother-in-law will be joining us tomorrow."

Nicky didn't bat an eye. "Cool. So why do you have the same look as when your boss texts you after hours?"

Ty tossed his phone on the coffee table and tucked Nicky back into the crook of his shoulder where she belonged. There it was again, thoughts he didn't want to be thinking right now. Shit. "And my two cousins. And their spouses."

She stiffened against him. Parents were one thing. But this had become the whole damn family all of a sudden. He couldn't blame her for being tense.

"It'll be fine, babe." He crossed his fingers while he said it, for extra luck.

She shifted, tossed a leg over his hips, and straddled him. Her fingers slid down his chest, over his sides, then onto her own thighs, pushing the robe aside until it fell open, and her gorgeous body was on display, ready for him to feast on.

"So, make me not care about tomorrow," she said as she dropped the robe to the floor.

Ty was more than happy to accommodate that demand.

CHAPTER 20

She should have brought her clothes and everything with her to Ty's last night. Nicky glared at the time then back into the mirror, trying to decide between the dangly star earrings—as close as she was willing to get to anything patriotic, and did you wear patriotic stuff for Memorial Day? Maybe the sedate pearl studs were better. A backyard cookout called for fun. But Memorial Day, when Ty's folks had spent the morning at Arlington, called for respectful.

She went with the pearls and pulled her hair into a high ponytail. She should've toned down the hair. Dammit. Oh well, it was too late to fix it now. She eyed the outfit on her bed —bright yellow off-the-shoulder top and dark denim capris. She wasn't feeling it.

Nicky threw open her closet door and stared at the array of color. Crinolines. Vintage band tees. Everything that wasn't made for getting messy was a little, okay a lot, funky. Or too dressy for today.

She dropped to her bed and Facetimed Sabrina.

"I need help!" Nicky flipped the camera to show off her planned outfit. "I don't wanna…"

Sabrina's laugh had Nicky thumbing back to her friend's face.

"So don't. What are your other options?"

Nicky marched back to her closet and panned the phone over the contents.

"Ah. Your standard Cyndi Lauper, goth pinup girl, dryad mashup."

Nicky flipped her off. "Do you think high waist sailor pants are a bit much?"

Sabrina's scrunched up nose gave her all the answer she needed. Way too much.

"I don't know that I can do this," Nicky whispered. "I don't normally give a shit what anyone thinks, but…"

She sank to the floor in front of her closet, clothes and passing time forgotten. All the insecurities built in over the years and honed by Jeremy bubbling right to the surface. Ty was different. She believed that. Felt that.

"But you love Ty," Sabrina replied. "Which kinda means you need to do this."

Nicky didn't bother denying it. She did love him, and Sabrina was right, Nicky needed to do this. She pushed herself back up. She eyed her closet again, skimming past the funky stuff. A pair of slim pale peach ankle pants—cigarette pants her mother would have called them. A turquoise sleeveless shell top. She propped her phone on the dresser and held up her selections.

"We've gone from Cyndi Lauper to Jackie O." Sabrina nodded her approval. "With a twist, of course. You okay?"

Nicky tossed the new outfit onto the bed and rummaged

for a different pair of shoes... something... classic... there! A pair of beige espadrilles. Perfect.

"Thanks for your help." Nicky held up the shoes for Sabrina's approval. "I'm a wreck, but I think I've got this."

"You do," Sabrina said with a smile. "Have fun!"

The phone went dark, and Nicky turned her attention back to getting ready. She was only two minutes late heading out the door to meet Ty, and the universe must have been in a generous mood because she didn't run into her grandfather.

Ty's smile when she walked down the front steps made it all worth it. He gave a low whistle and wrapped an arm around her waist, bending her back into a deep kiss. She'd have to reapply her lip gloss.

"Lady," he breathed against her mouth, "you look amazing. Well, you always look amazing. Even when I've seen you covered in paint. No, especially then. You ready?"

The ride to his parents' place was a blur, as was meeting his family—his mother, Sandra, in white and pale blue; her sister wearing red, white, and blue. The other women in similarly patriotic colors. And the men all in some shade of khaki pants or shorts. Nicky suppressed a giggle, recalling her earlier musings on whether patriotic accessories were appropriate, and her snarky comment about khakis. She and Ty grabbed drinks and settled into their spots at the long table set up in the shade.

Everything seemed to go well. Until his cousin Don started talking about bringing his wife to Baltimore for the first time.

"So, Chelsea has never been here before, and she's thinking it's all like the TV show *The Wire*, y'know. Drug dealers and shootouts everywhere." The man leaned forward and winked, actually winked. He and his sister had grown up in the semi-rural suburbs of Hunt Valley—not the city. His wife grew up in some small town in Georgia and that's where they'd settled.

"We figured we'd take a bit of vacation and do a little sightseeing. Spring break and all. So, Chelsea looks up all the places to see—Fort McHenry, The Constitution, BMA, The Walters..." he nodded at Ty. "All the usual stuff. Then she asks me about the Visionary's Artist Museum, or something like that."

Nicky braced herself for whatever was about to come out of his mouth. She'd had this conversation with Ty—not everyone appreciated or even understood what the AVAM was about. Those who didn't could range from confused to cutting, like her grandfather.

"I thought it was sorta fun," Chelsea interjected. "I mean, kinda like going to those tacky roadside attractions."

Nicky froze her face into what she hoped was a pleasant smile and prayed for a rapid end to this conversation.

"Oh yeah," Don continued. "I mean, they've got a statue of Divine. And a model of the Titanic made of toothpicks. Definitely tacky."

Nicky bit her tongue. Most people assumed the Titanic. Correcting Don was probably not a good plan. She doubted he'd take it as well as Ty had. Nicky tensed as Ty's fingers closed on her knee. He squeezed gently. His expression looked almost as strained as hers felt.

"Says the man who tailgates on the regular," Ty said. His lips were smiling in that 'hey this is a joke' way guys could get, but his eyes were cold and hard. Nicky could have kissed him right in front of everyone.

"Hey, don't come after my football," Don replied with a laugh. "That's an American tradition. I mean, that place doesn't seem like a museum, and it's kind of a dump. The least they could do is be more commercial. Make it like that Ripley's Believe It or Not place. Now that was fun!"

Ty's mother cleared her throat. "Karen," she turned to Don's younger sister. "Aren't you starting graduate school in the fall?"

Karen practically preened. "Well, we can't have Ty being the only one of us cousins with an advanced degree, can we? This was my last week as a dental assistant." She leaned her head on her husband's shoulder for an instant and smiled "Luckily, this guy makes enough as a doctor so I can focus on school."

Ty's fingers tightened again, and Nicky stifled a groan. So far, this was painful, but not terrible.

"We've all been monopolizing this conversation," Ty's Aunt Bea spoke up. "Where did you attend school, Nicky?"

That was a question Nicky could answer easily. "I have a BFA and master's in art education from MICA."

"How exciting," Bea replied. "And what do you do? Where do you work?"

Shit. She should have seen that one coming. Ty's already strained smile faded. Nicky glanced down at her fingers, twisting her napkin in her lap, keenly aware of everyone's eyes on her. Had Ty really not told his parents where she worked? She couldn't think of any other reason for them staying silent during the cousin's tirade. She hauled in a shaky breath and cast an apologetic glance at Ty.

"I teach classes at both the Baltimore Office of Promotion and Arts and the American Visionary Art Museum."

The words landed like the bomb they were. Chelsea sucked in a sharp breath and looked down at her plate. Ty's parents both looked like fish gulping at the surface—their mouths opening and closing. His aunt and uncle had strained smiles stretched so tightly they looked like they were about to crack. Don muttered something that sounded like "I'm sorry." And Doctor and Mrs. Hubby-Makes-Enough-As-a-Doctor let out uncomfortable sounding chuckles.

And then there was Ty. His lips pressed into a thin line.

"Everyone has to start somewhere." Ty's laugh sounded stiff and forced. "Nicky is an amazing artist with a stellar education and she's brilliant at what she does. I'm sure this is only the beginning."

It should have been a compliment. She was sure he meant it that way. But his words stung, reminding her of every criticism her grandfather had heaped on her head growing up. Unable to process what just happened, and determined to not make a scene, Nicky pulled in a shaky breath and forced a broad smile onto her face.

"I taught for several years at a private school in DC, but only recently moved back to Baltimore." Her voice felt overbright to her, but the uncomfortable expressions around the table were slowly melting into sympathetic looks, and for now, she'd take that over disdain.

"I can imagine that's been a challenge." Sandra was the first to respond. "When did you move back?"

Nicky hated herself a little for taking the coward's way out and not standing up for herself. And she wasn't too thrilled with Ty's weak response. "Mid-March. It's been a whirlwind."

A collective sigh went around the table. As if the fact that she'd only been back for a couple months made everything different. Acceptable. But she'd felt their scrutiny change when they learned where she worked. Everyone had expected her to blow up. To act like trash. Because what they saw were the tattoos and the piercings and the colorful hair. And the job at some strange place they didn't understand.

And Ty had allowed it. His comment encouraged it. As if she was going through some wild phase that she would soon tire of and grow up. She breathed a sigh of relief as conversation turned back to safer topics—weather, baseball, and Aunt Bea announcing she was planning a big Independence Day picnic.

Nicky made polite comments but mostly listened, feeling suddenly completely ill at ease—as if she didn't belong. Not one thing they spoke of interested her and she found herself counting the minutes until she could make her escape.

She made no protestations when Ty begged an early exit and she even laughed off Don's limp apology for his thoughtless comments about that museum.

"Even you have to admit it's outside the norm." Don's laugh was hearty, like this was a big joke. "Like they're trying to be weird or something. Y'know?"

Nicky managed a polite smile and raised her eyebrows. "Not to everyone's taste to be sure. It was a pleasure meeting you."

Back in the car, Ty fixed her with an odd look. "What was that?" His tone sounded amused, but the look on his face was confusion.

"What was what?" She had no clue what part of the meal 'that' could refer to.

He twisted in the seat to face her. "That very formal sounding thing you did with Don. I don't think I've ever heard you be so..." He threw his hands in the air and blew out a breath. "I don't even have the words."

Nicky bit her lip and breathed in for a count of ten before responding. "Should I have yelled instead? Contradicted him? What I said is true. Not everyone enjoys the museum. But I'm not over here making value judgments based on that."

Ty's eyebrows shot up and he opened his mouth as if to reply. Nicky didn't want an argument. She couldn't handle that right now. She was already stressed and frazzled, and the last thing she wanted was to add an argument with Ty to the mix. She laid her hand on his chest, silencing him before he spoke and said something that she couldn't ignore.

"Look," she breathed the word quietly. "Meeting family is hard. We knew this could be awkward. And it was. I don't..." She paused. In the past, she'd have been flying off the handle by now, telling the guy to take a hike. Hell, they would likely have not even gotten to the car, and she'd be catching a rideshare home.

"I'm sorry." The quiet words from Ty surprised her. "I know that couldn't have been easy on you, my cousin is a dick, and I wasn't much help."

Nicky's breath came easier, and Ty's chest rose and fell on a long sigh. It wasn't the full discussion they needed to have. It wasn't her talking to him about the hurtful things he'd said—perhaps, no probably, unintentionally. But it was enough to avoid the blow up right now. It was enough to let her settle back into the comfort they always had between them.

It was enough she didn't ask to be taken home rather than go back to his place. And when his kisses turned passionate, and his fingers lingered on the zipper in her pants, it was enough that she nodded and kissed him back.

In bed, they were perfect. They flowed together, so close, blurring until they seemed as one. Nicky cried when the orgasm hit, when Ty ground out her name into her neck as he came. She wiped the tears with the back of her hand before he could see them.

Because no matter how close they were in this moment, when it was just the two of them naked and entwined, there was a chasm between them now. And she wasn't ready to face that.

TY—WEDNESDAY, MAY 29

"Shit." Ty muttered aloud and stabbed at his iPad; certain he must've messed up the dates when he filled in his big wall calendar. Nope. There it was. David Clyde's farewell dinner was scheduled for the same night he'd promised Nicky he'd attend a concert at Artscape with her. Well, shit. He couldn't very well not attend the going away party for the man whose job he'd be taking—assuming the board voted in his favor.

Between Nicky's work schedule and his increasing duties as he learned the ropes to the role he'd soon have if all went well, they were facing several weeks of very little time together.

She worked on his days off, and he had obligations on hers. For all of June. They'd have this Sunday and Monday free together, and then the rest of the month they'd be on almost exactly opposite schedules.

Was this how life was going to be? Was this what he wanted? He pulled up his email and skimmed the event details. Maybe there were meetings he could shift. He glanced at the big wall calendar again—and maybe there were events she could leave early from. Or if she came straight home after a class, she could still make it to the Walters' cocktail party.

Ty scoffed at that idea. Nice thought. But Nicky usually came home from her Thursday classes covered in glitter or paint or something messy. That was a hands-on kind of day. Though coming in late would be fine.

Then the scowling face of Richard Mason intruded on those thoughts. Add in Sebastian Knox and all the board members who leaned that way and it became a great big nope. He needed to keep his dating life quiet until after the board voted. Which wasn't happening until after the farewell party.

Maybe their conflicting schedules were a blessing in disguise for now.

He jumped at his doorbell going off. Fuck. He'd forgotten he had plans for basketball with Deke today. He unlocked the door and headed straight back to the iPad, open laptop, and pile of papers spread out on the kitchen counter.

"Wow. You're normally a neat freak." Deke gave a pointed look at the mess. "And did you forget Wednesday afternoon ball?"

Ty swept the papers into a pile, slammed the laptop closed and thumbed off the iPad. "My job, plus learning a new position without anyone knowing because it's not been officially decided yet." He stuffed everything into his briefcase and rolled his eyes. "I'll be ready in five. You driving?"

After a few games of one on one with Deke, Ty's brain finally felt at least a little clearer.

Deke tossed the ball at him. "So, spill it."

"I'm up for a promotion, but it hinges on a vote—the museum director has an iron fist grip on more than half the board and is Nicky's grandfather. They have a strained relationship at best and he's an asshole." That was skipping a lot. Like his own concerns about how Nicky would fit into his life. And how he felt like a complete dick for even thinking that kind of thing.

Deke snagged the ball from his hands and tossed it in his bag. "Fuck another game. That steaming pile of shit needs a beer to unpack. We're going to Cold Bottom."

Ty picked up his water bottle and they headed back to Deke's car and they headed to the bar where they'd both spent many hours helping out in college. The place belonged to Zach's parents. Ty held his tongue until they were settled on stools at the long bar, then he unloaded the whole Memorial Day fiasco.

"On top of that, I realized I've got a massive and unavoidable conflict on a date I had promised Nicky. My boss is telling me I need to keep the relationship on the down low until after the board votes. And... fuck." Ty shook his head and tipped his beer back.

This was a much bigger mess than he'd ever expected. He figured he and Nicky would have some differences, and he expected them to be centered on her grandfather. He'd underestimated how bad it could be.

"This is the woman I met. The art teacher? She's cool as fuck." Deke raised his eyebrows. "The fuck problem does anyone have with an art teacher?"

Leave it to Deke to miss important details. Or maybe it was Ty's fault. He hadn't told anyone what Nicky did. His parents gave him shit about that after the barbecue; if they'd known where she worked, they could have brought that conversation to a halt before it went so far and made everyone uncomfortable. His mother read him the riot act for not stepping in and sparing Nicky that embarrassment. And what the fuck did it say about him that he didn't.

"Nah man. She's... kinda unconventional. She works with the Baltimore Office of Promotion and Art, putting together Artscape and teaching mostly kid's classes. Plus, she does stuff with the American Visionary Art Museum."

He braced himself for Deke's reaction. For a polite 'oh that's nice'. So long as Nicky worked outside the box, so long as they were together, that's what he'd be doing. Every time.

"Whoa! Cool!" Deke's eyes were wide, and a big smile creased his face. "That place slaps!"

Not the response Ty expected. Not from Deke.

"Ah, I get it." Deke swigged his beer and leaned forward. "And you're going to let that get in the way of what you want? Who you want?"

Put like that, it cut deep, and Ty felt like an even bigger shit. "I'm trying to put my career first here."

Deke flung a paper coaster like a frisbee, bouncing it off Ty's chest. "That's a bullshit answer. I never imagined you were an elitist prick."

Ty threw the coaster back at his friend. "What the fuck? Don't even. This is my dream job we're talking about. I think a little temporary sacrifice is worth it."

"Eehhhhh!" The loud buzzer sound Deke made echoed even in the bar. "Try again, dickhead."

Ty batted the next coaster that came flying, then apologized to the bartender Reg as the thing landed in the sink. Ty had known the man since college—when he'd first met Deke and Zach. This wasn't the first time Reg had been witness to hiccups in Ty's life.

"Seriously," he said, scowling at his friend. "Nicky is great, but we've only known each other a couple months. I don't know where this is going. What happened to not even thinking of settling down until thirty?"

Deke lined up with another coaster, then let it fall back to the counter after a stern look from Reg.

"First off, you're a year away from that. Second, that's my goal," Deke said. "You're the one who's given up the friends with benefits thing. And stayed celibate for how long before this woman?"

Ty turned away. It had been over six months and Deke knew it.

"Fuck you," Ty said. "Why do you take your earrings out when you teach? Why do you make sure no tattoos show, even in shorts and a polo?"

Deke tossed bills on the bar and slid off the stool. "Because I work for a conservative school. And I chose to work there, knowing what I was getting into. But this isn't about me. It's about you and the woman you're in love with, even if you won't admit it. Because you can't ask someone to change—not if you love them."

Ty nearly choked on his next swallow. "I don't want her to change," he sputtered, still coughing at the beer that went the wrong way. "She's... fuck, she's perfect just as she is. That doesn't mean she's perfect for my life."

Deke laid a hand on Ty's shoulder, then leaned in close. "Bullshit. Try talking to her about the conflict—figure out a compromise. Otherwise, you're an asshole." He shouldered the bag and headed for the door. "Either you love and accept her, or you don't."

Ty gathered up the cash Deke had left and added his own, plus a hefty tip, then followed his friend.

Nicky was perfect. In every way. Except his job. Well, her job really. If she was working at a normal museum, maybe Richard Mason wouldn't be such a dick about it, and her, and well... everything.

That, really, was the problem. Because Mason was the man with the keys to Ty's career in his hands and there was no compromise when it came to that. Not even for Nicky. If that made him an asshole, well, it made him an asshole.

CHAPTER 21

NICKY—MONDAY, JUNE 3

Oh, this month is going to be a shit show. Nicky stared at the big calendar hanging on Ty's wall in what had become their weekly routine—comparing schedules. Nearly every day was filled in with at least one item, usually three or four.

The first time she'd noticed her schedule up there, it had given her happy little shivers. She mattered to him. He was making room for her in his life. Then one day he'd handed her a pen and asked her to fill in the next week. So, she had—after grabbing her own pen, a pink one. She pulled out her phone and checked that he had everything. It was going to be a tight month, but with all they both had going on, that was bound to happen.

She got through the month then hissed in a breath when she turned the page and got to the weekend of Artscape. She swallowed hard and checked her schedule again, even though she knew the exact dates.

Ty's arms circled her waist, and his lips caressed her bare shoulder, but she barely felt it. "What are you glaring at, babe?"

Nicky jabbed a finger at July 13. "I thought you were planning to be with me for the concert on Saturday."

His lips stilled on her skin, then he straightened. The tension in his body radiated through to her.

"That's David's farewell dinner," he said. Well, she couldn't blame him for that.

"Oh, that makes sense. Sooo... how do we want to do this? I mean, the concert is slated to go till nine. I'm not on duty that night, I could..."

She trailed off when he let go of her and leaned back against the kitchen counter. "It's going to be a late night, and I'll be exhausted."

Something in his tone sent a chill through her. Maybe it was the fact that he was looking down at his feet rather than at her. Or the way his hands clenched on the counter.

"That..." Nicky struggled to find the right words. This was an important event for him, and she wanted to be supportive, but they would barely have time throughout June and July. She hadn't realized the farewell dinner was during Artscape. And he had the next day blocked out.

"We could do brunch on Sunday." She tried to keep her voice steady. Tried not to whine or plead.

"The board vote for the assistant director position is that Monday, babe." He shrugged, still not looking at her.

"Okay. So, Sunday is... what?"

Again, with the shrug and not meeting her eyes. "I'm not going to be fit company that day. Not up for our usual activities."

Nicky scowled. And silenced the words that wanted to fly

out of her mouth without thought. Instead, she stepped closer. Placed her hands over his and angled herself so she could look up into his face.

"And you think that's all I care about?" She struggled to keep her tone even when all she wanted to do was yell. "Ty, I enjoy your company, no matter what we are doing. And I know what a big deal that vote is! I want to be here for you."

He shook his head. And Nicky heard his voice at the barbecue saying everyone has to start somewhere. As if her work was nothing more than a steppingstone to something bigger, better. An embarrassing note to be swept under the rug.

She turned and surveyed the calendar again, scanning dates and comparing their schedules with a critical eye. He'd penciled in two possible dates for the two of them—both at night. Both at home. And yet...

"You know," she said as she slid her finger along the calendar and shot him a flirtatious glance. Luckily, he was looking and caught it, as a slight smile crept over his features. "It looks like you've got some time in here... We're doing a staff night before the grand re-opening of the museum restaurant. You could come to that with me. I mean, instead of it just being a late-night thing."

The ghost of a smile on his face faltered. Nicky looked at the calendar again. "Or... well... most Thursdays. I could join you for the cocktail party at the museum."

His face when she turned back to him said it all. He didn't want to come to her work events, and he didn't want her at any of his.

"It's just until the board vote, babe." His voice was strained, tight. His knuckles blanched white from his grip on the counter, as if he was holding on for dear life. "Once they vote, if I've got the position, it doesn't matter anymore."

Nicky gathered up the ragged shreds of her control, refusing to lose it right now. Because she loved this man. Dammit all to hell. She'd gone and fallen for another Joe Preppy, and despite all her early misgivings, Ty had proven her wrong, time and time again. Except now... Now he seemed to be reverting to type. And she would not cry. She would not come unglued.

She would approach this calmly. She would try to understand. And if he would meet her halfway, she would believe they could make it through this.

She swallowed against the tears that welled up. She steeled her face into a calm mask. And willed her voice not to shake when she spoke.

"Aside from yesterday and today, you've got two nights for us this month. Until the board votes on July fifteenth. That's a month from now."

He mumbled something she didn't catch, and she asked him to repeat it.

"I know." His voice wasn't much louder, but at least she understood him this time. "I'm sorry. It sucks."

She wanted to shake him. Scream at him. Beg and plead with him. If they were important to him, if she was as important to him as he was to her, he'd find a way. He'd make the time. Instead, she leaned on the counter next to him and covered his hand with hers.

"Okay. It's a month of suck. We can deal with that. And then what?"

His hand slid out from under hers and then he pushed away from the counter.

"I don't know." It came out as a groan, and he shoved his hands through his hair. "I don't fucking know."

Nicky's gut twisted with ice. What did he mean he didn't know? The fragile hold on her control slipped. "Well, either you'll get the job, or you won't, so maybe that should be my first question."

Ty whirled to face her, confusion creasing his brow. "Meaning?"

"Meaning I am trying to be understanding that you have a lot going on, and we have busy schedules, and it appears you want to avoid being seen with me." She stabbed her finger at different dates on his calendar.

"That's what you think?" Ty's voice was tight. She'd hit a nerve there and she hoped she was doing the right thing by pushing this issue.

"And I'm willing to roll with that for now," she continued, ignoring the question he'd asked. "I'm willing to push all my questions aside for the moment and get through this month of suck. But I asked you a simple question: And then what. But you don't know. So, I'm trying to figure it out."

Yep, she was definitely losing whatever ability to stay calm and rational she had. She tried to rein it back in. Get her emotions in a choke hold and not let go. "A month from now, the Walters Board will vote on whether you get the position of assistant director. What does it mean if you get it? Does this month of suck suddenly become a life of suck?"

"That's not a fair question."

Nicky gave him a sad smile. "It's a very fair question. And so is this one: what happens if you don't get the job? Do you stay where you are? Do you leave the Walters? And what happens if my grandfather makes it clear that I am the reason you didn't get the position? What then?"

Ty's hands clenched in his hair, and he thumped back against the wall opposite her. "You can't know he'd do that."

Nicky laughed. "Can't I? I only grew up with the man. I know how he works. I know he already told me I'd ruin your career if I didn't straighten up and fly right. It's a safe bet he'd share that with you—because he'd want you to blame me."

Nicky stopped. Ty's look of horror froze any words in her throat. She swallowed hard, choking back a sob and forced her voice to work. "And you would. You'd blame me."

"Why didn't you tell me he did that?" Ty's voice echoed in the space. "You should have told me."

"What, that my grandfather is a manipulative asshole who wants to hurt me because he sees me as the reason he lost his daughter?"

Ty's horrified look only deepened, and Nicky's heart twisted until it cracked. She didn't need to know the details. Ty's look told her enough—Richard Mason had said something to Ty. Maybe not against her directly, but she'd be willing to bet Ty had gotten an ultimatum of some sort. And he was giving in to it.

He was just another Joe Preppy. And this was going to end the same way every other relationship she'd had with that type had ended—with her heart in pieces.

"Yeah, fucked up family dynamic." *Oh screw this shit.* She had one last chance to save anything with Ty, she might as well lay it all on the table. She had nothing left to lose. "Gramps never approved of my father. Then Mom got pregnant, and everybody's plans changed. All Gramps saw was failure—his daughter's chance for a bright future was gone because some irresponsible bohemian prick knocked her up. Yeah, I heard those words direct from Gramps' mouth."

Ty's expression softened, his eyes pleading. "I'm sorry. No one should ever hear things like that."

"It made me who I am. Hesitant to trust. Reluctant to love. But I love you, Ty. And I know that means some hard choices, and compromise. So, I'm asking you—after the board votes, what then? What do you want?"

The look he gave her was a sledgehammer to her already cracked and breaking heart, shattering it into millions of pieces.

His eyes were flat, and his lips pressed into a thin line as he faced her. Nicky hauled in a shaky breath and steeled herself for whatever he was about to say, knowing she would leave here, head held high, and go someplace else to fall apart.

Ty would never see her cry over him.

TY

"I don't know," Ty said. That was a lie. He wanted her. He wanted to hear her say she loved him again. He wanted to say it back, whispered in bed and shouted from rooftops. But that was the one thing he couldn't do.

Not even now that he knew she shared his feelings. His entire career hung in the balance, and he would not condemn her to a life where her grandfather was an ever-present and controlling force. Nicky's face was an expressionless mask, but her usual perfect façade failed when it came to her eyes. The hurt reflected in her beautiful blue eyes ripped into him and it would only get worse if they stayed together while he was at the Walters.

"You should have told me about your grandfather." Not that he was doing such a great job on transparency himself. He shoved his fingers through his hair again. If she would quit looking at him with those sad eyes. "Look, I'm sorry. When I learned David was leaving, and that I was up for the position, it was a huge opportunity. Then Mason told me I needed to watch my appearances."

The hurt look in Nicky's eyes flashed to anger and then to something far worse—indifference. She looked bored. Like she'd heard all this before.

"So, your boss—my grandfather—told you I was bad for your career?" Her tone was neutral, but Ty heard the mocking behind her words, and it made him cringe.

"Not in so many words, and not like that. Just…" He blew out a breath and tried again. "That until the board confirmed me for the job, I needed to play politics, keep up certain appearances. That's all."

Nicky's lips twisting into a crooked smile. "And you were bitching at me for not telling you about the conversation with him? When you were keeping that from me?"

The anger was back in her eyes, blazing at him from a few feet away. Challenging him. "It wasn't just him. Sebastian Knox had a few thoughts as well. Maybe if I'd known about your grandfather saying things like…" He stopped when she arched her eyebrows and crossed her arms, clearly ready to argue. Shit.

"What? You would have done things differently?" As quickly as it had flared, the anger receded and Nicky gave him a tight smile—thin, strained, and brittle, as if it would break at the slightest provocation.

"We can stand here talking if only and what if all day, but that won't solve the problem. I'm not asking you to do anything about the next several weeks. I'm asking you what happens after the vote. That question hasn't changed."

Her voice quivered on the last word and Ty reached for her, but she shook her head and moved farther down the counter, away from him. Her hair tumbled from the messy bun—the streak that a week ago had been bright orange had faded to a softer more pastel hue. She'd be touching it up soon. Or changing the color again.

"You want to know what's going to happen if I get the job. And what if I don't. I can't answer those questions. I don't know."

This was going all wrong. All he wanted was to make this easy on her, but somehow, he kept making it worse. In a strange way, maybe this was the only way to protect her from even deeper hurt—he had to be the asshole responsible for her broken heart.

"What about you?" He hated himself for those words, but he didn't seem capable of stopping the train now that it was going. "You mentioned compromise and hard choices. What compromises are you making?"

Nicky raised her head and for a moment, her pain and confusion hit him hard. He didn't want to ask her to change. He couldn't ask it of her. Goddamn Mason and his damn controlling nature. His dream career was at risk of being derailed because of some fairytale creature—who, oh by the way, happened to be the only woman who'd ever had such a deep hold on his heart.

The end result was the same, unless there were some big compromises all around, he'd have to choose his career, or her. All because of her grandfather.

"I can get rid of the brightly colored hair and ditch the piercings, but I can't get rid of the tattoos. I can play the game if I have to—I am Richard Mason's granddaughter after all, but I'll never blend in the way he wants. And do you really want me to do that? To be that? What choices should I be making to help make us work? Because I'm trying to listen, Ty. I'm trying to figure out where we went wrong, and how to fix it."

Ty swallowed hard. Every time he considered what it would take for Nicky to fit into his world, he avoided going too far down that path. The trouble was, he didn't want her to change. He loved Nicky because of who she was—wonderful and wild, passionate and provocative.

None of this would be an issue if Mason wasn't his boss.

Or she wasn't his granddaughter. He couldn't imagine anyone saying his girlfriend's jobs were the problem. Though maybe that was the core of Mason's problem with her. Her jobs.

"You could find a different job." He knew that wasn't the right answer. In fact, it was a shitty answer, but he needed something, anything to make her see things in a different light. "Maybe then your grandfather…" He stopped and looked at her. Really looked. Capri jeans and a midriff top. A pair of paint spattered white Keds sat next to his front door and the red and white polka dot scarf that had been holding her messy bun lay crumpled on his counter. There was nothing about Nicky that Mason and his followers would ever find acceptable. All the things Ty loved about her. Which put him in the world's worst position.

"So, you're telling me the same thing as my grandfather."

Ty looked up sharply. Shit. He had been. Kind of. But not for the same reasons. Her face was set in a tight mask and everything about her body language said she was ready to fight or flee. He couldn't tell if she was angry, deeply hurt, or a bit of both.

"That's not fair." Not the best argument, but all he could come with in the moment.

"I'd argue that it's accurate." She fixed him with a look of disgust. "You're no different than he is. No different than your cousin at the barbecue. I work in a field I love that introduces people—especially children—to art in fun, non-intimidating ways. What in the hell is wrong with that?"

He sighed and leaned back against the wall, stuffing his hands in his pockets to keep himself from grabbing her and telling her how wonderful she was. He needed to focus on his career. His dream. Telling her how much he loved her wouldn't do him any good and it would only set her up for more pain later.

He had to give her up.

"And your grandfather, my boss, is an asshole. We know that. But he's also not wrong. You have multiple degrees. You could be doing so much more with yourself."

Nicky bit her lip and Ty wanted to crawl into the deepest, darkest hole he could find.

"I see." Her voice was quiet. A dangerous whisper. "Are you forgetting that I was teaching at a private school? You know why I left? I lost that job because my ex decided to get revenge for me leaving him, then calling the cops when he got violent."

She snatched her scarf from the counter and whirled on him. "You want to know the whole story? Would that help?"

Every fiber of his being wanted to ask her to stop. Beg her not to go there. He didn't need her to justify herself—to him or anyone.

"My ex-fiancé shoved my past in front of the school board. No one helped me pay for school. I took on the entire burden of my education myself and I'm almost done paying off my student loans. How did you pay for your education? I did it by waiting tables, and when that wasn't enough, I did some pinup modeling and burlesque and I stripped for a semester. You wanna judge me for that, too?"

None of that was surprising. Or horrifying—except for the idea that someone she once loved and trusted had hurt her and betrayed her like that. But there were no words to make it right.

Nicky tore through his apartment, grabbing up the little things of hers that had migrated to his place. A hair tie here, a lipstick from the bathroom counter. The pink satin robe she'd hung next to his blue flannel one.

"I'm not judging you." He needed to mend at least part of the rift he'd created. "I'm trying to understand why you choose to be in this position. You talk hard choices, but you make choices every day that lead to people... well... saying these kinds of things."

She stopped in the middle of cramming her things into a tote bag and laughed. Just started laughing in the middle of his bedroom.

"Oh. My. God." The words shot out between laughs. "I convinced myself that you were different. That you weren't like every other Joe Preppy former jock I've ever known."

Now anger flared in him. "What the fuck does that mean?"

"Uptight." She spat the word. "Regimented. Restrained. When we met, I thought—oh, no, another preppy boy who's going to be boring. But then I thought—don't judge a book by its cover."

She flung open his closet and pointed to the ties neatly hanging on one door, and the open tray of perfectly folded pocket squares on the shelf. Bright colors in the sea of the blues and grays of his suits.

"This is your life. It's stylish and colorful, but in a very controlled way." She spread her arms wide, taking in the entirety of the closet. "And you like it that way. Which is fine. I am not over here trying to change you or complaining about you being so tidy you're fussy. But here you are suggesting I mold myself into this tightly constrained box."

"No, I'm suggesting that maybe you need to act more mature. I know plenty of women who are very colorful, but who don't look like... like..."

Oh no. Bad choice of words. He didn't mean to go there. This was all wrong. This wasn't what he meant.

"Like what, Ty?" Her voice had dropped back to a whisper. Dangerously soft. Under any other circumstances, it would have been seductive. At the moment, all it did was make him realize how deep a pile he had stepped in.

"Look, I'm so..."

"Save it. What you're saying is, if I'm wearing linen and silk, and draped in a hand-painted scarf that cost a thousand dollars and was made by some underprivileged artisan in the Himalayas, and my earrings are conflict-free gemstones... I can be as colorful as I want."

"That's not what I said..."

"No?" She laughed, long and hard. "But you did. You put a higher value on a particular aesthetic. Just as you put a higher value on a particular type of art. If I were teaching classes at the Baltimore Museum of Art, or the Walters, we wouldn't be having this conversation, would we?"

"Again, that's not a fair assessment..."

"But it is..." She dropped the tote bag by his front door. She had made it through the entire apartment and packed all her things and he'd done nothing to stop her. He couldn't. He had to let her go, even if it cost his heart.

Her hands cradled his face, and her eyes were soft, pleading, and so gentle and kind it hurt to look into them. That look shattered him.

"You say you don't want to ask me to change, but the key there is you don't want to ask. You instead imply I should want to change—for myself. That I should be more mature. But none of that is for me—it's for you. That's not compromise, Ty."

She dropped her hands. "I'm going to make this easy. I won't live in the shadows as if I'm something to be ashamed of."

She slipped on her Keds and shouldered the bag. "When the board votes and you know if you've got this job, you make a choice. If you want me in your life, we figure out a compromise that works for both of us.”

His stomach sank but a small part of his heart soared—there was a chance. They could weather this storm.

Until Mason acts like an asshole again. Tries to exert control over her again.

Ty hated himself for doing this to her, but better the pain now than later when he was even more firmly under Mason’s thumb. Better this hurt than the never-ending stream that would come if they stayed together and he took the position that had been his dream for years.

“Or what? That’s not a choice. That’s an ultimatum.” He knew it wasn’t. Knew she was right. The hurt and sadness and anger in her eyes ripped at him. And still he knew he wouldn’t back down. Couldn’t. He’d made his choice, and it was killing him.

“So, me setting a boundary and expressing a need is an ultimatum?” She shifted the bag, marched over to his calendar, and stood still and silent a moment. “I didn’t think I needed to articulate the other half of that choice—and if you want to see that as an ultimatum, you go right ahead.”

Her hands flew over the page. When she stepped back, a big black line ran through the two evening dates he had set aside for them. Nicky tossed the pen back into her bag and marched to the door. “I’ll make it even easier. You are being an asshole, and I don’t make time for assholes.”

In a blink she was gone; the door slamming behind her and echoing off the walls. The sound reverberated inside him long after she’d left. Ty stood there, staring at the door as if she would rush back in at any moment and they could talk, figure this all out.

Somehow, everything had gotten twisted. He didn’t plan to

ask her to change. He couldn't. She was amazing and perfect and he was in awe of her. Didn't she see that? She burned too bright for his world. It was like trying to dim a star. She was better off being angry at him. Where she made the choice to leave.

His one consolation was to believe she would get over him faster if she was angry. He, on the other hand, might never recover.

CHAPTER 22

A week without Ty. A week out of her grandfather's house, because no way in hell was Nicky going to stay under his roof after everything. And now, a full-time job offer from the Baltimore Office of Promotion and the Arts was in hand. She could finally get a place of her own and move on—leaving the past where it belonged. And that included Ty.

"You gonna stand out there all day?" Sabrina waited in the front door, arms over her chest, staring down at Nicky as she stood at the base of the steps. At last, she had made some good friends. The best. She shouldered her bag and headed inside.

"Oh, that's a face that has news!" Anne exclaimed as Nicky hung her things in the hall closet.

"Not until after I have coffee." Nicky headed for the kitchen to make it happen. She should be happy. Things were looking up. But she felt empty. Ever since she'd left Ty's place. She'd come straight to Sabrina, eyes so full of tears she couldn't see straight. She'd cried so hard she couldn't hold anything down—even water bounced back.

That lasted two days. Then the numbness hit. And it hadn't let go. Maybe this was better. Anything was better than the wrenching ache she'd felt.

She was dimly aware of a beeping and a moment later Anne slid a steaming mug into her hands.

"You've got coffee," Anne said. "Start talking!"

Nicky took a slow sip, eyeing Anne and Sabrina over the rim. Amazing friends. A tiny warm spot in the cold expanse of her otherwise frozen heart. She pulled out the official job offer and laid it on the table but kept her hand on it.

"I'm afraid I'm gonna have to switch to per diem at the museum." Nicky gave Sabrina a sad look.

Anne scowled, not quite grasping it yet, but Sabrina's face lit up.

"You got it?" She snatched at the paper and Nicky relinquished it. Sabrina's eyes flew over the page, then she let out a low whistle. "Hot damn! Full-time staff for the fall. Congrats!"

She dropped the paper and hugged Nicky while Anne pulled it to her and read, then jumped into the group hug.

When they both settled back, Nicky scanned the offer again—nearly pinching herself to prove it was real.

"I don't start the new duties until after Artscape," she said. "It's a semester-by-semester role, but the position is funded for the full year and will likely renew next fall."

The other two women gave hoots and Sabrina rose, grabbed a bottle of whiskey, and dumped a generous pour into each coffee cup.

"You know what the worst part of this is?" Nicky leaned back in her chair and stared at their perfectly restored tin ceiling. "Working at AVAM was part of the problem—for my grandfather and for Ty. But I couldn't afford to turn down the work."

"Yeah, I know." Sabrina squeezed Nicky's hand. "I'm sad to be losing you there, but I know you need more hours than we can give."

Nicky sipped her coffee, the whiskey adding a pleasant burn. "Now I can afford to get out of your hair."

Anne scoffed. "That's not necessary. Why don't you stay here for a while? At least until you get fully settled and can really focus on finding the right place, and not just any place."

"Agreed," Sabrina added with a nod. "Ideally something with art space, but applications are coming up for studio space at Creative Alliance. That's an option worth considering."

Practicalities bounced in Nicky's head. And the echoing of her grandfather's cautions, and Ty's attitudes. For the first time since they broken up, she wished she could take back things she had said. She wanted a do-over, where she could listen, really listen, to what he had to say, and respond calmly. If she'd know then that in less than a week one of the major stumbling blocks would be removed... She shook her head.

No. It wasn't just the job. It was a completely different set of values. That wasn't something that would go away with a change of job status.

"Have you decided what to do with your giant nude?" Sabrina eyed her over a coffee cup.

Nicky had packed all of her pieces up and stored them at Becca's for the time being. Except for that one. She didn't want to see it every time she went to pack canvases for shipping. Just looking at it made her think of Ty. Sabrina had wrapped it up and tucked it away somewhere at AVAM.

"And I swear if you say anything about painting over it, I will hurt you."

"Wouldn't dream of it." In truth, Nicky had considered it.

Briefly. Even though it was painful, it was part of her, and that was what her art was about. Apart from that, she loved the colors. The design. The feeling of the piece. Opposites. Fire and water coming together. Like her and Ty.

"Becca says Creative Alliance is doing a showing of nudes in September and she's sure I can get it in there. So that's the current plan. Right now, I need to sit and enjoy this." She tapped a finger on the offer letter.

Later, needing fresh air and space to just be, Nicky sat on their tiny roof deck that commanded a stunning view across the Inner Harbor to the Baltimore skyline. Home.

At one point, she'd believed she never wanted to see this city again. The truth was, when she'd left for DC, it was her grandfather she'd been running away from. Then life had thrown her right back under his roof—she'd hoped for a chance at reconciliation and look where that ended up. But this quirky city was her home and she loved it. And despite it all, she still dreamed of one day teaching at MICA.

It wouldn't matter what she did, she was never going to please Gramps. She had to just accept that and move on.

And there was Ty. He'd made it clear she didn't fit into his world. But he'd implied she could if she wanted to. She pulled her hair out of its bun and held the colorful strands up to the light. She'd done them blood red the day after she and Ty split up. It seemed appropriate.

She'd said she would compromise... and she would. Gladly. But only so far. She'd seen what too much compromise led to. Her grandfather liked to remind her all the harm her father had done to her mother, but Nicky had come to see it all differently.

Whatever Charles Bisset had been, he was not the sole cause of their little family's problems. Despite what her grandfather had tried to make her believe, her father was not to blame for her mother getting behind the wheel drunk. Nor was he to blame for her fatal accident.

Nicky had given up viewing her father through rose-tinted glasses, but she wasn't about to view him as the villain either. Nor could she see her mother as the bad guy. Her mother had tried to get out from under her father's thumb—Charles Bisset and the daughter she bore him were testimonies to that. But in the end, security drove her back to what she knew. No, the villain in Nicky's story was always Richard Mason. His constant scorn, unreasonable expectations, and heavy-handed control were omnipresent factors throughout her entire life.

Compromise? No, she'd be willing to make the effort to look more mainstream if necessary, but she would never compromise who she was for any man. Not even one as amazing as Ty.

"Figured you'd be up here." Sabrina handed Nicky a wineglass filled with garnet liquid. "And figured you'd like a pre-dinner glass of pinot since Anne is making salmon tonight. What's got you so contemplative?"

Nicky took a slow sip. "The age-old question: who am I?" She tried to laugh. To make light of it. But her laugh came out hollow. "I'm not even sure anymore." She took another sip of wine and smiled. "And the root of all my problems—classism. You of all people know how deep that runs in the art community."

Sabrina settled into one of the other chairs, her face placid. "Look at me. I'm never going to fit into the crowd that promotes that classism because it benefits them. I decided a long time ago to channel my anger at that into something productive." She spread her hands as if encompassing the house, her life, and the AVAM, just visible down the hill. Then she gestured at Nicky. "And isn't that kinda the source of your conflict with both your grandfather and Ty?"

"Ouch," Nicky said with a laugh. "You're not wrong. I went to an art school where I wasn't even close to the fringe. Then I got visible tattoos and people quit looking at my portfolio and made snap judgements based on my outward appearance."

Nicky let out a sigh that threated to become a sob. Right or wrong, good, or bad, Ty had made his choice—his career came first. She couldn't blame him for that. Not really. She could, however, blame him for being an asshole about it. She needed to change the subject. There was so much good in her life right now, she needed to focus on that.

"I should've brought my sketchbook up." Nicky glanced at the skyline view painted orange by the setting sun. Wordless, Sabrina rose and retrieved Nicky's canvas bag from the top of the steps then deposited it by Nicky's side.

"I'll let you know when dinner's about to go on," Sabrina said.

Nicky jumped to her feet and hugged her friend. "Thank you. You and Anne mean the world to me."

Sabrina gave her one last squeeze and headed down the stairs. Nicky dug her colored pencils out and surveyed the view.

TY—SUNDAY, JUNE 16

"Happy Father's Day! I come bearing take out." Ty kicked the door shut and held up the bags. He braced himself for the inevitable questions about Nicky. His mother had been trying to get him to bring her to dinner ever since the Memorial Day fiasco.

He was still in high school the last time he'd brought a date home. He needed to tell his parents what had happened. As much as he hated to admit it, maybe they'd have some advice for getting over it.

"Where's Nicky?" His mother swooped in on him, snagged the bags from his hands and disappeared into the kitchen. "I thought you'd bring her along."

By the time Ty made it to the kitchen, she was already transferring the food to serving dishes. Lord knew Sandra Lake would never put take out containers on her dining table. Ty grabbed the platters as she finished them and took them to the table, avoiding her question.

His dad had a wine bottle in hand and four glasses. "Where is that lovely young lady?" He looked at Ty with such intense scrutiny that for a moment, he felt he was a teenager again, caught drinking.

"We broke up." Ty cleared his throat. "About two weeks ago."

A full minute of silence stretched out seemingly forever. His father's face froze into an expression of concern, then he turned and wordlessly put the fourth glass away. His mother held a plate of food in one hand and a serving spoon in the other and stared at him as if he'd grown two additional heads and had spoken from both of them.

"I'm sorry to hear that." She recovered first. "Nicky seemed so pleasant."

Understatement of the century. Nicky was far more than pleasant. She just didn't fit.

"It wasn't that crap with your cousins, I hope?" Leave it to his dad to find the edge of the problem and dig into it. "That was uncalled for. Had we known, well... She handled an uncomfortable situation with remarkable grace. And I wouldn't blame her for..."

"It wasn't the cousins, Dad." Ty spooned saag paneer onto

his plate and kept his eyes on the table. "Not all of it, anyway. It's more job related. Politics. And it's complicated."

He'd thought he wanted advice, but now felt reluctant to share. He'd made the right choice—but why did it feel so rotten. His parents were good at getting things out of him, though and the whole mess spilled out between the lamb biryani and the kheer. His mother gasped and tsk'd when he told her what his boss had advised.

"It sucks, but this is my career. It's important to me."

His dad's eyebrows raised, and he sat back from the table, an expression of mute shock painted on his face.

"If you're hoping for tips on feeling better about that choice, you're barking up the wrong tree." His father laid his silverware down, placed his elbows on the table and leaned toward Ty. "I'm not saying you made the wrong choice—not saying it was right, either—it's the way you went about it. Own your decisions."

Not what Ty had hoped to hear. He'd been kicking himself over that already. He should have told Nicky he couldn't see her any longer. That he needed to focus on his career. It's not like he hadn't had that conversation with women before—hell, he'd been on the receiving end of that conversation. Still...

"She had a choice to make as well," he began, but stopped when his mother put down her wine glass so hard, he thought the stem would snap.

"Tyler Michael Lake!" She pointed a finger across the table at him and once again, Ty was whisked back to his teenage years. "I know we taught you better than that. You make your decisions based on what is right for you and you take the responsibility for them. You do not shift that onto someone else and then blame them when they don't make the choice you want."

The curse of being the child of a psychiatrist and a behavioral therapist. You could try deluding yourself, but if your parents found out—they'd call you on your bullshit so fast your head spun.

No matter how Ty tried to justify what he'd said to Nicky, how he'd handled the whole break up, his parents were right— he'd fucked up.

After dinner, his dad cornered him in the kitchen under the guise of helping clean up.

"Never mind the right and wrong of the situation. Nothing is ever perfect or purely black and white. You were faced with a dilemma. You had a career-making opportunity presented to you. But it came with cautions about your lifestyle choices."

His dad hung the towel, dropped a detergent tab into the dishwasher and slammed it closed. "You could continue living your life and let the chips fall where they may. That's certainly a choice. Or you could have simply broken things off with Nicky—whether you explained all the details or not. Also, a choice. Either of those would have been more honest than what you did."

As if Ty needed to feel any worse. He'd come here hoping his parents would help him find a way out of the guilt he was experiencing, and the constant battle of feeling like he was justifying himself. Instead, things went the other way and it rankled.

"But it's never this or that. Never just two choices." He hated the whine he heard in his tone, but there it was.

"No," his mom said. "There are always nuances that create infinite possible paths. Some more honest than others. The problem you're facing—the reason you're struggling with this isn't just that you are emotionally invested in Nicky. That was clear at the barbecue. It's the way you handled it."

Ty groaned. He knew what was coming. Should have known before he came here. Hadn't he heard this lecture enough growing up.

"You're trying to make excuses," his dad said. "To defend your actions. And you're feeling the way you do because your actions were poor choices. You don't need to be finding a way to excuse those. You need to be owning them and apologizing."

Yep. There it was. Exactly what he should have expected. Fuck.

"Even if the outcome is the same," his mother added. "The result could be exactly as it is now—you placing your career over your relationship with Nicky. That's a valid option. But you can't abdicate the decision making and expect her to do it for you."

Ty raised his hands in defeat. "Okay. Okay. I get it. I fucked up." He ducked as his mother swung a dish towel at him over the cuss word. "How do I stop feeling like shit?"

His mother shook her head and walked out of the room. His dad poured two cups of coffee and headed to the back deck.

"You don't," he said as they sat. "That's not saying you don't need to apologize. You should do that. But it's not going to change how you feel. What about the job? Have you given any thought over being tied to a position that..."

"Please," Ty interrupted. "Stop. I think about that every day. Every. Single. Day."

"That says something, don't you think." His mother stood in the doorway, mug of tea in one hand and her iPad in the other. "It sounds like you need to do some soul searching and decide what it is you want. And then consider if this is the right step for you—regardless of whether Nicky is in your life or not."

She laid the tablet on the table in front of him and Ty caught his breath as a picture of Nicky with a group of kids filled the screen.

"I got the BOPA newsletter in my email this afternoon," she explained. "They do free art classes for inner city students. It's something I suggest to quite a few of my clients—getting at-risk kids involved in extracurriculars helps give them a sense of belonging that can keep them out of gangs. And it looks good for school applications."

Ty leaned in and looked at the picture again. The kids looked to be middle school age, and Nicky stood front and center, a big smile on her face, but that smile didn't reach her eyes. There he saw pain. Or maybe he was imagining it. Punishing himself with it.

"They've been doing this program for years," his mother continued. "And the dropout rate among the program kids is far lower than the local average. It's not just arts and crafts."

Ty skimmed the email—the kids had made mixed-media self-portraits. The email went on to say Ms. Bissett encouraged the kids to create a portrait with materials they loved—it could be a realistic portrait, or abstract, just something that represented the best of what each kid saw in themselves. On the back of each portrait, she asked the kids to write three positive things about themselves.

"It's my hope," the email quoted Nicky, "No, it's my belief that by giving a young person a positive lens through which to view themselves, they will walk away from class feeling better about themselves, and the world around them. And that will breed hopes and dreams and goals. Through art, and self-expression, they will find both acceptance and motivation to be their best."

Well, shit. How easy it had been to buy into Mason's

attitudes. To join him and Sebastian in looking down on programs like this one.

Ty looked at the picture again, the faces on the kids. Some facing the camera with bright smiles that lit up their faces. Some turned to Nicky, expressions wide in wonder—as if no one had ever given them positive feedback before.

In that group could be a budding new artist. At the very least, this was a group of kids who would no longer laugh and scoff on a field trip to a museum. They'd be at least a little intrigued. Curious even.

Mason and Sebastian would look at this group of kids and discount them. None of them would likely grow to be patrons of the arts. But why couldn't they. What stood in the way of that. Only economics. And without exposure to arts— without accessible exposure—even if they gained the means, they would have no motivation.

Ty pushed the iPad back toward his mother and swallowed his pride. "Looks like I've got a lot of thinking to do before the board votes."

CHAPTER 23

W onder of wonders, Ceremony Coffee was open on the morning of the fourth. Nicky slipped into the coffee shop for the first time in weeks, bracing herself in case Ty was there. She'd been resisting, but she'd barely slept last night and woke up to find Anne had used the last of the coffee for her typical five in the morning wakeup. She could have gone to a different coffee shop, but she missed Ceremony's brew.

"Hey!" Jace greeted as she walked in. "Been a while. Figured you two had maybe moved."

It took a minute for Jace's words to penetrate Nicky's caffeine-deficient brain. "No, I didn't... wait... So... Ty hasn't been in either?"

She'd been denying herself her favorite coffee all this time to avoid him, and she didn't need to.

"Nope," Jace answered. "Oh..." The smile on their face fell as the pieces must have clicked. "Oh, I'm sorry. Tell you what, I'll have Gabe make up something special. On the house."

Nicky shook her head. "The something special sounds good, but you don't need to do that. I need a pound of the house blend and a pound of the vanilla, too."

Jace made a few taps and spun the keypad to Nicky—just the coffee beans. She swiped her card and dropped a few of bills into the tip jar. Then Gabe slid her coffee across the counter with a big smile.

"Guaranteed pick me up. It's a certain popular cookie in a cup," Gabe gave the cup a little tap that sent the whipped cream jiggling. "Espresso, steamed oat milk, salted caramel and chocolate syrups, topped with whipped coconut cream and toasted coconut."

Nicky eyed the beverage, almost afraid to pick it up for fear of spilling. "I think I gained five pounds listening to you describe it. Is this new on the menu?"

"I've been working on some cookie-inspired drinks. This one's brand new. If folks like it, it'll go into regular rotation."

Nicky finally got brave and picked the towering cup up slowly and took a sip. And her eyes about rolled back in pleasure. "Oh, good grief that's perfect!"

Gabe shot her a thumbs up and went back to the bar. Nicky grabbed a swizzle stick and stirred the frothy cream down, stuck a lid on and headed back to Sabrina and Anne's.

At work, chaos reigned as everyone scrambled with last minute prep a week and a half before Artscape. Unexpected road construction had meant a change to one of the vendor lanes, and two Kidscape performers had to back out. Luckily, Nicky had a list of alternates who were more than happy to jump on the opportunity. Sabrina was equally buried, so they'd collectively decided to enjoy a quiet day off then walk to the harbor for fireworks.

Nicky tossed the coffee beans on the kitchen counter and went in search of her hosts. She found Sabrina sprawled in the backyard hammock and Anne curled in a chair reading on her tablet. Nicky settled into the lounge, prepared to join them in a lazy summer morning.

Until Anne dropped her tablet into Nicky's lap. "Have you seen this week's Arts section?" Anne tapped a fingernail on the headline about Baltimore summer art programs.

"Haven't yet." Nicky sat up and focused on the article. "I knew it was coming at some point. Becca gave me a heads up before she sent the newsletter out last week."

She skimmed the article summarizing upcoming art events and venues, then caught her name mentioned in conjunction with both BOPA and AVAM. There was even a pic of her at one of her BOPA classes. She looked back up at Anne, eyebrows raised.

"You've got a fan club," Anne continued, dragging her fingernail down the article to where the writer commented on Nicky's dynamic presentation at an AVAM tour as well as the class they'd sat in on for BOPA. "Did you even know there was a reporter there?"

Nicky stared at the picture. "At the time? Hadn't a clue. I get so wrapped up in the kids that unless someone comes right up to me, I'm not likely to notice."

Her breath caught as she read the next paragraph. The writer had interviewed Ty. There was his picture—his lopsided smile shining out in full color. She resisted the urge to zoom in.

"Wondered how long it would take you to see that," Sabrina said from her position in the hammock.

Nicky skimmed the paragraph, then read it more slowly. Finally, she cleared her throat and read.

"'I think it's amazing to have so many thriving arts programs in the city,' says Tyler Lake, Development Coordinator at the Walters. 'Especially programs like the ones at BOPA and AVAM that reach people who might otherwise never get positive exposure to the arts.'"

Nicky put the tablet down and stared from Sabrina to Anne. The other women chuckled, and Anne pointed back at the tablet. "Keep reading," she whispered.

"Lake went on to praise children's programs that guide kids in creating their own works of art. 'It's been proven time and again, children who are engaged in art classes do better academically and socially. Mocking kids' programs as glorified arts and crafts is a mistake. Exposing kids to the arts by encouraging them to create it for themselves is building a lifelong appreciation of art and making art more accessible is never a bad thing.'"

Nicky wanted to believe what she was reading. She wanted to think Ty had changed his mind. But the reality was, he was playing politics again.

"Pretty words." She handed the tablet back to Anne. "Too bad his actions don't say the same."

Sabrina was all gooey eyes. "You don't think maybe he's had a change of heart?"

Nicky rolled her eyes. "In three weeks?" She laughed. "Hardly. Even him being interviewed for this article smacks of PR spin. They haven't officially announced David Clyde is leaving. This is an opportunity to make Ty look good—so that when it happens, everyone can think: oh yeah, he seemed so progressive and forward thinking. Whatever."

Anne snatched the tablet and slid into a chair. "How, in such a short time, did you go from broken hearted to cynical and cold?"

"This is nothing new to me." Nicky sat forward and pointed to the tablet. "I've lived my entire life with the knowledge that people are watching. That appearances matter. And saying the right thing is important."

She rubbed her hands over her face and groaned. "Right now, I'm working fifty-plus hours a week to do what needs done for Artscape, plus I'm putting in another twenty or so hours a week at AVAM. All so I can sock as much money into savings as I can. All so I can afford a place and maybe even have enough to furnish it and eat."

Anne leaned forward and grabbed Nicky's knee. "We keep telling you to stay here. Take six months. Take a year."

Nicky leaned back and shook her head. "You're amazing. I've made a handful of friends here—thank you for that. I love and appreciate you both, so much! But otherwise, I've been back in Baltimore for four months and there's been a whole lot more negative than there has positive. And yet, I'm not interested in giving up. Maybe I'm an emotional masochist. I dunno."

"You need a girl's night," Sabrina said.

"I don't have time for a girl's night. Like I don't have the emotional bandwidth to look at this article and believe that Ty had a change of heart and we can get back together."

She hauled in a shaky breath. She'd tossed and turned many nights because of him. Because she couldn't let go of what she thought was something special. Different.

"We were a fling," she said, finally, and the words ached to say. "It was fun and I stupidly fell for him. It's gonna take me a long time to get over that."

Sabrina sat up in the hammock, "But what if he did…"

Nicky smiled gently. Sabrina and Anne—both hopeless romantics. "I appreciate your optimism, but I can't go there. Too much of what Ty said echoed the same shit my mother used to say, and she was echoing her father."

She swallowed hard. She never spoke ill of Richard Mason in public. That wouldn't be wise in the Baltimore art scene, but these two weren't public. They were her friends. More than that, they were family.

"At best, my grandfather is a bully and a jerk. At worst, he's an emotionally abusive asshole. He said the same exact things Ty said to me about my work, my ambition and motivation, my direction in life. I don't care how much I love him. Or how much reading this article makes me hope that he didn't mean it."

She'd been down this road before and it never ended well. "It's gonna take a hell of a lot more than a few pretty words to make me believe it."

TY—THURSDAY, JULY 11

A knot twisted in Ty's stomach as he put the finishing touches on his CV for the board's meeting and vote. He skimmed over the document, struggling to focus on the words. The entire last month felt like that—he'd thrown himself into work but could barely remember anything. Not since Nicky had left. One month without her and his entire world had gone flat and gray.

Ty hovered his finger over the send button, a twinge of uncertainty making his finger shake. What made him qualified to step into the assistant director's shoes? Never mind that his master's was in museum studies and his thesis had been on the significance of historic houses in a museum setting—based on his work with the Hopkins Homewood Museum, and his proposed dissertation was all about museum ethics and funding practices.

He hit send. He was qualified. He'd worked hard to get where he was, and his CV showed it. Years interning at the Baltimore Museum of Art and working countless hours with the Hopkins Archaeological Museum. He didn't even want to consider what he'd sacrificed.

A knock on his door startled him, and he looked up to see Richard Mason looming in his office doorway.

"Do you have a moment?" Mason was already crossing to the chair in front of Ty's desk, as if he needed no answer. Ty supposed he didn't. He was the director, and before that, had been a board member for years.

"Always." Ty plastered a smile on his face. "What can I do for you?"

The older man sat with his elbows on the chair, leaning back slightly, ankle up on his knee—as if he owned the place. If recent events surrounding Ty's career direction at the museum were any indication, for all intents and purposes, Mason did own the place. Or at least its decision-making engine.

"I know it's been a challenging few months and there have been some stresses, but I believe it's best to put those in the past."

Ty took the only safe path—he nodded his agreement. He couldn't imagine the guy had a sudden case of protective instincts regarding his granddaughter's broken heart. Hell, if Ty knew anything about Nicky, it was a good bet her grandfather didn't even know about it.

"I'll be honest. I was a little concerned at the tone the newspaper interview took. Sebastian was livid. But public response has been overwhelmingly positive. The board feels you managed the right note of progressive ideology grounded in history. Well done."

Whatever the hell that all meant. Ty managed to say something. It may have even sounded like a thank you. He'd agreed to the interview after his mother showed him the email newsletter featuring Nicky. If he was going to take on this job, he was going to do it on his own terms. Otherwise, what the hell was he even doing here, aside from becoming yet another Richard Mason or Sebastian Knox?

"Obviously, I can't predict the future, but I've heard through the grapevine that you'll be taking over after David Clyde moves on."

Ty kept the smile firmly in place. "I've heard rumor that might be the case, but that's up to the board, of course." He tried to keep his tone light. He certainly didn't want to seem arrogant, or flippant, or whatever else might piss off his grumpy boss.

"Well, that vote could go either way." Mason mimed a scale weighing two sides. "I wanted to say I'm glad you came to your senses."

Ty's smile slipped. He coughed into his hand, tried to screw a neutral expression back into place, and hoped he succeeded. "I'm not sure what you mean, Dr. Mason."

The older man smiled and shook his head. "I've said it before. Much like her father, Moira is a very persuasive person. She's attractive and charming and entirely distracting. I watched the disaster that followed when my daughter fell for such a man. At first, I had hoped you might prove a stabilizing influence, then I saw history repeating itself. It seemed for a while you were succumbing to my daughter's fate."

Ty could certainly agree with most of those descriptions, including the disaster that was now the ruins of his relationship with Nicky. Though he was certain that he and Mason viewed it all through a very different lens.

"I uh..." Ty scrambled for what to say. How could he possibly respond to what Mason had spewed? "My only concern is the museum, and my career. That has to be my focus." True and neutral enough. He hoped.

"Well said," Mason replied with a hearty laugh. "A man

has to know what's important in life and not allow himself to be swayed by frivolous girls who refuse to grow up. She could be doing so much more with herself."

Ty nearly choked on his next breath of air. Fuck. He had said those same things to Nicky. No wonder she got pissed at him.

Mason rose and offered his hand and Ty took it reflexively, though the more the man talked, the more Ty wanted to shake him and tell him his granddaughter was one of the brightest most caring people he'd ever met. Instead, he swallowed all of that, smiled and stayed silent.

"I look forward to the two of us working together more closely," Mason said, with a laugh and a wink. "Assuming, of course, the board votes in your favor, but I have a hunch."

Then he was gone, leaving Ty with a strong desire to wash his hands. Had the man actually said that vile crap about his own grandchild? He logged out of his computer and left—he didn't trust himself to manage even vague polite responses if anyone else stopped and talked to him.

At home, he realized he hadn't turned the calendar to July. He flipped the page and stared at the weekend. Bright purple letters in Nicky's gorgeous handwriting: ARTSCAPE-All Day! And beneath that, in his own neatly printed block letters and black ink David Clyde Farewell Party. And on Monday, the board meeting.

Ty sank onto a kitchen stool; his eyes fixed on the calendar. If he looked back at the past months, the pages were filled with color and hearts and stars and exclamation points—as soon as he'd given Nicky the okay to put dates on his calendar and she noted that he not only marked future dates, but used it as a shorthand diary, she'd attacked the pages with a handful of colorful pens.

She had drawn a heart around the day they first met. Stars

marked their dates and their first kiss earned hearts and stars. There was the glorious day in May that she had colored the entire square in pink highlighter, outlined the box in purple glitter, and drawn an elaborate kiss mark in the middle. The first time they'd had sex.

Her work events were penciled in with pink, to make it easy for him to see them, but everything personal, she had decorated in a rainbow of sparkly colors and images. It was like looking at a timeline of their whirlwind relationship.

Then it came to an abrupt halt. His breath caught looking at Memorial Day. He wasn't sure when she'd done it—probably the day she'd left and scratched out the dates he'd set aside, but the red, white, and blue flag she'd originally put there was colored in black and dripping red—was that blood, or tears? June had only a couple Nicky doodles.

Two months. How could someone have such a deep impact in not even a full two months of dating? Richard Mason's words came back to him: attractive, and charming, and entirely distracting. No, it was more than that. Nicky was so much more than that. She was an absolute force of nature packed into a human body. A very sexy human body.

He'd described her to Deke as perky. Hell, he'd thought it repeatedly—he liked her brand of perky. Nicky brought something vital into his life. Something amazing. Something he missed now that he didn't have it. And he wanted it back. He needed her back.

He was madly, irrevocably, head over heels in love with her. With everything about her. The only problem was, he'd fucked it all up. He'd made a complete mess of everything, and it was one hundred percent his fault. So, it was on him to fix it, and he could think of only one way to do that.

He had to show Nicky that she was his world.

It would mean disappointing Richard Mason, and

possibly losing the job opportunity, but... well... he was just succumbing to his fate.

First things first, he opened his email and drafted a letter to his academic advisor stating he wanted to change his dissertation. He had an idea, not quite fully formed yet, and he needed to know if it was possible. Screw funding practices. What he wanted to consider now was the social impact of museums and how to change young people's perceptions of them from boring places for old, rich people to exciting, interactive, educational, and affordable resources. Why couldn't a museum be a great date night. Or a place kids wanted to go.

He paused as he considered next steps. He'd have to notify Mason and the board of the change in focus. Even if they agreed, which was questionable, it would set him back. Once he set these wheels in motion, he'd be on a new path. It could cost him the promotion at the Walters and everything that meant about achieving his dream career.

Except that dream had proven to be a nightmare and he didn't want to imagine a future without Nicky in it. Even if she never forgave him, he was forever changed. Nicky had opened his eyes to things he'd never considered and it had taken him too long to realize it. Whatever the outcome, he knew he had the right idea.

Mason might have a chokehold on top staff at the Walters, but there were other museums. Ty finished and sent the email with the first genuine smile since Nicky had left.

CHAPTER 24

A sea of bodies pulsed to the music and the smell of alcohol and possibly some pot wafted through the air, overpowering even the food trucks behind him. Down near the stage, a guy in a tutu, a cape and not much else swayed and swirled to the driving Zydeco beat. Right next to an older couple in matching tie-dye tees doing some pretty complex swing dance moves.

Quintessential Baltimore, where quirky was a way of life, and Nicky fit right in.

He had no clue how or where to find her in this crowd. Or if she would want to see him, but he had to try. The choices he'd made to be here tonight had sealed his fate career wise, at least at the Walters, but he didn't care. He could find a job anywhere. He couldn't find another Nicky.

"Well, fancy meeting you here." The rich voice came from behind and Ty turned. Sabrina's braids were even more colorful than usual, with bright beads on the ends that clicked together as she shook her head at him.

"Yeah." He gave a weak chuckle and looked down at his own outfit—chinos and a short-sleeved linen shirt. He was the odd man out in this crowd.

"You wanna tell me what you're doing here? And why I shouldn't shoo your ass away before she notices you?" Sabrina planted one hand on her hip and fixed him with a glare he was sure could weld steel. He had no doubt that she not only could but would escort him all the way back to his place if he didn't offer up an acceptable answer. He also kind of liked the protective streak she had going for Nicky.

"Well..." He shrugged and decided to lay it on the line. "I can say I'm sorry, and I was an asshole all day, but it doesn't mean anything unless I'm willing to put my words into action."

Sabrina's expression melted into something surprisingly soft and sweet. She leaned close, pointed to a bright blanket at the far edge of the grassy slope. "She's over there with Anne. Wait at least until the song is over."

By the time he'd navigated the crowd, the song had finished, and the band launched into a rocking version of "On a Night Like This". Nicky jumped up, pulling Anne with her to dance, and Ty caught his breath. Had he really forgotten how beautiful she was?

Her hair was in its usual high ponytail with a broad streak of the hottest pink he'd ever seen shining in the lights. Matching bits of lacy stuff fluffed her ponytail into a wild array. A black and pink sequined crop tank top showed off her bellybutton ring, complete with hot pink jewel. Black cut off shorts with some sort of sparkly black and pink mesh tights and hot pink high-top Chucks finished the look. As if Rainbow Brite and some goth rocker decided to combine in a spectacular array that was one hundred percent Nicky.

All he could think was how much he wanted to kiss her.

This was Nicky. She was quirky. And wickedly smart. And funny. And... screams erupted right next to him as one of the band members took off his shirt. Nicky turned toward the sound, her eyes traveled the crowd, and she landed on him. She stumbled over her next step and almost crashed into another dancing couple.

She looked away, giving Anne a smile and the spell was broken. Her gaze strayed back to him. Ty schooled his face into a pleasant expression and soon found it wasn't hard. In fact, he was having a hard time not devolving into a goofy grin. The music was good and there was so much joy and positive energy around him.

In minutes it was all over. The song finished and Nicky leaned in, saying something to Anne, then made her way toward Ty, and suddenly he was nervous.

What if he fucked it up. What if she didn't want to listen. Or wouldn't give him another chance. All the negatives roiled in his head until he was ready to scream.

Then she was there, in front of him, looking at him expectantly, and Ty knew what he had to do.

"I'm sorry. I know I was an asshole, and I don't deserve your time, but..." He stopped. Her expression was bland, and he dared hope there was a chance. "I'd like to talk to you. With you. If you're willing."

"Not here. Your place. I'll give you five minutes to convince me to continue the conversation. My scooter's in the staff tent. Did you drive or walk?"

The carefully schooled expression on her face didn't bode well. "I took a rideshare. We can..."

She shook her head and led him through a tent flap into a dimly lit space filled with tables and boxes. Nicky waved at the security guard as she hauled her scooter out into the access way and climbed on. She tugged her helmet on and angled her head at the back. Ty didn't question whether she had a spare helmet. He got on behind her.

Then his hands touched her hips, and it was like touching a live wire. Every fiber of his being vibrated, crackling in response to her energy. Nicky grabbed her phone and typed something in and kicked the scooter into gear. "Hold on," she said and pulled away from the tent.

They rode to his place in silence; the whole way, Ty tried to decide what to say. How to say it. At his apartment, she stood next to the door, her arms crossed and an expectant look on her face.

"You don't want to sit?" Ty gestured into the apartment, but Nicky shook her head. Okay, not going the way he'd hoped. She was here, but looked like she was ready to bolt. There was only one thing he could think to share that might change her mind.

"I turned in my resignation at the Walters."

Nicky's eyes went wide. Her stiff posture loosened as she uncrossed her arms and stared at him. "Is that invitation to sit still open?"

"Would you like something to drink? Water or soda? Coffee?"

Nicky nodded and made her way to the living room as if in a daze and sat in the small side chair rather than the couch. Well. She was here and willing to listen. That was something.

"What do you mean you turned in your resignation?" She asked as he handed her a chilled soda can. "And didn't you have a farewell dinner to attend tonight?"

Ty's brain scrambled. He hadn't thought this part of things through. From the moment Richard Mason left his office on Thursday, his brain had been going what felt like ninety miles a minute but the one thing he knew he had to do was be here tonight and apologize. To beg Nicky for a few minutes of her time. After that, he didn't have any idea where to begin.

"Ty." Nicky's voice sounded as if it was coming from far away. "You convinced me to listen, but you kinda have to say something."

"I don't know where to start other than, I fucked up and I was an absolute asshole."

Nicky's lips tightened into a polite smile, and he could almost hear her voice telling him he'd already said that and to get on with it.

"Yeah, sorry." He shifted on the couch, wishing he could be closer to her. Touching her. "I changed my dissertation. For my PhD, I want to focus…"

The polite smile on her face morphed into a look of impatience. He wasn't going about this right, but everything hinged on something else—nothing made sense without at least three other things.

"I'm not going to bite your head off, y'know." Nicky shook her head and a small smile played at the corner of her mouth. "I nearly choked when I saw you in the crowd, so I get it. Start with why you're not at the dinner tonight. Or why you resigned. Pick one."

Ty laughed. If only it were that easy.

"Resignation first, I guess." He hauled in a deep breath and blew it out slowly, trying to gather courage from somewhere. "I did a whole lot of thinking after you left and I came to realize I'd been stupid and selfish as well as childish and cruel. I am sorry for that."

Her eyes softened and she swallowed hard. Maybe he was on the right path.

"I was feeling pretty shitty about myself and my actions when your grandfather paid me a visit." He tried to ignore her sharp intake of breath, but her cold glare made it tough to accomplish. "You of all people know what he can be like. When he left, it was... it was like all of a sudden, I had a clear vision of what I needed to do. First thing—I sent an email to my academic advisor. Friday morning, I had a meeting with Mason and Sebastian."

Ty pressed his lips together and forced himself to stay calm and neutral. That meeting had not gone well. They didn't support Ty's new dissertation concept and made it clear they didn't believe the board would stand behind it either.

"That day I became acutely aware that my worldview had evolved and was no longer aligned with theirs. I'm not sure I'd ever given it much thought before. I sure as shit did not want to spend the foreseeable future under the thumb of a certain museum director with a control streak a mile wide."

That brought a chuckle from Nicky. "It's actually about five miles wide and a good two miles deep. But continue."

"Not much to tell from there. After the meeting, I turned in a thirty-day notice of resignation. No surprise, by the end of the day, the museum executed my severance package and handed me my final paycheck."

He dared look at her. She sat, calm, cool, relaxed looking. She'd listened to that part. Ty sucked in a breath and crossed his fingers that she'd listen to the rest.

"I knew I had to be here. At the concert we were supposed to attend together. I had to tell you I'm sorry. More importantly, I wanted to show you that you mean more to me than anything else."

Ty reached across the seemingly huge divide between them and clasped her hand in his. She kept her eyes down, not looking at him, but she didn't pull away and he counted that as a win. Time for one more bit of courage.

"I love you."

Nicky's head snapped up, her eyes drilled into his and her

teeth sank into her lower lip. Tears welled in her eyes, and she sniffed. She stared at him for so long he forgot to breathe. She swiped at her eyes with the back of her hand and Ty worried he'd said the wrong thing.

"Nicky, I'm sorry," he said again but she slid out of the chair and sat next to him on the couch.

"Hush. Apology accepted."

They had a whole lot more to talk about, but for now, it felt good to be here with her again. He'd missed her company.

She bit her lip and doubt edged in. She'd accepted his apology. She'd moved onto the couch with him, but she still sat stiff and straight, keeping the distance between them. That few inches felt like a mile.

NICKY—SATURDAY, JULY 13

He'd said he loved her. Nicky's heart leapt. Her insides tumbled and twisted as she dared to hope, to believe.

"Can we..." Ty's voice broke, and he looked down, then took a deep breath, his shoulders rising and falling as if with great effort. "Can we try again? I'd like to. If you're willing."

Oh, the magic words she'd so longed to hear! And those gorgeous eyes, looking at her now full of uncertainty. Full of pain. And full of love. A toxic soup she knew all too well. How tempting it was to put all their misery to rest, to confess she loved him and kiss and make up.

He'd he wanted to try again, and she was more than willing. But first she had to be clear where she was right now.

"I accepted a full-time position for the fall semester at BOPA and I've applied as adjunct faculty at MICA for spring."

A tentative smile spread over his face, encouraging Nicky to go on.

"I'm staying with Sabrina and Anne. Renting their guest room for now." She swallowed against a dry throat. Why was this so hard. She'd imagined this countless times. Seeing him again. Talking to him. What would she say if... Well, here he was, saying all the right things and she was terrified to admit her own feelings.

"I considered going back to school, but the whole starving student thing gets old really fast. I'm not sure I want to go into administration. And there aren't that many opportunities in my field for..."

Nicky stopped talking. She was babbling. Nervously spewing words while Ty sat there watching her as if entranced.

"I think about that day. A lot." Nicky dared looking into his eyes and winced seeing her own pain reflected. "You hurt me."

"I know," he whispered. "I am so sorry."

The image of storming across Ty's kitchen to scratch out their two dates replayed in her head. She didn't know what to say, or where to even begin to explain what she was thinking.

"I don't think I would change my response." Nicky focused on his face and took a deep breath. "I am sorry, though. I know what I said had to be difficult. Hurtful."

Ty reached across the few inches separating them, capturing her hand, squeezing it. "It was more than deserved. I was a shit."

Nicky turned sideways on the sofa and took a good long look at Ty. His usually perfect beard was a little scruffy. His hair untidy. Dark circles under his eyes told a story of little sleep. She thought she'd enjoy knowing he was hurting as much as she was. But she didn't enjoy this at all.

He'd been hurtful, yes, but he didn't deserve this. He'd taken a risk, baring his heart. Now the ball was in her court.

"You said you'd like to try again." Nicky took in a shaky breath. "I'd like that, too."

The lines on Ty's face softened and he closed his eyes and breathed a thank you that had her aching to reach out to him, to climb into his lap and live and breathe his kisses.

Before she could do that, she had to be as open with him as he had been with her. He took the first step toward getting back together. The next step was hers.

"I said it before, and nothing has changed. I love you, Ty." As soon as the words left her mouth, Nicky's world felt right. The tightness left her chest and the frozen wasteland of her heart bloomed with fire.

His eyes opened wide and locked on hers as a smile spread across his lips, turning into that megawatt grin that had so enraptured her the first time they met.

He cradled her face in his hands, looking at her as if he wanted to memorize every detail. His tongue slid over his lips, making Nicky want to capture it between her teeth. He looked like he was trying to form words, but they weren't yet coming.

Nicky leaned into him, bracing her hands on his knees. "If you're thinking of kissing me, now would be a good time."

A low moan escaped Ty's lips and his fingers clenched into her hair. He tipped her head back until she stared up at him and here was the Ty who had turned her world upside down and driven her to heights she'd never before known.

"If I kiss you, I won't want to stop. Are you okay with that?" The words ground out, deep and hoarse, as if even voicing his desire required exercising great restraint.

Nicky wanted to break every shred of restraint he'd ever had until there were no walls or barriers between them. And she knew what he needed to make that happen.

"Yes, please," she whispered and melted when his hands clenched even tighter. When his lips pressed against hers.

When the smell of pepper and nutmeg engulfed her and the taste of him filled her mouth.

Nicky tugged at his shirt, desperate for more skin-to-skin contact. Ty broke the kiss only long enough to get his shirt off. Then his lips were on hers again and his hands cupped her ass as he lifted.

She shimmied out of her own top and bra on the way to his bedroom and was rewarded with his lips closing over her nipples. She grasped his hair and pulled up until she could see his eyes.

"I need to shower," she said. "I'm all sunscreen and sweat and glitter."

Ty changed direction, putting her down only to get the water running and finish stripping them both.

Under the hot spray, he cupped her face again, showering her with tiny kisses.

"I love you." His voice far surer this time. No question. No insecurity.

Nicky let the water wash over her right along with Ty's words.

Later she cried out her own love for him as his fingers hit sensitive spots, and again in bed as he slid into her, eyes locked on hers.

Much later still, she padded into the living room to get her phone and returned to find Ty sitting up.

"Everything okay?" His eyes roamed her body, heating her from the inside. As if they hadn't just had amazing sex.

"If I don't text Sabrina, she's probably gonna come hunting us down." Nicky flipped her phone to show him the string of texts from both Sabrina and Anne.

"Well, I don't ever want to be on her bad side. So, text her. Then come back to bed because I am not finished with you yet."

Nicky fired off a quick text and set her phone aside, then stood at the foot of the bed, hands on hips, admiring the man she loved.

"That sounded like an order."

Ty leaned back into the pillows, crossed his arms behind his head and arched an eyebrow at her. "Did it now? And how should you respond if that were the case?"

Those words went straight to happy places in her, making her breath catch and her nipples tighten. She flashed a big smile at him, placed her hands on the end of the bed and looked him straight in the eyes. Goodness, she loved this man!

"Yes, Sir."

EPILOGUE

Nicky's key clicked in the lock and Ty rushed to the door. He grabbed her bags before she even stepped into the apartment.

"Oof, sorry I'm late." She dropped a quick kiss on his lips and hung her coat. "It won't take me long to freshen up. I should've skipped the class today, and oh my god, I had a phone call right after...."

Ty stopped her with another kiss. "Don't worry about that." He dropped her bags in the office and caught her as she dug in the closet for her costume. "Go take a shower. You've got time."

Nicky whirled on him, and her eyes went wide. "Your mustache! Wow. That looks amazing."

The moment Nicky had agreed to do the Halloween event at AVAM, and they'd discussed costumes, he'd kept his beard closer than usual but left his upper lip alone. Today, he'd shaved everything except the mustache.

Nicky ran her fingers over the thin line on his upper lip. "I like it. Very Gomez."

If she didn't stop, they really were going to be late. "Tick tock, babe." He tapped his watch and Nicky scrambled to the closet again.

"We're due at the museum in half an hour," Nicky said as she tossed her Morticia costume onto the bed. "I'm..."

Ty rested his hands on her shoulders and kissed the back of her neck. "I already texted Sabrina. She knows we're gonna be late. So long as we're there by five, it's good. Go shower."

Nicky shot him a grateful glance and flew to the bathroom. Keeping his plans secret for the past month had killed him. It got even harder when he finally convinced Nicky to move in with him two weeks ago. Thankfully, Sabrina and Anne were in on the whole thing tonight.

"You're acting weird," Nicky called from the bathroom. "This isn't like you. You're acting like..." She trailed off and the door swung open. Nicky, half naked, stood in the door and glared at him. "You're acting like me. What's up?"

Sabrina had warned him she'd be like this. Hell, he knew she'd be like this. He also knew how to bring it to a screeching halt and get her to go along without further question.

"It's a surprise." Her eyebrows raised and he had her hooked. Now all he had to do was threaten to ruin it and she'd quiet down. A bit. "You can trust me, or if you want me to tell you..."

"No!" Nicky waved her hands at him then giggled and jumped up and down. "Don't spoil it. Really? You planned a surprise?"

He wasn't going to be able to keep his hands to himself if she kept standing there half naked and bouncing with excitement. He nodded and managed some degree of control when she threw herself at him and kissed him.

"Before five?" She was already moving back into the bathroom, dropping the rest of her clothes as she went.

By the time she was done in the bathroom, Ty had slipped into his Gomez costume—the black and gray stripes looked pretty good.

Nicky wiggled into the slinky black dress and smoothed her hair into a center part, somehow pinning her bangs out of the way. Miracle of miracles, they were out the door by half past four. *Making good time.*

At the museum, they found Sabrina and Anne—Sabrina dressed as the Black Panther, and Anne as Black Widow. Sabrina handed them flutes of champagne and Nicky's gaze flipped between the three of them.

"What are we celebrating?"

"There'd better be one of those for me." Deke's voice carried as he crossed to them. He embraced Nicky in a fierce hug before she held him at arm's length, then slowly walked around him with a low whistle.

"Captain America. Nice. I didn't know you'd be here." She glared at Ty and arched an eyebrow.

Ty squeezed her hand and leaned in close to whisper in her ear. "I already told you, it's a surprise." He straightened back up. He was reasonably confident about tonight. With Nicky, you could never be one hundred percent sure.

"I'll tell you one thing right now. The rest will have to wait until later."

Nicky scowled at him. "Okay. Spill it."

Ty sipped his champagne and leaned against a nearby pillar. "I am not rushing tonight. Not one bit of it."

Nicky made an impatient face and he relented. "My dissertation was accepted."

She clapped and her face lit up. "That is amazing. Congratulations. Record time. Now do I have to call you Doctor Lake?"

Ty glared at her, and she winked. "You can smack my ass

for that later," she said softly in his ear and his cock threatened to derail the evening with its own agenda—namely, getting Nicky naked as fast as possible. Focus. He had to stay focused.

"Not quite yet, but the hard part is done." He took another sip of champagne, enjoying the play of emotions on her face.

Nicky groaned. "Wait... everyone else here already knew?"

"About the dissertation? Only since this morning. I decided to wait till now to share with you."

Her eyes narrowed and she poked a finger into his chest. "This surprise better be worth it."

He loved it when Nicky got like this. Demanding. Determined. She would single mindedly focus until she'd solved whatever it was that was getting to her.

"Let's go mingle. We are part of the atmosphere tonight. Which means you two need to tango." Sabrina poked Nicky in the arm then turned to Deke. "And you need to prepare to be bombarded by kids and fangirls."

She gave Deke a slow once over then gestured for him to turn around. Deke obeyed without question and even Ty had to admit he made the costume look damn good.

"Lots of fangirls," Sabrina added.

They made their way into the main party space, already crowded with costumed guests. Predictably, Sabrina and Anne were mobbed by the younger set and Deke was surrounded by a group of admiring women.

When the band struck up a tango, Ty pulled Nicky onto the floor. The one thing he hadn't double and triple checked for tonight.

Ty relished every excited look he got from her. She loved surprises—she was like a kid at Christmas, practically vibrating with anticipation. She might complain and whine, but liked the drawn-out experience. Not unlike how she was in bed.

And he needed to get his mind out of the gutter if he was going to make it through tonight without doing something unspeakable like sex in the bathroom.

"Can you tango?" He whispered in her ear.

Nicky stuck her tongue out at him, then adopted a sexy pose and fixed him with a smoldering look from under her lashes. The perfect Morticia.

"Oui, mon cher."

And there went his cock again. Dammit. Who knew that would get to him. The beat picked up and Nicky followed him, smoothly gliding with his every move. He'd have to thank his mother for insisting on ballroom dance classes when he was a teen.

After their dance, they headed to the lobby for fresh drinks.

"And now for the rest." He led her to the stairwell and up to Reverend Wagner's Miracle at Midnight—the place where he'd first come to understand Nicky's point of view. "You know how we talked that my work might mean moving to another city?"

"You got a job offer," Nicky said. Ty nodded and Nicky took in a deep breath. "Where?"

Ty snagged her hands and pulled her down to a bench to sit. "See, here is where I have a big debate with myself over which comes first..."

He hauled in a shaky breath, giving silent thanks this room wasn't crowded. He was nervous. Ridiculously nervous. Then he looked at Nicky, and all worries disappeared. She held his hands and looked at him with a kind smile and eyes full of love.

"I love you," Ty said, and her eyes softened even more. "From the moment we met you shook up my life in remarkable ways. Good ways. Amazing ways."

Nicky's eyes narrowed. "You're about to tell me you got a job offer in someplace like Alaska."

Leave it to her to bring humor to the scene. That was her stock in trade when stressed.

"No. I'm about to propose to you."

Her mouth dropped open with a gasp and her eyes popped wide. He had a brief and horrible moment of thinking he'd fucked up and misread her and them and everything.

When her face transformed into little girl glee, Ty's chest eased.

NICKY—FRIDAY, OCTOBER 27

"Did you just ask..." Nicky stopped, unable to even voice the words for fear she'd misheard him.

"Well, I didn't ask, yet."

Her pulse pounded and butterflies went soaring around her stomach as Ty dropped to one knee. Those gorgeous green eyes fixed on hers. His fingers were steady as he curled them around her hands.

"I love you, Nicky, and I want to spend the rest of my life loving you. Marry me?"

Nicky never imagined herself crying at a proposal. Words failed her for a moment and all she could do was nod as happy tears coursed down her face.

Somehow, Ty stood, picked her up and settled her in his lap on the bench without a single fumble. His kiss was sweet and soft, his touch gentler than he'd ever been, as if he feared she would break or disappear.

"So," Nicky lifted her head and regarded him through slitted eyes. "Are you going to tell me where this job offer is?"

"Does it make a difference?"

Nicky gave it a moment's thought. "It could be Alaska for all I care, if we're together, that's all that matters."

She must have said the magic words because Ty sighed and her stomach tensed in preparation for the news.

"I've been offered the assistant director position at the Baltimore Museum of Art." The playful look on his face said he'd planned every bit of this.

"Seriously? You worked me up and got me all worried about moving and you've got a job offer here in Baltimore."

"Yeah, I'm evil like that."

"You just wanted to make sure I was all in before telling me…"

Ty's hands cupped her face seconds before his lips covered hers. "I don't care where we are, love, so long as I have you."

Nicky wriggled in his lap and was rewarded with the twitch of his dick under her thigh. She smiled and did it again, until Ty's fingers tightened on her leg.

"You never asked about the phone call that made me late," she said.

"I guess I assumed class went over, but you did mention a phone call."

"We have two more things to celebrate tonight. First, someone bought my nude at auction."

Ty's eyes crinkled as he smiled. "That's exciting!"

"Exciting is how much they paid for it. But that's not even the big news."

She hadn't processed it yet herself.

"I accepted a part-time adjunct faculty position at MICA for the spring semester. I can do that and BOPA. Then next fall, I go full-time staff at MICA."

Ty kissed her cheek. "Congrats! That's perfect."

Nicky smiled and raised an eyebrow at him. "The museum

director and the art professor. I like it. Though we might have to move—we're both going to need an office space."

He kissed her again long and slow. Goodness, she loved this man, and if he didn't stop soon, she'd be dragging him off to a dark corner somewhere rather than waiting till they got home.

"There's no rush," he said when he came up for air. "We'll find the right place. Together."

That was the one word she cared about. Together.

"Get a room!" Deke leaned against the wall next to the mural. "And congrats."

Another glass of champagne magically appeared in Nicky's hand, and she looked up to see Sabrina and Anne hovering on the other side of the bench.

"Aren't you forgetting something?" Sabrina nudged Ty whose whole body twitched.

"Oh!" Ty shifted her off his lap and dug into his jacket pocket. He pulled out a small velvet bag and dropped something shiny into his hand.

"I forgot this part. It took me forever to find something very special and a bit different, like you." He slid a sparkling black diamond onto her left-hand ring finger. "I love you with all my heart."

♥

ACKNOWLEDGMENTS

No author is an island and the list of people to thank for their help in getting this book out of my head and onto the page is long and varied, but there are a few I'd like to give a special shout out.

My former mentor turned crit partner Laura Brown has the patience of a saint for my never-ending "hey, does this work" questions. Also, check out her books!

The native Baltimoreans who helped hone some of the finer points about this city and its people: Christa, James, and Trey. Y'all rock!

This story has been through many hands along the way, including my former agent, Jana Hanson, who helped shape the unwieldy and slow thing into something far better.

My kids, Gabe and Marcie, are always on hand to help ensure my characters read like 20- and 30-somethings.

And a dizzying number of beta readers, editors, proofreaders, artists, designers, etc. You are so appreciated!

I will always acknowledge my husband–the man who enables and encourages me to focus on my writing. He is my real-life romance hero!

This could not have happened without every single one of y'all!

AUTHOR'S NOTE

While this book is set in Baltimore, and features many famous institutions in the city, the people and specifics are fictional. I did not give real behind-the-scenes details of places like The Walters, The American Visionary Arts Museum, the Baltimore Office of Promotion and the Arts, or events like Artscape and the Kinetic Sculpture Race.

Why?

Because this is a work of fiction, not an insider's look at those places and events. Because they are the setting and framework for a story about people who do not exist and things that never happened.

I am a huge fan of all of the places mentioned in this story, and this whole book is something of a love letter to my adopted hometown.

Anyone who lived in Baltimore after the pandemic will recognize this is a pre-Covid city—when Artscape was in July, the city and BOPA hadn't split, the CopyCat was still an active artist's loft, etc. The story was drafted pre-pandemic and faced with the options of "fixing"it all, and the resulting changes to the narrative, or leaving them and letting this story exist outside of time, I chose the latter. Again, because this is a work of fiction and not a Baltimore tour book.

Go to the link at the end and you'll find links to all of the places and events mentioned—if they still exist, of course, sadly, the awesome wine bar in Hampden closed during the pandemic.

If you ever find yourself in Baltimore—look these places up. They're worth a visit!

In short, any negatives, or "inaccuracies" are entirely works of my imagination and there for the purpose of the story—they are not reflections of the amazing events, places, and people who make Baltimore what it is—a surprisingly wonderful, and very quirky, city that I am happy to call home.

www.RoxanneBlackhall.com/locations

ABOUT THE AUTHOR

Roxanne Blackhall is the alter-ego of a former magazine and newspaper editor from San Diego, California, now living in the heart of Baltimore, Maryland. When not at her desk coming up with new ways to torment her characters, she can often be found in the kitchen, glass of wine in hand, cooking a meal for friends.

bsky.app/profile/roxyblackhall.bsky.social

facebook.com/roxanneblackhall

instagram.com/roxanneblackhall

threads.net/@roxanneblackhall

goodreads.com/Roxanne_Blackhall

COMING NEXT...

Here's a quick peek at **Intersecting Paths**, book 2 of Charm City Connections.

Note: this text is rough and unedited.

♥

Charlie—December 31

The soft breeze was a welcome relief after the crowd on the main level dance floor. Charlie Jones propped herself against the brick wall and stared down Frenchman Street. She hadn't had a New Year's Eve off in years and she intended to enjoy it.

A woman's throaty laugh floated through the air and Charlie glanced over to see a model-perfect platinum blonde draping herself around a smiling man leaning on the balcony railing.

Him again.

She'd spotted him early on. Even in the crowded bar, he was hard to miss. He looked like a Greek god decided to come to earth and walk among the mortals. Dark hair and

275

smoldering brown eyes sat in a ridiculously handsome face, and his shoulders strained the seams of a button-up shirt that looked custom tailored for his body.

It didn't hurt that he'd left more than the top two buttons open. Or that he'd rolled the sleeves up, showing off forearms that were the stuff of legends. The blonde was the third woman Charlie had seen him with—not that she was counting. Besides, she'd danced or hung out with an equal number of men, plus a couple of women. This was the last stop on a New Orleans bar crawl. Getting a little wild was expected.

Still, she had no desire to sit here and play voyeur if those two decided to start making out. She made her way back to the bar, found an open spot and caught the bartender's eye.

"Boulevardier, right?" He tossed a paper coaster in front of her as Charlie nodded.

"Good memory."

He took another order then made her drink and placed it on the coaster. "Like I'd forget that. You know how many sazeracs I've made tonight?"

"I can imagine. Never been my drink of choice." Charlie dropped cash in the tip jar and surveyed the room, letting the vibrant energy wash over her as she sipped her drink. This was why she liked running events—she loved helping people create happy memories.

She needed some happy memories of her own to wipe away the last few weeks. Hell, the last twelve months. Years of being staff had her used to being the observer—and that meant spotting potential problems before they blossomed. Fuck it, she was here to be social, not sit on the sidelines watching everyone else have fun. This wasn't work. She finished her drink and stood.

As she stepped away from the bar, she dodged a laughing

woman who wasn't looking where she was going and she backed into what felt like a wall that she was very sure had not been there before.

She turned and looked straight into the deep brown eyes of the Greek god. At five foot eight, she wasn't a small woman and her heels put her just under six feet, but she still looked up into his eyes. His mouth curled into a lopsided smile.

"I wondered when I'd bump into you again."

The warm, rich baritone of his voice sent pleasant shivers down Charlie's spine. *Down girl.* He was trouble she did not need. In her experience, if a man was as sinfully handsome as this guy, they were either toxic, terrible in bed, or both.

Then again, maybe he's just the right kind of trouble for tonight.

"Can I get you a drink?" He had leaned close to speak and the view only got better.

If she was being sensible, she'd switch to soda, or water. But nothing about the impromptu trip to New Orleans was sensible. Instead she nodded and the Greek god turned toward the bar and asked for a second of whatever she'd had and another for himself.

"You don't even know what I'm drinking."

"Nope." He followed that up with a chuckle and a widening of his grin.

"What if it's something awful?"

He shrugged as he pulled out his wallet to pay for the drinks. "Then it's an adventure. It's New Year's Eve. Gotta live a little dangerously, right?"

A week ago, she would have disagreed with that sentiment. Tonight, she wasn't living by rules. He scooped up both glasses and gave her a 'c'mon' gesture with his head. And damn if she didn't follow. She was a sucker for a little swagger and confidence. And this guy had them to spare.

He skirted the crowd and headed for the small patio in the back. Miraculously, they found two chairs. He waited for her to sit then handed her a glass and raised his own.

"To new friends," he said as he clinked his glass against hers then took a sip. "Oh, whiskey girl. Nice. Good choice. I'm Deke. Good to meet you."

Not for the first time, she wondered if name tags might have been a good idea.

"Pleasure. I'm Charlie."

Deke sat back and eyed her over the rim of his glass. She couldn't help feeling like he was appraising something.

"You're a bit of a social butterfly. I've seen you all over tonight." His eyes traveled from her face, down her body, and back up.

"I could say the same of you," she countered.

"Touché." He stretched long legs out and crossed them at the ankles. "Isn't that the point of this kind of event? Meet people. Make friends. Have fun."

If he could check her out, she figured turnabout was fair play. She let her gaze roam down his body. She suspected that was why he'd positioned himself the way he had—it gave her an unfettered view of broad shoulders and chest, flat abs and narrow hips. The slim-fitting pants he wore did nothing to conceal a very prominent bulge. Plus those long legs.

She got back to his face and he winked. Yeah. He knew damn good and well she was looking. And he knew she'd liked what she saw. *Definitely trouble.*

"So, we're in a tourist town and everyone here is from somewhere else, but I can't place your accent. Where are you from?" He leaned forward, his drink cupped in one big hand and an expression of rapt attention on his face.

Charlie shifted in her seat, a move that put her legs in contact with his. Not that she was complaining.

"Blame college in Massachusetts and working literally all over Europe for the lack of accent. I'm another tourist—just in town for the holiday."

His eyebrows arched up. "Yeah, me too. Flying back home tomorrow."

The last thing she wanted to think about was the world outside of this bar tonight. He was hot as fuck and just as charming, and that was all that mattered right now.

She nudged his knee with hers and shook her head. "Quid pro quo. I don't hear an accent from you."

He threw his head back and laughed, then leaned forward until he was very close. "Catholic school—the nuns were sticklers for diction and proper pronunciation." He tipped his head and smiled. "I always give at least as good as I get. Often better. Your turn. What do you do?"

The smirk he gave her as he sat back needed no translation. He'd meant every bit of that as an innuendo. Then he had to go and ask that question. Reality rearing its ugly head.

"I make people's dreams come true." That was how she viewed planning a wedding—she helped each couple bring their romantic ideas into reality. Deke gave her a quizzical look and Charlie flashed a smile. "I'm a wedding and events coordinator. You?"

"Cool. I'm a teacher."

He reached forward and snagged her empty glass. She hadn't even realized she'd finished her drink. Deke set them on the table and offered his hand.

"Dance?"

Why the hell not.

She slid her hand into his and he pulled her to stand. The song ended as they came back inside and the band slowed things down when they stepped onto the dance floor. Charlie didn't hesitate when he opened his arms. She laid one hand on his shoulder and Deke leaned close to her.

"You okay if I touch your waist?"

"As opposed to...?" She trailed off and batted her eyelashes at him and got a hearty laugh in return. He stepped closer and laid his hand high on her waist.

"So tell me more about you." His breath ruffled her hair as he spoke.

Another couple bumped into Charlie and Deke turned so they'd hit him if they did it again.

"Who says chivalry is dead? I think I'm gonna need more detail first. What do you teach? What's your subject? And what grade?"

"High school students, and I teach advanced math."

Should not have asked that question. Get back to flirting. Maybe another drink.

"Huh, I'd have pegged you more as an athlete."

She trailed her hand down the bulge of his bicep.

"I did play sports—pretty much all of them—but was never anything special as an athlete. I like being active, but it's not my life."

The firm muscles under her fingers said he was being modest. She gave his arm a squeeze. "Uh huh. You maybe wanna try that again? This says otherwise."

That pulled another laugh out of him. "I work out to maintain a body I feel good in and that I know women find attractive—fit, but not too fit. Well muscled, but not gym-bro bod."

"I mean, you're not wrong." She gave another squeeze to his bicep then slid her hand back up to rest on his shoulder. "I do yoga and swim. I'll never look thin, no matter what weight I'm at. Some people don't like that, and that's okay. There are plenty who do."

He stepped back a little and his eyes roamed her body top to toe. When he got back to her eyes, he gave a slow smile and pulled her close again.

"Count me among those who like that."

The rough rumble of his voice sent another cascade of shivers through her and conjured up images of getting him out of his clothes. A subtle shift in the music said the band was about to change things up again. Deke tipped his head and his lips brushed her ear.

"Think we can find a quiet spot?"

She stepped closer, bringing her body into full contact with his and it was electric. The beat dropped and the crowd around them cheered. Charlie made a face and Deke laughed again.

He pulled her away from the dance floor they climbed the stairs, bypassing the crowd on the second floor and turning up narrow stairs to the roof deck. The universe must have been smiling on them because it wasn't as packed as the rooms below.

"You wanna grab a table back there and I'll get drinks?" She pointed at the far end of the deck where a few tables sat in a dimly lit corner. More importantly, most of the people on the roof were clustered around the bar. Deke gave her a thumbs up and she turned to get drinks. Miracle of miracles, the wait wasn't too bad and she quickly joined Deke with fresh drinks in hand and two bottles of water tucked under her arm.

He stood by a tiny table tucked away from the others but only one chair. When she approached, he took the drinks from her and sat them on the table, then circled his hands around her waist and dropped into the chair. Gentle pressure from his hands encouraged her to sit.

She wasn't about to complain about getting closer to him,

but she'd never just sat on a man's lap. She did what she'd always done—half sat and half perched on his knee.

"Really? You're just going to prop yourself up like that?" Deke tipped his head toward the foot she had braced for balance. "When a man invites you to sit, he doesn't mean hover. May I?"

He held his hands out and she nodded, trying not to think about all the possible meanings of what he'd just said. Deke leaned forward, scooped one hand under her knees and the other around her waist then lifted. Charlie let out a little yelp of surprise then sighed as he settled her onto his lap.

"Better? There are reasons I work out that have nothing to do with looks."

Oh, it was better. And worse. Or at least more distracting. That little shift meant she was close enough to catch whatever combination of sandalwood and spice he was wearing and to feel that his legs were as well muscled as his arms. Not to mention that bulge she'd noticed earlier was now pressed against her hip.

He reached around her and retrieved the bottles of water, handing one to her before he settled back in the chair.

"So why here for New Year's?" Deke uncapped his water and took a long swig. The muscles in his throat flexed as he swallowed. "And why a bar crawl instead of a big party?"

"Would you believe me if I said it was cheap?" Charlie shook her head and laughed. "It was last minute. I knew I wanted to get away and just... be. Have fun. Not have to think. If any of that makes sense. I got a good deal. What's your excuse?"

He tapped the unopened bottle in her hand and watched until she twisted the lid off and drank a quarter of it.

"Like you, last minute thing. I had other plans but if I'm

being honest, my friend with benefits got pissed that I didn't propose at Christmas. Not gonna lie, I came to party."

At least he's honest. Not like I wasn't thinking the same.

He swapped his water for the cocktail and took a long sip. His eyebrows went up and he took another taste. "What the hell are we drinking? It's good, but I'm not sure what it is."

Charlie sipped more water, hoping staying hydrated would minimize the inevitable hangover she was going to have at this rate.

"Basically Scotch and soda meets whiskey highball, with a kick. The rest is honey and fresh ginger. And it's Glenmorangie. Which is probably why you couldn't figure it out."

She turned her head and found him closer than she thought. Another hint of spicy wood filled her senses. She switched her water for her cocktail and took a deep drink. It was that or wrap her arms around Deke and kiss him. Tempting as that was, she wanted to catch the fireworks at midnight. She was damn well going to enjoy the whole event.

The crowd on the roof grew and the music pumping through the speakers changed, making conversation difficult. Not that Charlie wanted to talk, anyway. Judging from the way Deke's eyes kept traveling to the vee of her dress, then down her legs and his hand, warm on her knee and the other curled around her hip, he didn't care either.

She wasn't sure at what point he'd put his drink down, but she sure as hell didn't mind his hands on her. Her own glass was half empty already. She was going to pay for this in the morning, but she did not care.

A handful of staff members spilled onto the roof, handing out glittery bags of NYE accessories and plastic flutes of champagne. They deposited two on the table in front of Deke and Charlie.

Someone blew a paper horn and Charlie laughed and snagged the bags. She pulled out beads, a glittery headband adorned with feathers and an equally glittery top hat. Without a word, she stuck the top hat on her head, then leaned in and secured the headband on his. She tossed the beads and glow stick bracelets back in the bags and did the same with the paper horns.

Someone pointed a camera at them and they both broke into broad smiles as the flash went off.

"It's getting close to midnight," Deke said into her ear. "Do you want to get closer to the front for a better view? Will we be able to see the fireworks from here?"

Charlie scanned the crowd now pressing at the front of the roof deck and had no desire to move. She tipped her head back and tried to recall the last time she'd been in New Orleans for New Year's Eve. She'd still been in college.

"I think we'll catch a bit of them from here. Do you want to..."

She didn't finish. The countdown started and the crowd was yelling along. Deke took the glass from Charlie's hands then wrapped his arms around her waist.

The first firework went off at the end of the countdown and Charlie half turned toward Deke. Her lips were a breath away from his. She whispered, "Happy New Year" and then closed the tiny distance.

She had thought to give him a quick kiss, nothing wild. The kind of thing people exchanged at times like this. But if his voice had sent shivers through her, his kiss was like an electric current. Charlie wasn't sure if the fireworks she felt were coming from inside her or the ones booming over their heads.

Deke's hands clenched on her waist. His tongue traced her lips until she opened her mouth to him. The sounds of the crowd and the thumping music faded as he filled all her senses. He tasted like honey and whiskey and he smelled like all things masculine and sexy. She was certain she could hear their heartbeats, or maybe it was just her own.

He pulled away, just a fraction of an inch, but Charlie wanted to reach up and grab him back. Deke pressed his forehead against hers and she knew what was coming. He'd said he'd come here to party, and she wanted to have fun and forget herself for a night. Deke seemed like the perfect way to do just that.

The last fireworks went off and some announcement came over the speakers about the band continuing for another hour. The crowd on the roof started to thin out.

"I think this is where I ask your place or mine." Deke cupped her head in his hands and Charlie was ready to agree to anything he suggested. "The street is gonna be a madhouse for a bit. Why don't we give it a few, then get out of here?"

The downside of quitting her job at the Ritz, no more employee discounts on rooms, but her bestie had scored her a stay at the Four Seasons. That seemed like a better idea than going to wherever he was staying.

Honking horns and cheering echoed from the street below. Getting a car now would be a nightmare.

"Mine," she replied. "We'll have to call a car."

DEKE

The look on her face had his cock throbbing in anticipation. *Fuck.* He'd had his eye on Charlie all night—her lush curves and the sparkly outfit had caught his attention, sure. The cascade of dark red curls and gorgeous smile didn't hurt. But it was the way she carried herself that had him entranced.

Her dress hugged her body like a glove and showed off

impressive cleavage and even more impressive legs that he was looking forward to wearing as earmuffs.

"Sounds like a plan," he replied.

Charlie shifted off his lap and stood. Her gaze traveled his body and the slow smile that curled her lips left no doubt that she'd noticed the effect she had on him. Deke didn't bother trying to hide anything. He was pretty sure they were on the same page and he'd make damn sure before things went too much further.

She strolled over to the balcony and leaned on the rail. Her skirt rode up, exposing creamy skin that he wanted to touch. The streets were crowded with people, most of them very drunk and shouting "Happy New Year" at anyone and everyone.

He'd come down here with every intent of kicking off the last year of his twenties with a hell of a good time. And he got the impression Charlie had a similar idea. It wouldn't be the first one-night stand of his life. After the debacle of trying a long-term friends-with-benefits thing, a one nighter had its appeal.

Not things he cared to think about when he was standing next to a goddess in human form. In her heels, she almost looked him in the eye. Almost. He knew from holding her in his lap, she was soft in all the right places.

Charlie shivered and Deke wrapped his arms around her. It was the most natural thing in the world to dip his head a tiny bit and kiss her. She ran her hands up his sides then around his back and pressed her body against his.

Fuck she feels good.

Back in college, he'd have been suggesting they find a bathroom and seeing how freaky they could get before people started pounding on the door. Those days were behind him, but damn she was tempting. She rose on her tiptoes and leaned over the rail and his view got even better.

"It's a busy night; we'll have a long wait for a car. We could walk it, but…" She held up a foot encased in a silver sandal with sky-high heel.

"No need." He caught her hand and turned her to face him, then hooked his thumb at the now almost empty rooftop. "Another minute and we'll have this space to ourselves. Looks like everyone's going back in for the band."

Every time the door opened, the music got louder. Charlie peeked around him then chuckled and pointed at the bar. The bartender was shutting down and telling folks the roof would remain open but they'd have to go downstairs for drinks.

"That's your reason."

"C'mon." He took her hand and moved away from the brightly lit balcony area. Instead of returning to the table they'd occupied, he pulled Charlie to a dark corner created by the stairwell and the adjacent building.

As soon as he stopped, Charlie brought her hands up, curled them behind his neck and pulled him to her for a kiss.

All thought left his brain as his blood headed for points south. In seconds, he had her backed against the brick wall, his leg pressed between her thighs and his mouth on her neck. He reached down and cupped her ass, shifting her tighter against him.

Charlie clung to his shoulders and let out a tiny gasp as his teeth skimmed her skin. Then she lifted one leg and wrapped it around his waist. He slid a hand under her dress, up smooth skin and the curve of her hip until his fingers grazed a barely-there thong.

It would take seconds to get that off of her. He could be inside her warmth with a few tugs of clothing and the condom in his pocket. In years past, he'd have been doing just that.

She arched against him, her fingers coiled in his hair and pushed down. He took the hint and trailed kisses along the swell of her breasts, nudging the fabric aside until he could pull a nipple into his mouth.

"Oh fuck, yes."

That and the rocking of her hips against him was all the encouragement Deke needed. He cupped her ass and lifted her higher, pressing her harder against the wall. Her dress slid down, exposing more of her magnificent breasts and Deke wasted no time lavishing them with attention. He shifted his grip to slide his arm under her leg.

She trembled at the first touch of his fingers over the smooth fabric of her thong. He hooked a finger under the edge of the material and found wetness. She rolled her hips as if trying to get closer to his hand and Deke chuckled.

"Don't stop. That feels so good."

Nothing in the world could make him stop right now. He sucked her other nipple between his lips, eliciting another soft cry of pleasure. Then he slid his finger along her silken folds—warm and slippery wet with want.

The thought of sinking to his knees and burying his face between her thighs was tempting, but this was not the place. He wanted to feast on her until she begged him to stop. Instead, he stroked his fingers over her, coaxing her open while he treated her nipples the way he wanted to treat her clit.

She rolled her hips again and his finger slipped between her pussy lips. Her hands clenched in his hair, holding him tight against her breasts. He teased his finger along her entrance and she moaned softly. He didn't care that they were a few feet from a handful of stragglers still on the roof, or that anyone who came around the corner would see them in the shadows.

Deke pressed a finger into her and was rewarded with a

clench of her muscles around him. At this rate he'd be having to count backwards from a hundred to keep from coming about two seconds after he entered her.

"Oh yes. Fuck yes."

Charlie rocked her hips against him, grinding down onto his hand until Deke slid a second, then a third finger into her. Her moans got a little louder and she clamped one hand over her mouth. She was so fucking hot that Deke was about ready to come in his pants.

He rotated his hand until he could press his thumb over her clit while his fingers still pumped into her. The swollen bud was hard under his touch and he pushed the hood back a bit more.

"Harder! Oh my god. Harder please."

Deke wasn't sure if she meant sucking on her nipples, finger-fucking her tight pussy, or the thumb on her clit, so he opted for all three. He let his teeth graze her skin and flicked his tongue over her nipple then rubbed her clit in time. Then he curled his fingers forward until he found her g-spot and he stroked hard.

Charlie's entire body arched. Her head tipped back and she let out a cry before stifling it with both hands over her mouth. Her pussy walls clenched around his fingers. He was pretty sure he had her on the verge of orgasm. Hopefully, the first of many tonight. He just needed to keep it up and push her over that edge.

Someone set off firecrackers in the street and Charlie stiffened at the popping sounds. Her hands came out of his hair. Deke lifted his head and eased his fingers from her, using his body to shield her from view, even though the roof was deserted.

She straightened her dress and grabbed her phone.

"Lemme check on a car." She tapped the screen then

scowled. "Um… shit. It's gonna be a while." She held the screen for him to see the estimated forty-minute wait.

The look she gave him had him wanting to say screw the car, I want you right here, right now. Her eyelids were heavy and her lips swollen and red as if she'd been biting them. He could imagine those lips wrapped around his cock, and he wasn't even all that enamored of getting head.

He should ask if she was okay. He was usually all about clear consent and always asked. Tonight, he had assumed. *Not drunk enough to blame the alcohol.*

Her body language made her desire clear, but that didn't make it right. Still, something told him if he checked in, she'd take it the wrong way.

Deke cupped her head in his hands and pulled back. Her pout was almost his undoing.

"Show me what you want."

He let go of her and spread his arms wide. Charlie tilted her head to the side and smiled. She trailed one hand up his leg, then leaned in and pressed her lips to his throat. Her fingers teased over the buttons of his jeans then along the length of his cock—hard and throbbing and aching to be let out.

She nipped his ear with her teeth as she worked her hand into his waistband and down. Slim fingers slid around his shaft. Charlie sucked in a sharp breath then let out a whispered "fuck." Her grip tightened and she groaned a little.

"You're… that's umm… a lot."

It wasn't the first time he'd heard that. He'd had more than a few women change their minds after seeing him—he had no problem with it and was always happy to make sure they still had fun. Charlie didn't look worried. In fact, she looked like she was ready to get naked right where they stood.

Her fingers tightened on him again, then loosened and slid

until she circled the head of his cock. She teased along the ridge until he was gritting his teeth to keep from pinning her against the wall and fucking her senseless.

Instead, he leaned his back into the corner and pulled her closer.

"Let's play a game. Put your back against me."

He opened his arms and she nestled her deliciously round ass against his crotch. *Fuck me.*

"Spread your legs."

Charlie's legs parted and Deke draped one arm around her shoulder, letting his fingers trail down inside her dress. He pushed a leg between hers, nudging until she spread even wider. He brought his hand up Charlie's leg and brushed his finger over the soaking wet fabric of her thong.

"Don't come. No matter what. We're going to play until the crowd thins out, then we're going to your room and I plan to lay you back on the bed and make you come with my mouth."

Charlie shivered and let out a soft gasp.

"Tell me if you want that."

"Yes." There was no hesitation and she shifted against him, bringing her breasts higher and spreading her legs even more.

"Good girl." Deke teased her nipples with one hand as he slipped his fingers into her thong. She was still slippery wet and arching against him. He pinched her nipple and thrust fingers into her in one stroke. Charlie covered her mouth with her hand and her whole body tensed.

Fuck, she likes it rough. This was going to be an amazing night.

He alternated between feather light touches and hard, almost punishing pinches and strokes as more firecrackers and small fireworks went off and the noises from the street got louder. Deke nipped her ear lobe and she whimpered.

Everything about her responses said her brain was shut off and she was lost in the sensations. As much as he loved and craved that, he wasn't sure how much was conscious choice and how much was alcohol. Tempting as it was to fuck her right here, that wasn't going to happen.

He brought her hand around and pressed her palm over his hard on. Charlie squeezed and wriggled her ass against him.

"To be clear," Deke whispered in her ear. "Once we get to your hotel, I want to make you come, repeatedly. Then I want to fuck you. Are you okay with that?"

She turned in his arms, pressed her lips against his. Her fingers tightened on his cock.

"I am very okay with that," she replied. "I want you, and I don't care how long the wait for a car is."

In seconds, she had her phone in her hand and the ride app open. The universe must have been smiling on them because the expected wait was less than ten minutes. Charlie wiggled the phone and gave him a grin that confirmed again— they were on the same page.

"Take off your thong." He held his hand out and waited.

Charlie tucked her phone away and took half a step back. Her eyes never left his as she reached under her skirt and slid the barely-there thing down her legs then put the scrap of fabric in his hand.

Deke pocketed the thong and pulled her closer, then spun so she was pressed into the corner. He slid his hand between her legs and cupped his fingers over her mound, squeezing gently, relishing the feel of skin on skin. Charlie moaned and lifted a leg to curl around his waist.

"You've got five minutes before we need to get downstairs. What do you want?" Deke knew what he wanted. More than anything in the world, he wanted to feel her wrapped around him with no clothing in the way.

Charlie lifted her other leg and locked her ankles behind his back. *Fuck me.* His pants were the only thing between him and the delicious softness of her pussy. He slid his fingers into her, eliciting a moan of pure pleasure. Charlie curled her hips up and Deke settled into a slow rhythm with his palm flat against her and his fingers pressing deep inside.

She arched and ground against his hand, her head thrown back against the bricks and her lips parted as little gasps escaped her. The frantic energy of earlier had mellowed into something richer, deeper, and Deke was all for it.

"Oh, that's so good."

He didn't care how long it took, he wanted more of that. Hell, he wanted more of her. She was lost to the world as she rode his hand. If he shifted and paid more attention to her clit, she'd probably come in seconds.

Not yet.

He'd promised to make her come with his mouth, and he had every intention of keeping that promise.

Her phone pinged and Charlie's eyes opened. She blinked, smiled at him, and slowly lowered first one leg, then the other.

"Guess we should get downstairs."

Her grip on his hand was tight as they navigated the steps. She paused on the second floor and pointed at the bathroom.

"No line. It's a miracle. Be right back." She disappeared through the black lacquer door and Deke turned for the other bathroom. Washing his hands seemed like a good idea.

Their ride pulled up just as they stepped into the street. Charlies stumbled getting into the big SUV, but Deke managed to steady her before she went down. He wasn't sure whether it was the state he had her in, her shoes on the uneven pavement, or the drinking.

He'd damn sure find out before getting naked. She settled against his side in the backseat, then tipped her head back to kiss him and all thought left Deke's head. They bumped and jostled at a snail's pace along the crowded street. Tempting as it was to continue what they'd started, the driver had the interior lights on—probably to discourage that behavior—and Deke wasn't into putting on that kind of show.

Charlie shifted in the seat and her head rested on his shoulder.

Sleepiness has hit.

He chuckled and curled his arm around her, pulling her closer. He had sisters and had dated enough women in college to know the pattern of tipsy to sleepy.

By the time they pulled up at the hotel, Charlie was half asleep. Deke helped her out of the SUV, into the lobby and to the elevators. All thoughts of sexy times got shoved to the back of his mind. Sure, he loved the idea of making her lose herself, but he wanted her awake and fully aware to start.

"What floor?" Deke pushed the button and waited for an elevator to open.

"Six twenty," Charlie replied. Inside the elevator, she pulled out a keycard and handed it to him. She was steady on her feet as they walked down the hall, then stumbled again as he unlocked her door and ushered her inside.

"I may have had too much to drink." Charlie sank to the bed. She reached up and pulled something out of her hair, sending a riot of curls tumbling around her face.

Deke knelt and took off her shoes. By the time he rose with the sparkly sandals in hand, she was asleep.

Well, shit.

He had an early morning flight, so the idea of staying until she woke up and then picking up where they left off wasn't on the table. Plus he didn't imagine she'd wake up in the sexiest of moods.

Instead, he placed the shoes in the closet, then pulled her

up so she was in the bed and tucked a blanket over her. She didn't move during any of it. He found a notepad and pen and tried to decide what to say.

She'd never told him where she was from. Or where she lived. He'd taken his cue from her and been equally evasive. Maybe she wanted strictly anonymous sex. He glanced at the bed—her curls spilled over the pillow. Her lips were puffy from kisses and he'd left a few red bite marks on her neck.

Shit. Didn't mean to do that.

On closer look, they were minor and would likely fade by morning. He turned back to the empty notepad.

Charlie,
Thank you for making my night. Meeting you was an amazing end to one year and an even better start to the next. If you're ever in Baltimore, give me a call.
Deke

He added his cell number, folded the note in half and stuck it under a bottle of water on the nightstand. He found her phone and plugged it in, stuck her panties next to it and the water bottle, then turned off the lights and let himself out of the room.

The door snicked shut behind him and Deke made his way down the hall as if in a dream. She had to be some figment of his imagination. He should have gotten her number earlier. He should have made her come. That was his only real regret of the night—that he hadn't gotten to experience her orgasming from his touch.

The elevator opened and Deke checked the time. It wasn't too late. He could probably go out and find some willing woman. But as he walked back to his AirBnB, every woman he passed paled in comparison to Charlie. He climbed the steps to his room. Despite washing his hands, he could still smell her on him. Her scent was in his clothes. Some floral perfume that had an edge to it and the intoxicating scent that was her. If there was a heaven, this is what it would smell like.

Deke stripped for bed. His cock still throbbed and he'd have to do something about that before he could sleep. And he knew what he'd be imagining as he came—Charlie with her head thrown back, tits in his face, and his cock buried in her wet pussy.

Fuck.

He closed his hand around his cock and stroked.